WAR ON THE STREETS

SAS
OPERATION

War on the Streets

PETER CAVE

Harper
An imprint of HarperCollins*Publishers*
1 London Bridge Street,
London SE1 9GF
www.harpercollins.co.uk

This paperback edition 2016
1

First published by 22 Books/Bloomsbury Publishing plc 1995

Copyright © Bloomsbury Publishing plc 1995

Peter Cave asserts the moral right to
be identified as the author of this work

A catalogue record for this book
is available from the British Library

ISBN: 978 0 00 815536 0

Set in Sabon by Born Group using Atomik ePublisher from Easypress

Printed and bound in Great Britain

MIX
Paper from
responsible sources
FSC™ C007454

FSC is a non-profit international organisation established
to promote the responsible management of the world's forests.
Products carrying the FSC label are independently certified
to assure consumers that they come from forests that are managed
to meet the social, economic and ecological needs
of present and future generations.

Find out more about HarperCollins and the environment at
www.harpercollins.co.uk/green

1

Lieutenant-Colonel Barney Davies, 22 SAS Training Wing, cruised slowly down the Strand and the Mall, then turned into Horse Guards Road. It was not the first time he had been summoned to a Downing Street conference, and he'd learned a few of the wrinkles over the years. Finding a parking space was the first trick. You had to know where to look.

Finding his objective, he slid the BMW into a parking bay, climbed out and loaded the meter to its maximum. These things had a nasty habit of stretching out for much longer than anticipated. What might start as a preliminary briefing session could well develop into a protracted discussion, or even a full-scale planning operation. Failing to take precautions could prove expensive.

He turned away from the parking meter and, glancing up to where he knew the nearest security video camera was hidden, treated it to a lingering smile. Every little helped. If they knew he was coming it might just cut down the number of security checks he'd have to be stopped for. Picking his way between the buildings, he ducked into the little labyrinth of covered walkways which would bring him to the back of Downing Street and ultimately to the rear security entrance of Number 10.

In fact Davies was stopped only twice, although he suspected he had identified at least two other plain-clothes men, who had allowed him to pass unchallenged. He preferred to assume that this was due to his face having become familiar, rather than security becoming sloppy. There could be no let-up in London's fight against terrorism.

The final checkpoint, however, was very thorough. Davies waited patiently as the doorman checked his security pass, radioed in his details and paused to await clearance. Finally, he was inside the building and climbing the stairs to Conference Room B.

He pushed open the panelled double doors and stepped into the room, casting his eyes about for any familiar faces. It was always a psychological advantage to re-establish any personal links, however tenuous, Davies had always found. It gave you that little extra clout, should you find yourself out on a limb.

Of the five people already in the room, Davies recognized only two: Michael Wynne-Tilsley, one of the top-echelon parliamentary secretaries, and David Grieves from the 'green slime'. Davies decided not to bother with Wynne-Tilsley, other than to give him a brief nod. On the single occasion he had had any dealings with the man before, Davies had found him to be a close-lipped, somewhat arrogant little bastard, and far too protective of his job to give out any useful information. He would be better off having a preliminary word with Grieves. The man might be MI6, but he would probably respect Davies's grade five security clearance enough to give him at least an inkling of what the meeting was about. And forewarned was forearmed. Davies hated going into things blinkered, let alone blind.

He sauntered over to the man, smiling and holding out his hand. 'David, how are you?'

2

Grieves accepted the proffered hand a trifle warily. 'Don't even ask,' he warned, though there was the ghost of a smile on his lips.

Davies grinned sheepishly. 'Come on, David, you're here and I'm here, so somebody's got to be thinking of a joint operation.'

Grieves conceded the point with a vague shrug.

Davies pushed his tactical advantage. 'So where in this benighted little world are we going to get our feet wet now?' he asked. 'First guess: central Africa.'

Grieves smiled. 'Wrong,' he said curtly. 'A bit closer to home and that's all I'm telling you until the Home Secretary opens the briefing.'

It was scant information, but it was enough to tell Davies two things. First, if the Home Secretary rather than the Foreign Secretary was involved, then it was a sure bet that it was a purely internal matter. Second, Grieves's guardedness suggested that he had been called to another one of those 'This Meeting Never Happened' meetings. It was useful information to have. Briefings conducted on a strictly need-to-know basis were invariably the stickiest.

Wisely, Davies decided not to press the military intelligence man any further. He looked around the room, trying to guess at the identities of the other three occupants. The youngest man looked pretty bland and faceless, and Davies took him to be a minor civil servant of some kind. The other two were a different breed. Both in their late forties or early fifties, they had the unmistakable stamp of those used to exercising authority. The senior of the pair was tantalizingly familiar. Davies felt sure that he ought to recognize the man, quite possibly from exposure in the media. But for the moment, it just would not come.

Grieves followed the direction of his gaze. 'I take it you recognize McMillan,' he muttered.

It clicked, finally. Alistair McMillan, Commissioner, Metropolitan Police. Davies must have seen the man's picture a dozen times over the past few years. Seeing him out of uniform had thrown him off track.

'And his colleague?' he asked.

'Commander John Franks, Drugs Squad,' Grieves volunteered. 'Now you know almost as much as I do.'

'But not for much longer, I hope,' Davies observed. The Home Secretary had just entered the conference room, flanked by two more parliamentary secretaries. Davies recognized Adrian Bendle from the Foreign Office, and wondered what his presence signified.

The Home Secretary wasted little time. He moved to the octagonal walnut conference table, laying down his papers, and nodding around the room in general greeting. 'Well, gentlemen, shall we get down to business?' he suggested as soon as he was seated. He glanced over at Wynne-Tilsley as everyone took their seats. 'Perhaps you'd like to make the formal introductions and we can get started.'

Introductions over, the Home Secretary looked at them all gravely. 'I suppose I don't really need to remind you that this meeting is strictly confidential and unofficial?'

Davies smiled to himself, momentarily. Just as he had suspected, it was one of those. That accounted for the absence of an official recorder in the room. Pulling his face straight again, he joined in the general nods of assent around the table.

'Good,' the Home Secretary said, and nodded with satisfaction. He glanced aside at the young parliamentary secretary who had accompanied him. 'Perhaps if you could close the curtains, we can take a look at what we're up against.'

The young man rose, crossed the conference room and pulled the thick velvet curtains. Pressing a remote-control panel he held in his hand, he switched on the large-screen video monitor in the far corner of the room.

As the screen flickered into life, the Home Secretary continued. 'Most of you will probably have seen most of these items on the news over the past few months. However, it will be useful to view them all again in context, so that we can all see the exact nature of the enemy.'

He fell silent as the first of a series of European news reports began.

Davies recognized the first one at once. It was the abduction of the Italian wine millionaire Salvo Frescatini in Milan, some three months previously. The report, cobbled together from amateur video footage, police reconstructions and television news clips, covered the kidnapping, in broad daylight, the subsequent ransom demands of the abductors and the final shoot-out when the Italian police tracked the gang down. It was a bloody encounter which had left eight police officers dead and a score of innocent bystanders wounded. The film ended with a shot of the hostage as the police had finally found him – his trussed body cut to shreds by over two dozen 9mm armour-piercing slugs from Franchi submachine-guns. The kidnappers had been armed like a combat assault team, and were both remarkably professional in their methods and utterly ruthless.

The sequence ended, the venue switching to Germany and more scenes of murderous violence. Angry right-wing mobs razing the hostels of immigrant workers to the ground, desecrated Jewish cemeteries and clips of half a dozen racist murders.

A student riot at the Sorbonne in Paris came next, with graphic images of French riot police lying in pools of their own blood after protest placards had given way to clubs, machetes and handguns.

The screen suddenly went blank. Daylight flooded into the conference room once more as the curtains were drawn back. The Home Secretary studied everyone at the table for a few seconds.

'France . . . Italy . . . Germany,' he muttered finally. 'The whole of Europe seems to be suddenly exploding into extremes of violence. Our fears, gentlemen, are that it may be about to happen here.'

There was a long, somewhat shocked silence in the room, finally broken by Adrian Bendle. 'Perhaps I could take up the story from here, Home Secretary?' the Foreign Office man suggested.

The Home Secretary agreed with a curt nod, sitting back in his chair. Bendle took centre stage, standing and leaning over the table.

'As you're probably aware, gentlemen, we now work in fairly close co-operation with most of the EC authorities,' he announced. 'Quite apart from our strengthened links with Interpol, we also liaise with government departments, under-cover operations and security organizations. Through these and other channels, we have pieced together some highly unpleasant conclusions over the past few months.' He paused for a while, taking a breath. 'Now the violent scenes you have just witnessed would appear, at face value, to be isolated incidents, in different countries and for different reasons – but not, apparently, connected. Unfortunately, there *is* a connection, and it is disquieting, to say the least.' There was another, much longer pause before Bendle took up the story again.

'In every single one of the preceding incidents, there is a common factor,' he went on. 'In those few cases where the authorities were able to arrest survivors – but more commonly from post-mortems carried out on the corpses – all the participants in these violent clashes were found to have high concentrations of a new drug in their systems. It is our belief, and one echoed by our European counterparts, that this is highly significant.'

Commissioner McMillan interrupted. 'When you say a *new* drug, what exactly are we talking about?'

Bendle glanced over at Grieves. 'Perhaps you're better briefed to explain to the commissioner,' he suggested.

Grieves climbed to his feet. 'What we appear to be dealing with here is a synthetic "designer" drug of a type previously unknown to us,' he explained. 'Whilst it is similar in many ways to the currently popular Ecstasy, it also seems to incorporate some of the characteristics, and the effects, of certain of the opiate narcotics and some hallucinogens. A deliberately created chemical cocktail, in fact, which is tailor-made and targeted at the youth market. Initial tests suggest that it is cheap and fairly simple to manufacture in massive quantities, and its limited distribution thus far could only be a sampling operation. If our theories are correct, this stuff could be due to literally flood on to the streets of Europe – and this country is unlikely to prove an exception.'

'And the connection with extremes of violence?' Commander Franks put in.

'At present, circumstantial,' Grieves admitted. 'But from what we know already, one of the main effects of this drug is to make the user feel invulnerable, free from all normal moral restraints and totally unafraid of the consequences of illegal or immoral action. Whether it actually raises natural aggression levels, we're not sure, because we're still conducting tests. But what our boffins say quite categorically is that the use of this drug most definitely gives the user an *excuse* for violence – and for a lot of these young thugs today, that's all they need.'

The Home Secretary took over again. 'There are other, and equally disquieting factors,' he pointed out. 'Not the least of which is the appalling growth of radical right-wing movements and factions which seem to be popping up all over Europe at the moment. Many, if not all, of the incidents you have just seen would appear to be inspired by such ethology. The obvious conclusion is both inescapable and terrifying.' He broke off, glancing back to Grieves again. 'Perhaps you could explain our current thinking on this, Mr Grieves.'

Grieves nodded. 'In everything we have seen so far, two particularly alarming factors stand out. One is the degree of organization involved, and the second is the degree and sophis-tication of the weaponry these people are getting hold of. We're not talking about kids with Stanley knives and the odd handgun here, gentlemen. We're dealing with machine-pistols, sub-machine-guns, pump-action shotguns – even grenades.'

Commissioner McMillan interrupted. He sounded dubious. 'You make it sound as though we're dealing with terrorists, not tearaways.'

Grieves's face was set and grim as he responded. 'That may well be the case, sir,' he said flatly. 'We have reasonable grounds for suspecting that a new type of terrorist organiza-tion is building in Europe, perhaps loosely allied to the radical right. If we're right, they are creating a structure of small, highly mobile and active cells which may or may not have a single overriding control organization at this time.'

Commissioner McMillan was silently thoughtful for a few moments, digesting this information and its implications. Finally he sighed deeply. 'So what you're telling us, in effect, is that a unified structure could come into being at any time? That we face the possibility of an entirely new terrorist force on the rampage in our towns and cities?'

The Home Secretary took it up from there. 'That is *exactly* what we fear,' he said sombrely. 'And we believe that conventional police forces may be totally inadequate and ill-prepared to deal with such a threat.' He paused, eyeing everyone around the table in turn. 'Which is why I invited Lieutenant-Colonel Davies of the SAS to this briefing today,' he added, quietly.

There was a stunned silence as the implications of this statement sank in. Of the group, no one was more surprised than Barney Davies, but it was he who found his voice first.

'Excuse me, Home Secretary, but are you saying you want to put the SAS out there on the streets? In our own towns and cities?' he asked somewhat incredulously.

The man gave a faint shrug. 'We did it in Belfast, when it became necessary,' he pointed out. He looked at Davies with a faint smile. 'And it's not as if your chaps were *complete* strangers to urban operations.'

Davies conceded the point, but with reservations. 'With respect, sir, an embassy siege is one thing. Putting a full anti-terrorist unit into day-to-day operation is quite another.' He paused briefly. 'I assume that's the sort of thing you had in mind?'

The Home Secretary shrugged again. 'Yes and no,' he muttered, rather evasively. 'Although personally I had seen it more in terms of a collaboration between the SAS and the conventional police forces. A joint operation, as it were.'

Davies held back, thinking about his response. Finally he looked directly at the Home Secretary, shaking his head doubtfully. 'Again with respect, sir, but you are aware of the rules. The SAS does not work with civilians.'

The Home Secretary met his eyes with a cool, even gaze. 'I think you're rather stretching a point there, Lieutenant-Colonel Davies. I would hardly call the police civilians.' He thought for a second, digging for further ammunition. 'Besides, the SAS Training Wing works with various types of civil as well as military groups all over the world, so why not on home ground? Think of it more in those terms if it makes you feel better. A training exercise, helping to create a new counter-terrorist force.'

The man was on dicey ground, and he knew it, Davies thought. Nevertheless, his own position was not exactly crystal-clear, either. They were both dealing with a very grey area indeed. For the moment, he decided to play along with things as they stood.

'And how would the police feel about such a combined operation?' he asked.

McMillan spoke up. 'We have discussed similar ideas in principle, in the past, of course. But obviously, this has come as just as much of a surprise to me as it has to you.' He paused for thought. 'But at this moment, my gut feeling is that we could probably work something out.'

The Home Secretary rose to his feet. He looked rather relieved, Davies thought. 'Well, gentlemen, I'll leave you all to think it through and come up with some concrete proposals,' he said, collecting up his papers from the table.

'Just one more thing, Home Secretary,' Davies called out, unwilling to let the man escape quite so easily. 'We'll have full approval from the relevant departments on this one, I take it?'

The man smiled cannily. He was not going to be tempted to stick his head directly into the noose. 'Grudging approval, yes,' he conceded. 'But of course you won't be able to count on anyone with any real authority to bail you out if you come unstuck.'

It was more or less what Davies had expected. He returned the knowing smile. 'So we're on our own,' he said. It was a statement, not a question.

'Aren't you always?' the Home Secretary shot back.

It wasn't a question that Davies had any answer for. He was silent as the politician left the conference room, followed by his aides. There was only himself, Commissioner McMillan, Commander Franks and David Grieves left around the table. No one said anything for a long time.

Finally, Franks cleared his throat. 'Well, it would seem to me that the first thing you are going to need is a good, straight cop who knows the drug scene at street level,' he said thoughtfully. 'No disrespect intended, but it really is foreign territory out there.'

It made sense, Davies thought, taking no offence. Franks was right – the theatre of operations would be something completely new and unfamiliar to his men, and they didn't have any maps. They would need a guide.

'Someone with a bit of initiative, who can think for himself,' Davies insisted. 'I don't want some order-taker.'

Franks nodded understandingly. 'I'll find you such a man,' he promised.

2

The blue Porsche screamed round the corner into the narrow mews entrance at a dangerous angle, clipping the kerb with a squeal of tortured rubber and wrenching the rear wheel up on to the narrow pavement. Bouncing back down on to the cobbled street, the car slewed erratically a couple of times before straightening up and slowing down, finally coming to a halt outside one of the terraced cottages. Like everything else in this part of south-west London, the house was small but expensive.

Glynis Jefferson glanced sideways out of the car window, looking at the number on the house to check the address. There was no real need. The sounds of rave music and general merriment issuing from the house showed that the party was still in full swing, even at three-thirty in the morning. Relief showed on the girl's strained face as she opened the car door and stepped out.

Her knees felt weak, buckling under her. She leaned against the side of the car for support, trying to control the violent shudders which shook her whole body in irregular and involuntary spasms. It was a warm night, yet she was shivering. Her young face, though undeniably attractive, was taut and lined with tension, ageing her beyond her years. Her eyes

were wide, apparently vacant, yet betraying some inner distur-
bance, like a helpless animal in pain.

She pulled herself together with an effort and dragged herself
up the three stone steps to the front of the mews cottage. She
rang the bell, fidgeting impatiently as she waited for someone
to answer it.

The door was finally opened in a blast of sound by a young
man in his early thirties. Glynis did not recognize him; nor
did it matter. Names were not important to her.

Nigel Moxley-Farrer lolled against the door jamb, appraising
the young blonde on his doorstep. His eyes were glassy, the
pupils dilated. He was either drunk, or stoned – probably both.
An inane, vacant grin on his face showed that he approved of
his attractive young vistor.

'Well hello, darling. Come to join the bash? You're too
gorgeous to need an invitation. Just come on in.' He lurched
backwards, inviting her into the house.

Glynis shook her head. 'I'm not partying. I'm just looking
for Charlie.'

Despite his befuddled brain, Nigel's face was instantly
suspicious. His eyes narrowed. 'Charlie? Charlie who?'

Glynis shuddered again. Her voice was edgy and irritable.
'Aw, come on, man. Don't piss me about.' She paused briefly.
'Look, I was at Annabel's tonight. A guy called David told
me I could score here tonight.'

So it was out in the open; no need for any further pretence.
They both knew exactly what Charlie she was looking for.
C for Charlie – the code word for cocaine among the Sloane
Ranger set.

Still grinning, Nigel shook his head. 'You're too late, darling.
Charlie's been and gone.' He spread his hands in an expansive
gesture, giggling stupidly. 'Hey, can't you tell?'

Another violent spasm racked Glynis's body. A look of despair crept over her face. 'Oh, Jesus!' she groaned. She looked up at Nigel again, her eyes pleading. 'Come on, somebody's got to be still holding, surely? The money's no problem, OK?'

Nigel shook his head again. 'Not a single snort left in the place. We all did our thing a couple of hours ago.' He reached out, grasping her by the arm. 'But don't let that bother your pretty head, darling. We've still got plenty of booze left. Why don't you just come in and get chateaued instead?'

Glynis shook free of his grip with a sudden, violent jerk. The sheer intensity of her reaction wiped the grin from Nigel's face for a second. He stared down at her more carefully, noting the perspiration starting to show through her make-up, the nervous twitching of little muscles in her face.

'It's really that bad, huh?'

Glynis nodded dumbly. She looked totally dejected and pathetic. Nigel looked at her dubiously for a while, finally coming to some sort of a decision.

'Look, I'll tell you what I'll do. Got a pen and paper?'

Glynis nodded again, this time with a flash of hope on her face. She rummaged in her handbag and fished out a ballpoint pen and an old clothing store receipt.

Nigel took them from her trembling fingers. Holding the scrap of paper against the door-frame, he began to scribble.

'Look, this guy is strictly down-market, and he charges way over the odds on street prices . . . but he can usually come across, know what I mean?'

The girl nodded gratefully. 'Yeah. And thanks.'

She turned to go back down the steps. Nigel called after her. 'Hey, look, don't forget to tell him Nigel M sent you. It puts me in line for a favour, know what I mean?'

Glynis didn't answer. Nigel remained in the doorway for a few moments, watching her as she climbed into the Porsche and backed hurriedly out of the narrow street. A slim female hand descended on his shoulder, and a pair of red lips which smelled strongly of gin nuzzled his ear.

'Hey, come on, Nigel. You're missing the party.'

Nigel turned away from the door, finally.

'Who was it – gatecrashers?' his companion asked.

Nigel shook his head. 'No, just some junkie bird chasing Charlie. I sent her to Greek Tony.'

His girlfriend pulled an expression of distaste. 'Ugh, that slimeball? She must have been pretty desperate.'

Nigel nodded. 'Yes, I think she was,' he muttered.

Detective Sergeant Paul Carney sat at his desk, sifting through a growing pile of paperwork. Several empty plastic cups from the coffee machine and an ashtray filled with cigarette stubs testified to a long, all-night session. There was a light tap on his office door, and Detective Chief Inspector Manners let himself in without waiting for an invitation. There was a faintly chiding look on his face as he confronted Carney.

'Didn't see your name on the night-duty roster, Paul,' he observed pointedly.

Carney shrugged. 'Just catching up on some more of this fucking paperwork, when I ought to be out there on the streets. Bringing this week's little tally up to date.'

Manners clucked his teeth sympathetically. 'Bad, huh?'

Carney let out a short, bitter laugh. 'You tell me how bad is bad. In the last four days we've snatched five and a half kilos of coke at Heathrow alone. That means a minimum of twenty-five kilos got through. This morning we pulled a stiff off an Air India flight. Two hundred grand's worth of pure heroin in his guts, packed in condoms. One of 'em burst during the flight. What you might call an instant high.'

'Jeezus, I thought those things were supposed to *stop* accidents,' Manners said.

'Not funny, Harry,' Carney muttered. 'Christ, we're under fucking siege here. Provincial airports, the ferries, commercial shipping, private boats and planes, bloody amateurs bringing back ten kilos of hash from their Club 18-30 holidays on Corfu. And we haven't got a fucking clue yet what's going to come flooding in through the Channel Tunnel. There's shit coming at us from all sides, Harry – and we're being buried under it.'

'We . . . or you, Paul?' Manners asked gently.

Carney shrugged. 'Does it matter? Caring goes with the job.'

Manners conceded the point – with reservations. 'Caring, maybe. Getting too personally involved, no. You're getting in too deep, Paul. Maybe it's time to think about a transfer out of drugs division for a while.'

Carney blew a fuse. 'Dammit, Harry, I don't want a bloody transfer. What I want is to get this job *done*. I want every dealer, every distributor, every small-time school-gate pusher out of business, off the streets, and in the nick.'

'That isn't going to happen, and you know it.'

Carney nodded his head resignedly. 'Yeah. So meanwhile I'm supposed to just tot up the casualties without getting uptight – is that it?' He paused, calming down a little. 'I suppose you know we've got a batch of contaminated smack out on the streets in the SW area?'

Manners shook his head. 'No, I didn't,' he admitted. 'How bad is it?'

'Bad bad,' Carney muttered. 'Two kids dead already and one more in a coma on a life-support system. That's just the tip of the iceberg. We don't know yet how much more of the stuff is out there, or how widely it's already been distributed. And on top of that, there's this new synthetic shit which has started to come in from Europe. Early reports say that it's really bad medicine.'

Manners smiled sympathetically. 'OK, Paul, I'll get you what extra help I can,' he promised. 'Meanwhile, you go home and get some sleep, eh?'

Carney grinned cynically. 'We don't need help, my friend – we need a bloody army. That's a fucking war out there on the streets.'

'Yeah,' Manners said, and shrugged. There was nothing he could say or do which would make the slightest amount of difference. He turned back towards the door.

'Oh, by the way,' Carney called after him. 'You think I get too personally involved. You want to know why?'

Manners paused, his hand on the door-knob.

'The kid on the life-support system,' Carney went on. 'His name's Keith. He's fifteen. His parents live in my street.'

Glynis Jefferson studied the row of sordid-looking tenements through the windscreen of the Porsche with a distinct feeling of unease. This was definitely *not* Sloane Ranger country. This was ghettoland. Under normal circumstances, she would have jammed the car into gear and driven away as fast as she could. But tonight she was not in control; all normal considerations were driven out of her mind by her desperate craving. She checked the address on the slip of paper, identifying the block in question. Glancing nervously about her, she stepped out of the car and walked up to the front door. Rows of bells and small cards identified the building as divided into numerous bedsitters and flatlets.

The door was slightly ajar. Cautiously, Glynis pushed it open, wrinkling her nose in disgust at the stench of filth and squalor which wafted out. She stepped gingerly over the threshold into a dark, dingy and filthy hallway, littered with junk mail and other debris. For a moment her instincts screamed out at her to turn back, run away. But then the shudders shook her body again, a pain like a twisting knife shrieked through her guts. She walked down the hallway past a row of grimy doors, most with bars or metal grilles over the glazed top half.

She stopped at the fifth one and knocked urgently. There was a long pause before the door opened a few inches and a pair of shifty eyes inspected her through the crack. Obviously they liked what they saw. The door opened fully to reveal Tony Sofrides, grubby and unshaven, with dark, oiled hair hanging down to his shoulders in greasy, matted strands. He was wearing only a soiled T-shirt and a pair of equally filthy underpants. His eyes ran up and down Glynis's body as though she were a prime carcass hanging in a meat warehouse.

'Well, you're a bit out of your patch, aren't you, princess?' he drawled, noting her expensive night-club apparel. 'What's the matter? Lost our way to the Hunt Ball, have we?'

Glynis thrust the piece of paper under his nose. 'Nigel M sent me. I need to score.'

Sofrides snatched the paper out of her hand, scanning it with suspicious, furtive eyes. 'Did he now? Presumptuous little bastard, ain't he? So what did he tell you?'

'That you were a reliable supplier. I need Charlie. You holding?'

Sofrides leered at her, revealing a row of yellowed teeth. 'I'm always holding, baby,' he boasted. 'Regular little mister candy-man to those who know how to treat me right.' He stepped back from the door, inviting her to enter. 'Come on in, sweetheart.'

Glynis hesitated, despite her urgent craving.

Sofrides shrugged. 'Look, you wanna score or not? I don't do business in hallways and I ain't got time to fart about. Now you either come in or you fuck off. Your choice.'

Glynis made her choice. Reluctantly she stepped into the sordid bedsit, glancing around at the filth and mess in disgust as Sofrides closed the door behind her.

Catching the look on her face, Sofrides glared at her. 'No, darling, it ain't your daddy's country house in Essex, but it's where I live. So don't turn your pretty little nose up, OK?'

Glynis rummaged in her handbag and pulled out a thin wad of notes. 'Look, can we get this over with? I just want a couple of hits to tide me over, but I'll take more if you want to make a bigger deal.'

Sofrides glanced at the money contemptuously, returning his eyes to her body. 'Actually, darling, I'm not exactly strapped for cash right now,' he said. He paused, jerking his head over to the grimy, unmade bed in the corner of the room. 'But I am a little short on company, if you know what I mean. Wanna deal?'

Glynis shuddered – but this time it was mental revulsion rather than the desperate need of her drug-addicted body. 'No thanks,' she spat out, turning towards the door.

Sofrides jumped across the room, cutting off her retreat. 'Wise up, kid,' he said, grinning wickedly. 'It's four in the morning and I'm your last chance. Do you really think you can hold out for much longer?' He raised his hand, extending one finger and running it slowly across her lips, down her throat and into the cleavage of her breasts. 'Now, are we going to play or not?'

3

The sex was quick, violent and sordid. Afterwards Glynis felt dirty all over, and it wasn't just the accumulated sweat and grime clinging to the grey bedsheets. Thankful that it was over, at least, she dressed hurriedly as Sofrides lay back on his pillow, grinning with post-coital pleasure.

Glynis glared at him, undisguised loathing in her eyes. 'Right, you've been paid in full. Now what about my score?'

Sofrides leered at her. 'I got bad news for you, princess. Apart from having me tonight, you're right out of luck. Ain't a snort of coke in the place.'

It took several seconds for the words to sink into Glynis's mind. When it finally did, her first reactions were of shock and sheer panic, quickly followed by a wave of pure hatred. 'You lousy little bastard,' she screamed. 'You told me you were holding.'

She hurled herself across the room in a blaze of fury, her arms flailing wildly. Sofrides uncoiled from the bed like a snake, warding off the attack by grasping her by the wrist and twisting her arm savagely. Drawing back his free hand, he smashed her across one side of her face and backhanded her on the other. He pushed her to the floor, where she lay sobbing.

The dealer looked down at her without pity. He crossed slowly to a chest of drawers, opened it and pulled out a flat tobacco tin, which he tossed on to the bed. 'I got some smack, that's all. Take it or leave it.'

Glynis crawled to her feet, shaking and in pain both from the violence of his attack and her appalling craving. Uncertainly, she moved towards the bed and opened the tin. She stared dumbly at the loaded hypodermic syringe it contained.

'Well, come on, darling. I ain't got all night,' Sofrides challenged her, seeing her hesitation. He moved up beside her, taking out the syringe and thrusting it into her hand. 'Shoot up and get out, before I change my mind.'

Glynis stared at the syringe in horrified fascination. Her face was a mixture of desperation, fear and bewilderment. She glanced up at Sofrides, her eyes almost pleading.

His lips curled into a scornful sneer as he identified her problem. 'You little silver-plated spoon-sniffers. You've never shot up before, have you?'

Glynis could only nod.

'Here, I'll show you,' Sofrides said. He clenched his fist, pumping his forearm up and down half a dozen times. He pointed to his slightly throbbing vein. 'Just there, see? Just stick the needle in and push the plunger. That's all there is to it.'

Awkwardly, Glynis copied his movements, holding the syringe clumsily in a trembling hand, almost at arm's length. Fumbling and shaky, she pushed the gleaming point of the needle towards her arm.

Sofrides looked away, letting out a little snort of disgust. 'Oh Christ! Go in the bloody bathroom and do it, will you?'

Still unsure, Glynis slunk into the poky bathroom and closed the door behind her. Sofrides threw himself back on the bed, propped himself up with a pillow and lit a cigarette.

He plumed smoke up at the ceiling, grinning. He felt very pleased with himself.

The cigarette had burned down to a stub before he thought about the girl again. After crushing it out in the ashtray he pushed himself off the bed and strode to the bathroom door, rapping on it with the back of his hand. 'What the hell are you doing in there?' he demanded irritably. There was no answer.

He tried the door handle. It was unlocked. Sofrides pushed the door open to find Glynis sitting stiffly on the toilet, her head lolling back against the pipe from the cistern. The empty hypodermic dangled loosely from her fingers at arm's length. Her face was ghostly white, her eyes wide and staring and her body twitching convulsively and obscenely.

Sofrides looked at her without sympathy. 'Feel rough, huh? Don't worry. A couple of minutes and you'll be high as a kite.' He reached down to seize her by the elbow, and hauled her roughly to her feet. The empty syringe dropped from her fingers, shattering on the tiled floor.

'Come on, I want you out of here,' Sofrides told the girl curtly, as he tried to drag her out of the bathroom.

Glynis took a couple of shuffling steps and stopped, her legs sagging beneath her. She would have collapsed to the floor but for the dealer's grip on her arm. He pushed her back against the bathroom wall, propping her up. There was the first trace of concern on his face as he noted her wildly rolling eyes, the tremors which rocked her body and the shallowness of her breathing. Even as he watched, Glynis seemed to be torn by a convulsion of pain which caused her body to jack-knife and made her clutch at her abdomen with her free hand. She let out one long, shuddering groan and went limp, before sliding down the wall to sit on the floor like a puppet whose strings have just been cut.

'Oh shit!' Sofrides spat out in anger – but it was fear that registered on his face. He dropped to his knees, staring into the girl's wide, but unseeing eyes. They were completely still now, and her body was totally motionless. Panic rising in him, Sofrides snatched up her wrist, feeling for the faintest hint of a pulse. There was nothing.

Sofrides pushed himself to his feet and stood there shaking for a few seconds, his brain racing. He turned towards the telephone, thinking briefly about calling an ambulance but rejecting the idea almost immediately. The girl's face was already puffy and showing signs of bruising where he had struck her. He remembered the bite marks he had put in the soft flesh of her breasts during their brief sexual encounter. With his criminal record, reporting the girl's death was tanta-mount to placing himself on a manslaughter charge at the very least.

He tried to think, as he paced round the small bedsitter several times, trying not to look at the girl's lifeless form slumped just inside the bathroom door. He crossed to the room's single window and stared out into the dark and deserted street.

There was only one choice, he realized finally. Somehow, he had to get the girl's body into his car without being seen. After that it would be easy. London had hundreds of back-streets and alleyways where the body of a drug addict, drunk or vagrant turned up every so often. With nothing to connect the girl to him, she would be just another statistic.

His mind made up, as quietly as he could Sofrides began to drag Glynis's body towards the door.

Paul Carney tidied up the paperwork on his desk and switched off the Anglepoise lamp. Rising, he crossed to the door and switched off the main light, plunging his office into darkness.

Locking the door, he strode across the deserted main office towards the outer reception area.

The desk sergeant looked up at him, grinning, as he walked past. 'Barbados for our hols this year, is it, Mr Carney? Or a world cruise, with all this overtime you've been putting in?'

Carney smiled at the man wearily. 'Oh yeah, at least,' he muttered. 'Goodnight, Sergeant.'

The man nodded. 'Goodnight, sir.'

Carney walked out into the night air, taking a deep breath before heading for the rear car park. On reaching his Ford Sierra, he climbed in and drove slowly to the main gates. He was exhausted, yet in no hurry to get home. Or at least back to the Islington flat, Carney reminded himself, thinking about it. It had ceased to be a home when Linda had walked out, over six months earlier. She'd even taken the dog.

The roads were almost deserted. Carney cruised past the rows of darkened office buildings for a couple of miles before turning off into the residential back-streets around Canonbury. He passed a small row of shops, some with their windows still lit or showing dim security lights in their rear storage areas.

The grey Volvo took him by surprise, shooting out from a small side road only yards ahead of him. Carney stamped on the brakes instinctively, allowing the car to complete its left turn and accelerate away from him with a squeal of rubber on tarmac.

Crazy bastard, Carney thought, reacting as a fellow road-user. Then the copper in him took over, asking the obvious question. What could be so damned urgent, at four-thirty in the morning? He stamped down on the accelerator, making it his business to find out.

Carney caught up with the Volvo at the next set of traffic lights. He pulled across the vehicle's front wing and leapt

out of his own car. He wrenched the driver's side door of the
Volvo open.

'All right, you bloody moron. What the hell do you think
you're playing at?' he growled, before he had even seen who
was sitting at the wheel. There was a long, thoughtful pause
as he recognized the driver.

'Well, well, well,' Carney said slowly. 'If it isn't Tony the
Greek. And what particular form of nastiness are you up to
tonight, you little scumbag?'

Sofrides looked up at him with a fearful expression, cursing
the cruel vagaries of fate which had thrown Detective Sergeant
Paul Carney across his path this night of all nights. They'd
had run-ins before – almost every one of them to his cost.

'I ain't done nothing, honest, Mr Carney,' Sofrides whined,
desperately trying to bluff it out.

Carney grinned cynically. 'You don't have to do anything,
Tony. Just being in the vicinity constitutes major environmental
pollution.' He held the door back, jerking his head. 'Out.'

Reluctantly, Sofrides climbed out of the car, still protesting
his innocence. 'I'm clean, Mr Carney – honest.'

Carney shook his head. 'You wouldn't be clean if you
bathed in bleach and gargled with insecticide,' he grunted.
He paused, staring at the young man thoughtfully. There
was something wrong, something out of character. Sofrides
was not displaying his usual arrogance. He looked frightened,
guilty.

'What's wrong with you tonight, Tony?' Carney demanded.
'Where's all the usual backchat, the bullshit? You're scared,
Tony – and that makes me very suspicious indeed.'

Increasingly desperate, Sofrides tried to force a smile on
to his face. 'I told you, I ain't done nothing. I just don't feel
so good, that's all. Must have been something I ate.'

It wasn't going to wash. Carney was convinced he was on to something now. He peered at Sofrides's face more closely.

'I do have to admit that you don't look so good,' he muttered. 'In fact, Tony, you look as sick as the proverbial parrot.' He paused momentarily. 'Know what I think, Tony? I think you've just made a collection and I've caught you bang to rights. I think you're carrying a major consignment of naughties, that's what I think. The question is: what, and where?'

Carney suddenly seized Sofrides by the arm, forcing it up around his back in a savage half nelson. He frogmarched him over to his own car, opened it and pulled a pair of handcuffs out of the glove compartment. Snapping the cuffs around the young man's wrist, he pushed him back to the Volvo, wound down the window a few inches and clipped the other bracelet to the door-frame.

'So let's take a little look-see, shall we,' he suggested, returning to his own vehicle for just long enough to grab a powerful torch.

The Volvo seemed clean, much to Carney's disappointment. Sofrides watched him search thoroughly beneath and behind the seats, in the glove compartment and underneath the dashboard.

'See, I told you I ain't done nothing. So how about letting me go, Mr Carney?' Sofrides suggested hopefully.

Carney shook his head. 'We've only just got started, Tony. It'd be a pity to break the party up this early now, wouldn't it?' He straightened up from searching the interior of the car. 'Right, let's take a little look in the boot.'

A fresh glimmer of panic crossed Sofrides's eyes. 'Look, tell you what. Suppose I make you a deal?' he blurted out.

Carney sounded unimpressed. 'Oh yes, and what sort of deal would that be, Tony?'

Sofrides snatched at his slim remaining chance eagerly. 'I know a couple of new crack houses which have just opened up. I can give you names . . . places . . . times.'

Carney grinned wickedly at him. 'But you'll do that anyway, once I get you nailed,' he pointed out. 'You'll sing your little black heart out just as soon as you see the inside of the slammer. You'll have to do a bit better than that, Tony.'

Sofrides was really desperate now, clutching at straws. 'How about if I set someone up for you – someone big?' he suggested. 'I'm only a little fish, Mr Carney – you know that.'

Carney paused, tempted. 'And who might you have in mind?' he asked.

Sofrides picked a name at random. 'How about Jack Mottram? He deals in ten Ks at a time.'

Carney sighed wearily. The little bastard was trying to wind him up, he thought. 'Jack Mottram wouldn't piss on you if your arse was on fire,' he said scathingly. 'Now stop jerking my chain, all right?' He pulled the key to the hand-cuffs from his pocket, releasing them from the Volvo door. He grabbed Sofrides by the scruff of the neck, dragging him round to the back of the car and nodding down at the boot.

'Right, just so we don't hear any little whinges about planted evidence,' he muttered. 'Open it up and we'll take a little look in Pandora's box.'

For a moment, Sofrides was tempted to try to struggle free and run for it. As if sensing this, Carney tightened his grip. 'Don't even think about it, Tony. I could outrun a little lardball like you in twenty yards flat. Besides, you might have a little accident resisting arrest, and we wouldn't want that to happen, would we?'

Sofrides sagged, realizing he was beaten. His heart pounded in his chest as Carney turned the key and opened the boot, then shone the torch inside.

Carney was not prepared for the sight which greeted his eyes, and he was visibly shaken. It was revulsion, quickly followed by a wave of rage, which washed over him as the beam illuminated the girl's contorted body, her sightless eyes staring up at him out of her pale, bruised face.

'Jesus,' Carney muttered, with a long, deep sigh. His body quivered with shock and anger.

The desperate urge to run washed over Sofrides again at that moment. Not really thinking clearly, he twisted his body to break free from Carney's grip and jerked up one knee at his groin.

Carney's reactions were fast, but not quite fast enough to avoid contact altogether. Twisting his body, he winced with pain as Sofrides's savage blow connected with the side of his hip bone. That, on top of his grisly discovery, was enough to make Carney snap. His mind exploded in a red mist of pain and rage. Suddenly, everything came out – his tiredness, his frustration with the job, his total loathing of little low-lifes like Sofrides. He raised the heavy torch and smashed it against the side of the dealer's head, shattering the glass. Sofrides screamed in agony as Carney drove a full-blooded punch deep into his solar plexus and then cuffed him across the ear as he began to double up in agony. Several more blows followed as the policeman went berserk, venting the full force of his frustration in a few moments of blind, senseless violence. Finally he pushed Sofrides over the lip of the boot until he was half lying across the girl's body, and brought the heavy lid crashing down.

There was a last, agonized scream from Sofrides, then silence.

Mentally drained and utterly exhausted, Carney fell back against the side of the car, breathing heavily and cursing himself under his breath. Sanity had begun to return now, and he knew he'd gone too far.

There was no smile of greeting on the desk sergeant's face as Carney strolled into the station later that morning. 'Excuse me, sir, but the DCI asked me to tell you to report to his office as soon as you came in.'

Carney nodded. He had been expecting it. 'Thanks, Sergeant.' He headed straight for Manners's office and tapped lightly on the glass door.

'Come.' The man's tone was curt and peremptory. He stared grimly at Carney as he walked in. 'Sit down, Carney,' he snapped, pointing to a chair.

Carney did as he was told, his heart sinking. Harry Manners's use of his surname had given him a pretty good clue as to the severity of the dressing down he was about to receive. He looked across at his superior with what he hoped was a suitably contrite expression on his face.

There was a moment of strained silence before Manners spoke. 'Tony Sofrides is in the Royal Northern Hospital,' he announced flatly. 'He has two skull fractures, a broken arm, ruptured spleen and three cracked ribs.'

Carney could not resist the only defence he had. 'Christ, sir, did you see that girl?'

Manners nodded. 'I saw them both.' He paused for a moment, sighing heavily. 'Goddammit, man, what the hell got into you? Don't you realize you could have killed him?'

Carney hung his head, although there was a spark of defiance left. 'So what should I have done? Slapped his wrists and told him he'd been a naughty boy? Look, Harry, I know I blew my stack, and I'm sorry.'

Manners was shaking his head doubtfully. 'I don't think that's going to be enough – not this time.'

Carney realized for the first time that he was looking suspension, possibly dismissal, in the face. He could only presume upon their years together as colleagues, and as friends. 'Aw, come on, Harry. You can cover for me on this one, surely. There's a dozen shades of whitewash. Resisting arrest, assaulting a police officer, injured while trying to escape . . .' He tailed off, studying his superior's face.

Manners shook his head again. 'I'm not sure I can – and what's more to the point, I'm not sure that I should,' he said. 'The bottom line is that you had a chance to make a right-eous arrest and you blew it. Not only that, but you beat the shit out of the suspect as well. That's bad policework, and we both know it. It was sloppy, it was excessive – and it was dangerous.' He paused, sighing. 'And it's not the first time.'

There was a pleading look in Carney's eyes. 'Oh Christ, Harry. Don't throw that crap at me as well. Three isolated incidents, spread over fifteen years in the force. I've been a damn good copper, and you know it.'

Manners nodded regretfully. 'Yes, you have been a good copper, Paul. But you've got a touch of the vigilante in you, and that makes you a risk. One that I don't think I can afford to take any more.'

There it was, out in the open at last. Carney sighed heavily. 'So, what happens now? Are you going to suspend me? Or would you prefer me to do the honourable thing, and resign? Hand over my card and go the way of all ex-coppers and take a job as a private security guard?'

Manners fidgeted awkwardly. He was not finding his task at all pleasant. 'That's not your style, Paul – and we both know it.'

'Then what?' Carney demanded. 'Is there any kind of choice?'

Manners looked uncertain. He shrugged faintly. 'I don't know . . . there might be,' he murmured.

Carney snatched at the thin straw of hope. 'Well what is it, for Christ's sake?'

Manners looked apologetic. 'Sorry, Paul, but I can't tell you anything more at the moment. It's just something which has filtered down from the boys upstairs. I'd have to look into it more closely, and it might take a bit of time.'

'And meanwhile?' Carney asked.

'Meanwhile you take a rest, on my direct recommendation,' Manners said firmly. 'You're suffering from stress. Overwork, the sheer frustration of the job, you and Linda splitting up. Let's just call it a period of enforced leave for the time being, shall we?'

4

Maybe it wasn't such a crazy idea after all, Davies thought, on the drive back to Hereford. He'd spent the remainder of the previous day and most of the evening hammering out the bones of a workable scheme with Commander Franks and Commissioner McMillan, and they had made surprising progress.

What had particularly impressed him had been both men's total commitment to the job, and their willingness to be flexible. While he had not been given a total *carte blanche*, most of his ideas and suggestions had been listened to and given serious consideration. By the end of the day, they were all more or less in agreement as to the general size and structure of the unit they would create, and had a good idea of the sort of personnel who would make it up.

This factor alone had allowed Davies to take some vital first steps. After leaving the two policemen, he had checked into the Intercontinental Hotel and spent the rest of the night making a series of telephone calls. Most of the key personnel who would help set up the new force were already either on recall to active duty, or about to receive transfer orders. For obvious reasons, SAS officers with experience on the streets of Northern Ireland had been high on the list, along with individuals with particular skills or interests which might be required for such an unusual operation.

Now he was on his way back to Stirling Lines to start the tricky process of recruiting his foot soldiers, leaving Commander Franks to fulfil his promise to provide a nucleus of hand-picked police officers. It now seemed more than feasible that together they could merge the two interests and peculiar skills into a single, if somewhat hybrid, task force which could transpose the disciplines and tactics of a military force into a civil environment.

Only one thing had changed from the Home Secretary's initial briefing. For try as he might, Davies had been unable to share the man's conviction that the job could be seen as an operation for the SAS Training Wing. It had become increasingly clear to him that the task was in fact almost tailor-made for the Counter Revolutionary Warfare Wing. In many respects, the CRW team had already been doing that very job for a number of years. Davies intended to place the day-to-day operations of the new unit under their jurisdiction at the earliest opportunity and then duck out, remaining available solely as a liaison officer between SAS commanders and the Home Office should such contact prove necessary. That was the theory, anyway. But first came the people, for a unit was only a collection of individuals moulded to a common purpose. And finding the right individuals was crucial.

It would take a very special kind of young man to do the job properly, Davies was well aware. And young they would have to be, if Grieves's theories were correct and their enemy was deliberately targeting the youth culture. Infiltration might well prove their best weapon, at least in the early days, which effectively ruled out anybody over the age of twenty-five.

But they would also need to be sufficiently mature and stable enough to cope with the pressures and possibly the temptations they might be exposed to. They needed to be resourceful as well as tough, disciplined yet independent thinkers.

Davies nodded to himself thoughtfully as he pulled off the M4 at the junction which would bring him into the north-east suburbs of Hereford. Yes indeed – a very special breed of young man, for sure!

The white Escort shot through the red light and came screaming out of the side road into the main flow of traffic along Oxford Street. A collision was inevitable. The driver of the mail van stamped on his brakes and attempted to swerve, but was unable to avoid clipping the offside front wing of the Escort and spinning it round in a half-circle. The car bounced up the kerb, scattering terrified pedestrians in all directions, glanced off a bus stop and finally came to a halt half on and half off the pavement, facing the oncoming traffic. The squeal of brakes and the heavy thumps of a multi-vehicle pile-up continued for a full fifteen seconds. It was a nasty one. The shunts finally stopped, and there was a blessed few moments of silence before a concerto of angry car horns began to blare out.

Constable John Beavis slapped his forehead with the flat of his hand and let out a weary groan. It was only his second week of traffic duty and something like this had to happen. Even worse, he'd been due to go off duty in less than fifteen minutes and his daughter's school sports day started at twelve-thirty. He'd promised to be there to cheer her on in the three-legged race. He began to walk towards the long snake of crashed vehicles, counting them gloomily. This little mess looked like it would take a couple of hours to sort out.

He hurried past the line of irate drivers, ignoring the dozens of shouted complaints and curses which were hurled in his direction. The sight of a uniform seemed to give them all a scapegoat, someone to blame. Finally reaching the end of the line, he approached the white Escort which had started it all and peered in through the closed passenger window.

There were two occupants, both young. A male driver and a blonde female. Both sat rigidly in their seats, gazing fixedly straight ahead of them through the windscreen.

Constable Beavis rapped on the passenger door with his knuckles. There was no reaction from inside the car. The couple continued to stare blankly ahead, ignoring him. He banged the window again, more angrily. Neither occupant even glanced sideways. It was as if they were both totally oblivious of what was going on around them.

Beavis felt his anger rising. They were probably both dead-drunk, he thought, and it made his blood boil. It was a miracle that no one had been seriously injured, let alone killed. As he wrenched open the car door the girl turned to face him slowly, like a video replayed in slow motion. Her face was blank, utterly devoid of expression. Beavis felt the hairs on the back of his neck prickle slightly as he stared into her eyes. They were wide open, but vacuous, almost dead. Like two small green mirrors, they seemed to reflect back at him. Beavis noted the dilated pupils, the strange facial immobility, and came to a revised decision. Not drunk, worse than that. They were both stoned on drugs, blasted out of their minds, the pair of them.

His anger reached a peak and he thrust his hand into the car, grasping the girl by the arm. He wanted to pull her out, shake her, slap some life and some sense into her pretty, but stupid little face.

The girl's lips curled slowly into a scornful smile, which was almost a snarl. 'Fuck off, pig,' she hissed, with sudden and surprising vehemence. Then, sucking up phlegm from her throat, she spat full in his face.

The young man also came to life. As Beavis staggered back, clawing at his face and trying to clear the sticky spittle from his eyes, he reached forward to the car's dashboard locker, opened it and reached inside. His hand came out again holding a 9mm Smith & Wesson 39 series automatic pistol. With cool deliberation, he leaned across his passenger and brought the pistol up, taking careful aim. Then, with an insane little giggle, he shot the policeman straight through the forehead, between the eyes.

The youth lowered the gun again and unhurriedly opened the driver's side door. He climbed out, dragging his girlfriend behind him. Hand in hand, they crossed the paralysed road to the far pavement and began to stroll casually in the direction of Marble Arch, firing shots indiscriminately into the crowds of panicking shoppers.

Two hours later, Commissioner McMillan had a full report on his desk. He read it gloomily, digesting the horrific facts. The constable had died instantly, of course. Of the four subsequent victims, one young woman had been dead on arrival at hospital and an older woman was on life support and not expected to make it. The two other bullet wounds were serious, but not critical. The Escort, stolen two days earlier in West Hampstead, had contained several bundles of right-wing pamphlets and propaganda material, along with a Czech-built Skorpion machine-pistol in the boot. The couple had eventually disappeared, unchallenged, into the underground system. By now, they could be anywhere.

McMillan finished reading the report with a heavy, sinking feeling in the pit of his stomach. All the pieces seemed to fit the pattern. Pushing the document across his desk, he sighed heavily. So it had started already, he reflected bitterly. He'd been hoping they'd have a little more time.

5

Sergeant Andrew Winston took a careful and calculated look at the pot on the table before flicking his eyes over his hand again. It was not an easy call. Seventy-five quid in the pot, a fiver to stay in the game and he was holding a queen flush. Winston hesitated, feeling vulnerable. Three-card brag wasn't really his game; he was more of a poker man. He'd only allowed himself to be suckered in out of boredom.

'Come on, Andrew,' Andy Collins taunted him from across the table. 'Put up or fold up. Or are you chicken?'

Winston never got a chance to answer the challenge. A strange hand plucked the three cards from his hand, dropping them face down on the table.

'He's not chicken – he's just sensible.'

Winston whirled round, ready to jump to his feet and ready for a fight. Interfering with a man's gambling hand was serious business. He recognized Lieutenant-Colonel Davies at once, instantly relaxing. His face broke into a surprised grin. 'Hello, boss. What a coincidence, seeing you in this boozer.'

Davies shook his head. 'Not really. I was looking for you.'

Winston was still puzzled. 'How did you know I'd be here?'

Davies smiled. 'I didn't. But I've already been to just about every other pub in Hereford.' He nodded at the cards. 'Pick up your money. I need to talk to you.'

Winston looked uncertainly at the two players remaining in the game.

'Don't even worry about it,' Davies assured him. 'Collins wasn't your real threat, except he'd have kept you both in the game longer and cost you more money. Pretty Boy's the danger. My guess is that he's holding a run – or better.'

It was a prediction which was about to be put to the test. Emboldened by the fantasy that he had bluffed Winston out of the game, Collins dropped his jack flush triumphantly. 'See you, Pretty. Got you, I reckon.'

Pretty Boy Parrit shot him a scornful glance. 'You got to be fucking joking, my old son.' Slowly, deliberately, he laid out the king, queen and ace of spades and reached for the ashtray full of money.

Collins's face dropped. 'You spawny bastard. I thought you were bluffing.'

Pretty Boy grinned wickedly. 'Who dares wins,' he joked, scooping up the pot.

Impressed, Winston looked up at Davies. 'How did you know?'

Davies shrugged. 'Probably from playing a damned sight more games in the spider than you've had hot dinners. And from knowing men, being able to read faces.' It was an expression of quiet confidence, rather than a boast.

Winston pushed himself to his feet. 'But what if you'd been wrong?' he asked.

Davies grinned. 'I'd have paid you myself,' he said – and Winston had no doubts at all that the man was perfectly sincere.

'So, what did you want to talk to me about, boss?' Winston asked, after Davies had bought fresh pints and led the way to an empty table. Davies took a sip of his bitter, eyeing Winston over the top of the glass. 'Something's coming up,' he said flatly. 'And I want you in on it.' He paused for a few moments, savouring his beer. Finally, when the glass was half empty, he launched into a slightly edited account of the events of the past two days.

Winston listened carefully until Davies had completely finished. There was a slightly ironic smile on his face when he finally spoke. 'Excuse me for pointing it out, boss, but aren't you forgetting something rather important.'

Davies looked puzzled. 'What?'

Winston laughed. 'For Christ's sake, you're looking at it. Or are you getting colour-blind in your old age? I'm black, in case you hadn't noticed.'

Davies stared at the big Barbadian's grinning features with a perfectly straight face. 'Fuck me – are you?' he said, in mock surprise.

Both men shared the joke for a few moments, before Winston spoke again. His face was more serious now. 'No, seriously though, boss. If we're really talking about mixing with a bunch of these crazy fascist bastards, having me around ain't going to help much, is it?'

It was Davies's turn to be serious now. He felt a little awkward, knowing that he had to step on sensitive ground. 'Maybe *you're* forgetting something, Andrew,' he pointed out. 'Like it or not, the fact is that a high proportion of London's drug abuse occurs within the black community,' he went on, almost apologetically. 'You'll be able to get to places, gain the confidence of people who wouldn't give us poor honky bastards a chance.'

Winston conceded the point with a nod. 'Yeah, you're right there, boss. I hadn't thought of that.'

There was a moment of thoughtful silence. 'Well, what do you think?' Davies asked eventually. 'Do you want in?'

Winston didn't really need to think about it. He was normally a mild, easy-going man who never made a big thing out of race, and he was well aware that some of his more militant brethren would probably refer to him disparagingly as a white nigger for doing the job he did. But he had a quiet, but unshakeable pride – both as a man and as a black man. All extremes of bigotry offended his sense of decency and humanity. As he would sometimes say, if pressed on the matter: 'We all bleed the same colour.'

He looked Davies in the eyes, nodding his head firmly. 'I'm in,' he muttered. 'All the way.'

'Good.' Davies raised what was left of his pint by way of a toast. 'I'm calling a briefing in the Kremlin for 0900 hours on Thursday. Meanwhile, I'd like you to come up with a few names, if you can. You're closer to ground level than I am these days.'

'Who have we got so far?' Winston wanted to know.

There seemed no reason to withhold the information, Davies thought. He felt totally confident that he could count on the man's discretion. 'I've already called in Major Anderson from Belfast. And Captains Blake and Feeney will be at the meeting,' he said. 'With you on board, that should take care of the officer level. What we need now is a couple of dozen young but reliable troopers with plenty of recent experience in the Killing House. If we're putting combat-armed men out on the streets, they're going to need bloody fast reactions.'

Winston nodded in agreement. Davies was right about the last point. Knowing the difference between friend and foe was preferable in combat, but not absolutely crucial. Mistakes could, and did, happen – a death by 'friendly fire' was an unfortunate but accepted risk that every trooper took. If it happened, there would probably be an enquiry, but not a major scandal. The same could not be said for a mistake being made among the civilian population. One innocent person shot by mistake, and at least seven different flavours of shit would hit the fan.

That was where the 'Killing House' came into its own. Officially known as the SAS Close Quarter Battle building, it created remarkably lifelike situations in which mock battles could take place – often demanding lightning-fast reactions and split-second judgement by the combatants. At any moment they might be confronted by a dummy or pop-up target which could be anything from a terrorist with an Armalite to a blind man wielding his stick. Hesitate and you were dead, losing valuable points. Shoot too hastily and you risked being sent back to basic training, or worse. More than one SAS hopeful had been RTU'd purely on poor performance in the Killing House.

'You'll also be needing at least four specialist snipers, of course,' Winston added.

Davies nodded. 'And a couple of men with Bomb Squad training, and at least two good demo men,' he confirmed. 'But the fundamental requirement is going to be youth, which will probably mean a fairly high proportion of probationers. That's why sheer quality is so vital on this one. We won't have any leeway for any guesswork, or don't-knows. Every unit boss will have to have absolute and implicit trust in every single man under his command.'

Winston thought about it for a few seconds, finally whistling through his teeth. 'That's a pretty tall order, boss.'

Davies nodded at him. 'I know – a shitty job with a lot of responsibility. That's why I'm asking you for your personal recommendations.'

'Well, thanks, boss,' Winston muttered, grinning ruefully. Being put on the spot like that was something of a backhanded compliment. He nodded discreetly over towards the table where the card game was still in progress. 'Off the cuff, I'd say that Pretty Boy would be a rather good contender. He seems like a real laid-back bastard at times, but he's got the reactions of a bloody mongoose.'

Davies cast a brief glance in the man's direction. 'Any specials?' he wanted to know.

Winston nodded. 'Explosives and demolition. That man can blow a hole in a building wall without rattling the windows.'

It was a wild exaggeration, but Davies knew what he meant. 'Age?' he asked.

Winston shrugged. 'Twenty-eight, but he looks younger. And his accuracy scores on the range are impressive.' Winston broke off to grin. 'Despite his nickname, he's not just a pretty face.'

It was time for a more direct and important question, and Davies asked it. 'Would you want him covering your back?'

There was not a second of hesitation. 'Rather him than a hundred others,' Winston stated unequivocally.

Davies took the personal recommendation at face value. 'All right, bring him in,' he said quietly. He drained his beer and pushed himself to his feet, adding: 'Well, I'll leave you to go and lose some more money.'

Winston looked at him sheepishly, then grinned. 'Your confidence in me is totally underwhelming, boss.'

6

Paul Carney's telephone rang. It was by far the most exciting thing that had happened to him in two days. He virtually jumped across the flat to snatch it up.

'Paul?' The voice on the other end of the phone was hesitant, almost apologetic.

And so it ought to be, Carney thought, recognizing the caller as DCI Manners. The man had, after all, virtually suspended him. His response was somewhat less than enthusiastic. 'Yeah?' he grunted. 'What is it?'

There was a long sigh on the other end of the line as Manners got the message. It was more or less the reaction he had been expecting. 'Look, Paul, about that special job I mentioned to you,' he muttered, finally. 'They want to see you.'

'They? Who's they?' Carney asked guardedly.

'Sorry, Paul, but I can't tell you that,' Manners apologized. 'But there are a couple of Special Branch officers on their way round to your flat now. I'm sure they will explain everything to you.'

Eagerness, and the air of mystery, had already raised Carney to a pitch of anticipation. A sense of frustration was not far behind.

'Special Branch?' Carney queried irritably. 'For Christ's sake, Harry, what's going on here?'

'Sorry, but that's all I can tell you for the minute,' Manners said flatly. He had only the sketchiest idea of what was going on himself, and he'd been pressed to secrecy. Whatever the full facts were, they were well above the level of a mere Detective Chief Inspector. Even as a friend, there was nothing he could tell his colleague on that score. There was, however, something he *could* say, and he needed to say it.

'There's one other good piece of news I think you ought to know,' Manners went on after a brief pause. 'You know that batch of contaminated heroin you were worried about? The stuff that killed the girl?'

Carney jumped on it immediately. 'Yeah. What about it?'

'We've pulled it in – hopefully the whole lot,' Manners told him. 'And you were right – it was real bad shit. Adulterated up to seventy per cent and cut with bleaching powder, among other things. Lethal.'

Carney let out a sigh of relief. 'Yeah, thanks, Harry. That is good news. How did you get on to it?'

'Sofrides talked,' Manners told him. 'He led us straight to his supplier. A callous little bastard out for a quick profit and damn the consequences.' He was silent for a while. 'Just thought you'd like to know, that's all.'

'Yeah, thanks.' Carney felt equally awkward, not sure what to say to his boss. The line was silent for a long time.

'Well, good luck – whatever happens,' Manners said finally, and hung up.

Carney slipped the receiver back into its cradle and began to pace about the flat, trying to figure out what was going on. He did not have to wait very long. Less than three minutes after the call from Manners, there was a light but firm knock on the door.

There were two men standing in the hallway as Carney opened up. They both looked businesslike and efficient. They were unsmiling.

'Paul Carney?' one of them asked.

Carney nodded. The two men exchanged a brief glance and took the admission as an invitation to enter. They stepped across the threshold, the second man closing the door behind him.

Minutes later, Carney was in the visitors' car, being driven south to New Scotland Yard.

McMillan gestured to a vacant chair at the table. 'Please sit down, Carney. Would you care for a drink?'

Carney felt himself tense up, both physically and mentally. Was this the opening move in some sort of test? he found himself wondering. Coppers weren't supposed to drink on duty. So did they want to see if he lived by the book?

He forced himself to relax, rationalizing the situation. All this secrecy was making him paranoid, he decided. The offer was probably an innocent and genuine one. Besides, he wasn't officially on duty any more, and he could certainly do with a drink. He nodded, finally. 'Yes, thank you, sir. A Scotch would be fine.'

The commissioner allowed the faintest smile to cross his face. So Carney was a man, and not just some order-following drone. Carney noticed the smile, realized that he *had* been tested, and could only assume that he had passed.

McMillan stood up, opened a filing cabinet and pulled out a bottle of Glenfiddich and a chunky tumbler. He splashed a healthy measure into the glass and carried it over to Carney before resuming his place at the table. He looked at Carney thoughtfully for a while. 'Well, no doubt you've been wondering what all this is about,' he said at last.

Carney allowed himself a small grin. 'You could say that, sir.'

Commander Franks consulted a slim dossier on the desk in front of him. He studied its contents for a few seconds before looking up at Carney. 'Your superior says you're a tough cop, Carney,' he said. 'You know the streets and you know your enemy.'

Carney shrugged. 'I just handle my job, sir.'

Franks nodded. 'But unfortunately you can't always handle your temper,' he pointed out. It was a statement of fact, not quite an accusation, but Carney was immediately defensive.

'I just hate drugs. And I hate the villains who are pushing them to our kids,' he said with feeling.

'As do we all,' Franks observed. 'But our job places certain restrictions upon us. We have to work to specific rules, standards of behaviour which are acceptable to society. You went over the top, Carney – and you know it.'

It was an open rebuke now, inviting some sort of apology. Carney bowed his head slightly. 'Yes, sir, I'm aware of that. And I'm sorry.' He did not attempt to justify his actions in any way.

It seemed to satisfy Franks, who merely nodded to himself and glanced across at McMillan, passing some unspoken message. The commissioner leaned across the table, resting his elbows on it and forming a steeple with his fingers. 'Right, gentlemen,' he announced in a businesslike tone. 'Let's get down to it, shall we?'

For the next forty-five minutes Carney faced an almost non-stop barrage of questions. Some seemed totally irrelevant, and a few were of such a highly personal nature that he found himself becoming irritated by what he thought were unwarranted intrusions into his private life. As the session drew to an end, however, he began to realize that the three men in that room now knew just about everything there was to know about Paul Carney the policeman and Paul Carney the man. His opinions, his personality, his strengths – and his weaknesses. It was a rather disconcerting feeling.

Finally McMillan glanced at each of his colleagues in turn, inviting further questions. There were none. He turned his attention back to Carney.

'Let's get to business, then. It would appear that you need a job, Mr Carney. We have one for you, if you want it. A very special job, I might add.' He paused. 'Are you interested?'

Carney was guarded. 'I suppose that would have to depend on what the job was,' he said.

'Ah,' McMillan sighed thoughtfully. 'Now that gives me something of a problem. Basically, I cannot give you any details about the job until you agree to take it. You will also be required to take a grade three security oath.'

Carney was flabbergasted – and it showed on his face. He gaped at McMillan for several seconds before finally finding his voice. 'With respect, sir, that's crazy. How can I agree to a job without knowing what it is? It might not suit me. I might not suit it. I couldn't be a pen-pusher, buried behind some pile of papers, for a start.'

McMillan smiled faintly. 'I appreciate your candidness, Mr Carney,' he murmured. 'But I can and do assure you that far from being desk-bound, you'd be out there fighting crime. In the very front line, so to speak.' He paused briefly. 'But that's all I *can* tell you at this point. It's now completely down to you. We can proceed no further without your agreement.'

Carney's head was spinning. In desperation, he looked over at Commander Franks. 'If I turn this down, sir, what are the chances of my being returned to normal duty?'

Franks shook his head slowly. 'None,' he said, bluntly. 'The very qualities which make you attractive to us also preclude your continued service in the conventional police force.'

The finality of this statement was enough to push Carney over the edge. He made his decision on impulse as much as anything. 'All right, so let's say I'm in,' he muttered, still slightly dubious.

McMillan nodded gravely and signalled to Grieves, who produced an official-looking document from his pocket and slid it over the table towards Carney. 'Read and sign this,' he said curtly.

Carney scanned it quickly, eager to find some clue as to what he was letting himself in for, but the document itself told him virtually nothing. Finally he looked up at Grieves again, who silently handed him a fountain pen. Hesitating for just a moment, Carney read the security oath aloud and signed the paper. McMillan and Franks added their own signatures as witnesses and Grieves returned the document to his pocket. It was done.

'Right. Now we can tell you what we have in mind,' McMillan said. He began to launch into a detailed account of the plans formulated thus far.

7

'I'll tell you right away that I have some serious reservations about this whole concept,' Barney Davies said candidly. 'But I agreed to treat it as a workable idea, and you're the man they've sent me. So if we can work something out, we will.'

Carney tried to think of a suitable rejoinder, and failed completely. An opening speech like that was a hard act to follow. And he was already feeling a little out of his depth anyway.

He'd been ordered to report to Lieutenant-Colonel Davies at SAS HQ in Hereford, and that's what he'd done. Merely passing through the gate guard had been like walking into the lion's den. Like most civilians, Carney had only a sketchy picture of the SAS and how they worked. Fact was thin on the ground, and the man in the street could only form his own mental image from the fiction and the legend. And that legend was of a special breed of super-heroes, just one step removed from Captain Marvel or Superman.

'I'll try to keep that in mind, sir,' he managed to blurt out eventually.

Davies smiled. 'Lesson one,' he said. 'We don't place a great deal of emphasis on rank in the SAS. A man is respected for what he is, what he can do, rather than the extra bits of material sewn on to his uniform. In your case, as you're basically an outsider, and a largely unknown quantity, you'll be just another trooper. So don't expect any deference from the rest of the men you'll be working with. To them, you'll be just another probationer.' Davies paused, his tone softening a shade. 'And you don't have to call me "sir", by the way. "Boss" is perfectly acceptable.'

Davies flipped quickly through the file which Commander Franks had faxed to him. 'So you think you're tough,' he muttered, without condescension.

Carney bristled slightly. 'I don't think anything,' he protested. 'But I can look after myself, if that's what you mean.'

Davies nodded, looking faintly pleased. 'Good. You don't allow yourself to be put down too easily. But don't get any inflated ideas. Keep in mind that any one of my men could probably fold you up, stick a stamp on you and stuff you in the second-class post before you even knew what was happening.'

Carney took this somewhat colourful piece of information at face value. It was delivered not as a boast but as a hard fact – and he found himself believing it.

'I assume Commissioner McMillan has already briefed you as to the general theory?' Davies went on.

Carney nodded. 'You want me to advise a special task force. Basically point you in the right direction.'

Davies nodded again. 'In a nutshell, yes. But you'll be more than just an adviser, more like a seeing-eye dog. We're going to need a man on the ground. Someone who knows the right people and the right places.'

'Or the wrong people and the wrong places,' Carney suggested.

Davies found this mildly amusing, and smiled. 'Whatever.' He was thoughtful for a while. 'Of course, in an ideal world you should never be required to get involved in a combat situation. However, we don't live in an ideal world. There may be times when you find yourself up front. What have you done in the way of weapons training?'

Carney gave a faint shrug. 'Standard police training. Revolver and some sniper rifle practice.'

Davies consulted Carney's file again. 'Not bad scores,' he observed, in a matter-of-fact tone. It was the nearest thing to a compliment he had given out so far. He made a note on the file. 'But we'll check it out in a minute.' He eyed Carney up and down like a piece of meat. 'When was your last physical?'

Carney had to think about it. 'I'm not sure,' he admitted. 'Probably about five or six months ago.'

Davies made another note. 'We'll have to do something about that, as well.' He looked at Carney appraisingly. 'You look reasonably fit. Do much in the way of training, working out?'

Carney shrugged. 'Just regular health club stuff, once or maybe twice a week. Weights, bike machine, a couple of miles on the rolling road.'

'Sports? Pastimes?' Davies asked.

Carney smiled ruefully. 'Don't get a lot of time these days. I used to climb a bit, and I was junior squash champion at school.' He studied Davies's eyes carefully, noting that the SAS man was unimpressed. 'Actually, all this raises something I wanted to talk to you about,' he said.

Davies raised one eyebrow. 'Which is?'

Carney paused for a second, framing his thoughts. 'Look, I have a pretty fair idea of the sort of men I'm going to have to work with,' he started out. 'And I'm prepared for the fact that there's quite likely to be a certain amount of resentment – me being an outsider and all.'

Davies made no attempt to deny it. There would have been no point. However, it was good that Carney appeared to have a realistic viewpoint. He eyed him thoughtfully. 'So what's the point you're trying to make?'

Carney took the bull by the horns. 'If I'm to stand any chance of gaining the men's respect, I know I'm going to have to earn it,' he said quietly. 'That's why I'd like to get involved at ground level, if it's at all possible. What are the chances of my joining some of the men in basic training?'

Davies was impressed – both with the man's accurate assessment of the situation and with his bottle. He smiled thinly. 'Have you got the faintest idea of what you might be talking yourself into?' he asked.

Carney was perfectly truthful. 'No,' he admitted. 'But I'd still like to give it a go.'

Davies's smile broadened. 'Look, it's fairly obvious that, like most members of the general public, you have a somewhat simplistic view of how we operate,' he said, without sounding patronizing. 'It's not a question of "six weeks basic training and you're in the SAS". All our volunteers are already highly trained soldiers. Our selection training is short, brutal and perhaps the most intensive in the world – but it doesn't just stop there. Basically, an SAS soldier never stops training from the day he joins the Regiment to the day he leaves. It's an ongoing thing.'

Carney digested all this information stoically. 'All right, I concede that I'm not prime material to start with. But I'd like to get some time in with the men.'

Davies was more and more convinced that Franks had sent him the right man, but he wasn't giving anything away. He merely nodded faintly. 'OK, I'll see what can be arranged,' he promised as he rose to his feet. 'But right now, let's get you down to the range and see what you can do.'

He ushered Carney out of the room and along a long corridor, eventually stopping by a steel-shuttered door. Producing a security key from his pocket, Davies unlocked the heavy door and swung it open, revealing a flight of concrete steps which led down into the basement. As the door opened, a barrage of loud noise echoed up the stairs. It took Carney a few seconds to identify it as the sounds of gunfire in an enclosed space. He followed Davies down the stairs and through another security door, finally stepping into the vast underground indoor firing range.

The sudden appearance of Lieutenant-Colonel Davies seemed to act as some sort of signal. The half a dozen or so troopers using the target range discharged their weapons quickly, put them down and walked away. Davies led the way over to a shooting booth next to the armourer's office, summoning the man with a click of his fingers.

The armourer stepped over smartly, slipped a fresh clip into a handgun and laid the weapon down.

'What have you used in the past?' Davies asked, glancing at Carney.

'Standard-issue army Webley .38 revolver,' Carney told him.

Davies nodded, picking up the semi-automatic in front of him. 'We tend to use these,' he explained. 'The Browning 9mm High Power handgun. They've been around for a good few years now, but we find they do the job.' He picked the gun up and thrust it into Carney's hand.

Carney weighed the weapon, assessing its feel. It was somewhat lighter than the heavy pistols he was used to, yet oddly it felt somehow more solid, more real. Instinct told him that this was not a gun which had been designed, or ever intended for, making holes in paper targets. This was a weapon expressly created to kill people.

Davies quickly ran through the weapon's operation, finishing with basic safety instructions. 'You've got eight shots in that magazine,' he said, 'although normally it'll hold up to thirteen. Don't put it down, or point it away from the target area, until you've emptied it.'

Carney moved into the firing position, spreading his feet slightly and balancing his body. Holding the gun in the approved two-handed grip, he squinted down the sights towards the black silhouette at the end of the range.

'Carry on,' Davies muttered.

Carney squeezed gently on the trigger, loosing off the first three rounds before checking the target. All three shots were high – the semi-automatic had a greater kick than he was accustomed to. Lowering his aim to compensate, he tightened his grip and fired off three more rounds. They were better – both body hits. He put the final two slugs smack in the middle of the target's blank black face and laid the gun down again.

'Not bad,' Davies said, with grudging approval, as the armourer slid over and inserted a fresh clip into the magazine. 'But don't be too obsessed with going for head shots. The traditional "double tap" through the forehead isn't quite as fashionable now as it used to be.'

Carney looked at him in some surprise. 'I thought a guaranteed kill was the object of the exercise?' he said.

Davies nodded. 'Oh, it is. Basic SAS philosophy is that you don't point a gun at someone unless you fully intend to kill him. But there can be other factors.'

Carney was intrigued. 'Such as?'

Davies shrugged. 'Suppose we were dealing with a hostage situation, involving armed terrorists,' he suggested. 'The prime consideration would be to neutralize the gunmen before they could do any harm and to protect the hostages as much as possible. Think about it, Carney – a head is a small target, and the human body is a bigger one. Accurate, sustained fire to the body is going to put your man down just as efficiently, but with less loose bullets flying about the place.' He paused, nodding down at the the gun in front of Carney. 'That's why the Browning is a good weapon. It has real stopping power.'

There was a sudden crash from behind them as the inner steel door was kicked open. It was followed, almost immediately, by the roar of an angry voice. 'I warned you, Davies – you bastard!'

Carney whirled round, to take in the burly figure of the soldier who had just burst into the underground range. His eyes were blazing cold rage, and his mouth was contorted into a mask of fury. They were looks that could kill – and the L1A1 self-loading rifle that he carried slung at his hip gave him the capacity to do exactly that.

'I told you what would happen if you turned down my transfer,' the man raged on, moving purposefully towards Davies. 'Now I'm going to kill you, you bastard.'

Out of the corner of his eyes, Carney was aware of the armourer trying to edge towards the arsenal. The movement was also noted by the armed intruder, who barked out a warning: 'Don't even fucking think about it.' He advanced upon them inexorably, his finger curled lazily around the trigger of the rifle.

Perhaps foolishly, the armourer made a quick and desperate grab for a gun. The rifle bucked twice in the soldier's grip. The armourer let out a brief cry of pain as the two shots cracked out, then began to sink to his knees, clutching his hand to his belly.

Carney's guts churned over. He had no doubt now that he was going to die. It was so stupid, so pointless, that he felt a seething, blinding anger more than anything else. It was this, and a sense of desperation, which made him act instinctively, without thinking.

He pivoted on the balls of his feet with grace which would not have disgraced a Russian ballet dancer. In one smooth movement, he snatched up the loaded Browning and dropped to the floor, rolling away from Davies and bringing the gun up into position.

The sudden action took the soldier unawares. He had not been prepared for the intervention of a civilian. In the fraction of a second it took him to recognize the threat, and to swing the rifle in its direction, Carney had fired off three shots. The soldier stopped dead in his tracks, the rifle dropping from his hands. Then, soundlessly, he collapsed to the floor.

Carney was trembling all over. He found it hard to catch his breath. The jolt of adrenalin which had surged through his system had put his mind and body into overdrive. He could not think clearly, other than register the fact that he had just killed a man. Wide-eyed and questioning, he could only gape at Davies's face as though the man could offer him some sort of an explanation.

None was offered. Davies's face was impassive, composed. He seemed perfectly calm, as though nothing out of the ordinary had happened. Carney's brain reeled. It was as if the man had no emotions at all, nerves of absolute steel.

Then Davies began to smile, to Carney's further astonishment.

'Good, you have no compunction about killing in a crisis situation,' he murmured with quiet satisfaction. 'Quite a few people won't, you know – even when their lives are directly threatened. They tend to freeze up – until it's too late.'

Carney could understand none of it. Still bemused with shock, he tore his eyes away from Davies's face to the soldier on the floor.

The man was scrambling to his feet now, a broad smile on his black face. The armourer, too, had miraculously recovered and was once again standing calmly beside the gun store.

'Blanks, of course,' Davies said casually. 'Just a little test, you understand. You passed, by the way.'

Carney felt like hitting him. Instead he forced himself to breathe slowly and deeply until he started to feel reasonably normal again. His victim was standing beside him now.

'Mr Carney, meet Sergeant Andrew Winston,' Davies said by way of introduction. 'You'll be working quite closely with him. Winston writes poetry and kills people – and does them both very well indeed.'

Winston extended a hand. 'Hi,' he said.

Carney had no choice but to take it. He received a warm, hearty handshake. 'You were fast,' the big Barbadian complimented him. 'Bloody fast, as it happens.'

'I said you'd be working closely together. I don't expect you to fall in love with each other,' Davies said mockingly. He clapped his hands together, rubbing them in a gesture of satisfaction. 'Well, gentlemen, now that's all over, perhaps we should retire to the Paludrine Club for a drink.'

8

Three weeks later, Paul Carney was a much fitter, wiser man, and bore a deep and lasting respect for the men of 22 SAS, along with a fierce pride in his involvement with them.

True to his word, Lieutenant-Colonel Davies had cleared it for him to train alongside his military colleagues. The first few days had been sheer hell, the next two weeks worse, but Carney had come out of the experience with a whole new perspective on things. He now knew that it was possible to push the human body, and the human spirit, to the limits of pain and beyond the boundaries of endurance. And he was beginning, slowly, to understand the almost mystical sense of group pride and loyalty which bound together the men of the finest combat regiment in the world.

His initial fears about his acceptance by the rest of the men had been proved right. For the first few days he had simply been ignored. And when that had ceased to be a feasible proposition he had been treated with guarded suspicion, even hostility. Then came the jokes at his expense, the insults and the humiliation, culminating in a series of cruel practical jokes, many of them bordering on the savage. For days after the ragging finally ceased, Carney found it difficult to readjust himself to the taste of tea which had not been enhanced with the flavour of piss.

But he'd stuck through it all, with dogged determination. He'd learned to survive a twenty-mile route march across rugged hill country with a 24-lb bergen strapped to his back. He'd faced extreme weakness from near-starvation and learned how to appease his hunger by eating raw slugs and snails and the roots of certain wild plants and grasses. But most of all, and perhaps most importantly, he'd learned the strange exultation of knowing himself to be a survivor against adversity and a rare breed of man. A strong individual – and yet an even stronger member of a team, a unit. Carney felt he had been granted a great privilege afforded to few men.

He had won the men's respect, if not yet their full acceptance. That would take time; perhaps it might never fully occur. It didn't really matter. What did matter was that the team had been formed, and it worked: a quartet of four-man patrol units, forming a full troop, which would serve as the sharp end of the operation. With intelligence backup and a further eight troopers on standby, they were all set up and ready to go. Davies had already granted them their autonomy, as he had always intended. Having fulfilled his original brief, he no longer had an active role to play, and the SAS had little use or regard for padding.

There remained only a final briefing, and their first assignment. That, as it happened, was closer than anyone yet suspected.

They were all assembled in the Kremlin, the SAS Operations Planning and Intelligence cell at Stirling Lines. Major Mike Anderson, recalled from undercover work in Northern Ireland, had been assigned Troopers Phil 'Jumbo' Jackson, Eddie Mentieth and Pete Delaney. All were recently badged, having completed their fourteen weeks of Continuation

Training only two months earlier. The second unit, headed by Captain Barry 'Butch' Blake, also consisted of three probationers and was the stuff of an 'Englishman, Irishman and Scotsman' joke, cockney Mike Peters, Jimmy Phelan and Ian 'Aberdeen' Angus.

Captain Brian Feeney's unit was complemented by another mixed bag, with the mercurial blend of Scouser Ted Brennon, Cornishman Miles Tremathon and the sole Welshman of the troop, Hugh Thomas. The 'North–South' split of the group was largely held in check by Hugh, who had already earned himself the nickname of the Lethal Leek, from his prowess in CQB, close-quarter battle.

Officially Carney was not attached to any particular unit, his role being somewhat vaguely defined as adviser to all four. Yet he found it almost impossible not to associate himself with Andrew Winston, with whom he had established a strange bond which was not quite friendship, not quite trust. Backed up with Pretty Boy Parrit, the unit was brought up to full strength by the addition of young troopers Terry Marks and Tony Tofield, the pair of them known throughout the Regiment as Tweedledum and Tweedledee, from their habit of staying close together. A few years older than most of the others, Winston had picked them mainly because he knew and trusted them implicitly, both of them having accompanied him on a particularly hazardous mission in the mountains of Kazakhstan, in the former Soviet Union, several months previously.

The assembled men waited for David Grieves, the man from the 'green slime', to give them a briefing update and final clearance to go into operation. After that, they would largely be on their own, and the meeting would open out into a 'Chinese Parliament' in which every man, regardless of rank, was free to have his say.

Grieves arrived and took the rostrum, facing them squarely. 'Gentlemen, we now have a name for our enemy,' he announced, a trifle melodramatically. 'The drug goes under the street name of Nirvana.' He paused, a thin and rueful smile on his lips. 'For those of you not clued up on oriental religions and mysticism, it's a word which Buddhists use to describe a state of supreme inner peace. Particularly ironic, since this drug has the exact opposite effect.'

'You mean like a bloody laxative?' Ted Brennon shouted out, raising a guffaw of laughter from the rest of the men.

Major Anderson shot him a withering glance. Until Grieves had finished, he was still nominally in charge by virtue of rank. Bullshit from the men would only be tolerated once the Chinese Parliament was under way.

Grieves took the brief interruption in his stride. 'With what limited tests our forensic scientists have been able to conduct, it is estimated that the use of this drug raises natural aggression levels by between fifty and sixty per cent,' he went on. 'In other words, anyone under the influence of this substance is at least one and a half times more likely to commit an act of violence, even sadism. Of course, this rough guide becomes somewhat meaningless if the user happens to be of a violent nature to start with. Even worse, we don't yet know what the build-up factor is likely to be. Continued use may well raise these aggression levels on an exponential, and possibly permanent, scale.'

Carney put up his hand, attracting Grieves's attention. 'Form and administration?' he asked.

Grieves knew exactly what he meant. 'Currently we believe it is being produced as a pill, the active chemicals contained within an inert and largely harmless base compound. However, because the drug works in incredibly low dosages, and has a high absorption factor in humans, it may also occur in microdot form.'

Carney accepted the information stoically, although from his point of view it was probably the worst possible scenario. Pills were the most popular form of drug-taking with thrill-seeking kids, especially the very young. Current drugs such as Ecstasy had made massive inroads into new markets by virtue of the fact that they appealed to a whole new genera-tion of kids who might balk at injecting themselves or inhaling crack. Pills and microdots had a perceived image of being 'clean', even fashionable.

There was another negative factor. Given quite moderate production facilities, pills were quick and easy to manufacture and simple to distribute. And tracing that distribution network would be more difficult, since the established and fairly well-known chain of needle-users was virtually useless.

As Carney pondered on these problems Grieves continued his briefing.

'We're pretty sure that the drug originated in Germany, and the initial distribution through mainland Europe was controlled from there,' he went on. 'However, that is no longer the case. Production facilities are now beginning to pop up all over the place.' Grieves paused for some time before coming to the main point of his address.

'And here's the good news, gentlemen,' he announced finally. 'We are pretty sure we have already identified one of these factories operating from a disused farm in Norfolk. Busting that factory will be your first assignment.'

Grieves stepped back from the rostrum, indicating that he had said what he wanted to say. The meeting was now open.

Major Anderson climbed to his feet. 'But surely that should be a job for the conventional police forces?' he queried. 'Isn't sending us in rather like taking a sledgehammer to crack a walnut?'

Grieves shook his head grimly. 'The German police, fully armed, tried a similar operation just over two weeks ago,' he said. 'They lost five men. We don't want to take that sort of risk, and besides, it gives you an early chance to try yourselves out. Hopefully, it will also serve as a warning to these bastards that we're not going to take the soft approach. It may be a slim hope, but if we could frighten them off before they get really established in the UK, we might save ourselves a whole lot of trouble.'

'So basically what we're talking about here is sending one load of psychotic bastards in after another load of psychotic bastards?' Pretty Boy observed facetiously.

The comment evinced a wave of groans and protest.

'You speak for yourself, Pretty Boy,' Aberdeen Angus shouted out. 'I'm as sane as the next man.'

This claim was hotly disputed by most of the other troopers, several of them pointing out the fact that he was, in fact, sitting next to the lethal Leek, who was widely known to be as barmy as a bedbug. The Welshman's predictable arguments of self-defence were in turn rubbished by various accusations of sheep-shagging and other unsavoury practices in the Black Mountains.

Major Anderson let the men enjoy their few moments of good-natured ragging. It was something of a tradition, if not standard SAS procedure, to indulge in a bullshit session after a briefing. Rising from his chair, he strolled over to Carney, who was sitting beside Winston.

'Look, you're the nearest we've got to an expert on drugs abuse,' he muttered. 'Why the hell should kids want to dose themselves up on something which is going to drive them crazy. That's what I fail to understand.'

Carney could only shrug. It was a question he'd been asked many times before, and he still didn't have an adequate answer.

'Why not?' he asked. 'They've been doing equally stupid things for years. Shooting shit into their veins which they know to be addictive and physically destructive. Popping amphetamines which turn brain tissue into something resembling gruyere cheese. Deliberately tripping out into the world of nightmares and insanity.' He paused, letting it sink in. 'So why not this new drug? Something which raises violence into a near-ecstatic experience would seem almost a natural for some of these kids. It's the ultimate trip for the nineties. Just look at a bunch of football hooligans on the rampage.'

Anderson stared at him piercingly. 'You're a cynical bastard, aren't you?' he observed.

Carney merely smiled bitterly. 'Let's put it this way, Major. You've fought on your battlegrounds; I've fought on mine.'

There wasn't much to offer in the way of a rejoinder, Anderson thought, remembering nights on patrol in the Shankill Road. Nodding faintly, he turned away and made his way over to Grieves for further information on the location of the suspected drugs factory.

Carney turned to Winston. 'So, what's my position on this one?' he asked.

The Barbadian grinned at him. 'Your position is that you don't have one,' he said firmly. 'This little jaunt will be strictly down to us death or glory boys.'

Carney nodded. It was exactly the answer he had been expecting, but he still looked disappointed.

'Hey, listen, you've still got an important job to do,' Winston reminded him. 'Out there on the streets, that's where the real battle's going to be fought. You're our eyes and ears

out there. We're still going to need information on the distribution network for this stuff.'

The little speech made Carney feel better, as it was intended
to do. Winston was right. He *did* have a job to do – and he
fully intended to do it to the best of his ability.

9

'I don't know about you, boss, but I feel a right prat,' Pretty
Boy complained bitterly. Known as something of a snappy
dresser when he was in mufti, he was currently clad in khaki
shorts, thick brown socks, heavy walking boots, a padded
blue checked shirt and carrying on his back a bright blue
and yellow rucksack which boasted the legend 'Hiker's
Friend'.

Winston, similarly dressed, looked at him with a vaguely
peeved expression. 'Stop bloody moaning and just enjoy yourself,' he said. 'We're just a couple of country-loving ramblers
out for a nice quiet stroll. What could be better than a leisurely
stroll in the open air on a nice day like today?'

Pretty Boy grunted, unconvinced. 'Well, I think we look
like a couple of bloody poofs,' he muttered. 'Fancy holding
hands to make it a bit more convincing?' Changing his trudging
walk into a mincing gait, he sidled up to Winston's side, slipped
his index finger into the man's huge palm and tickled it.

Winston shrugged him away with an exaggerated gesture.
'Fuck off,' he growled good-naturedly. 'Otherwise I'll start
believing all those rumours about you that float round the
shower rooms.'

Pretty Boy laughed, moving away again and falling into normal step beside the big sergeant. They continued walking up the rutted lane, which curved around to the right of a cluster of derelict barns about a hundred yards ahead of them.

'Right, now keep your eyes peeled,' Winston hissed, suddenly becoming very serious. 'According to my information, the farm's just around that bend, between the outbuildings. And look casual, for Christ's sake. It's a ten-to-one shot they'll have someone on lookout, and they're bound to be suspicious of strangers, even at a distance.'

Pretty Boy nodded, now equally businesslike. 'You got it, boss,' he said quietly.

The abrupt change in dialogue betrayed the true nature of their mission. Far from being on an innocent ramble in the country, they were carrying out a vital reconnaissance of the suspected farmhouse, which had now been under intensive surveillance for three days. The SAS rarely jumped into anything without extremely careful preparation – and this mission would be no different. Detailed information as to the position and structure of the main building and outbuildings was of supreme importance, as was any information which could be gathered about personnel, guards and possible defensive positions. Although Major Anderson had established a concealed observation post on the far side of the farm, and conducted round-the-clock surveillance using high-powered zoom cameras and night-sight binoculars, this was the closest anyone had yet ventured to the buildings themselves. Aerial reconnaissance had furnished valuable plans of the general layout of the farm, but Winston and Pretty Boy needed a good view from ground level. They were hoping to pick up information on any vehicles which might be parked out of sight among the barns and outbuildings, besides checking out the lane as a possible attack point.

They were less than sixty yards from the nearest barn when Winston tensed suddenly, his keen ears picking up the low growl of engines in low gear grinding up the lane some way behind them.

Pretty Boy had heard them too. He cast a quick look over his shoulder. 'They ain't in sight yet, boss,' he said hurriedly. 'What do we do – dive for cover?'

Winston stopped, considering the suggestion in a flash. His eyes darted from side to side, taking in the limitations of the open terrain around them. Short of hiding in a narrow rain culvert on one side of the lane, there was no decent cover to speak of.

'Forget it,' he hissed. 'Just keep walking. Whoever it is may have bumped us already, and it would look fucking suspicious if we suddenly disappeared, wouldn't it?' He began to move again, deliberately slowing his pace as the sound of the approaching vehicles drew nearer.

There were two, his keen instincts told him. A fairly small 4WD vehicle such as a Land Rover or a Shogun, and a much heavier lorry. He hissed aside at Pretty Boy. 'Right, discreet surveillance as they go past. I'll concentrate on the car, you check out the truck.' He broke step momentarily to let Pretty Boy move a foot or so in front of him, so that they would both have clear and unobstructed side vision. The vehicles were right on their heels now, less than thirty yards from the turn-off to the farm buildings.

They stepped to the side of the lane, waiting to let the vehicles go past.

The smaller vehicle was in fact a Jeep Cherokee. Winston eyed it covertly as it rolled past him, counting its occupants.

Driver and passenger in the front, one more man sat on the back seat.

The lorry which followed it was older, and probably a four-tonner, Winston estimated. He looked away from it, letting Pretty Boy fulfil his side of the deal. The lorry's brake lights flashed on almost as soon as it had ground past.

'Bingo,' Pretty Boy breathed. Up to that point neither of them had been sure whether the two vehicles had any connection with the farm at all. But now they were definitely slowing, preparing to turn in between the buildings.

Winston and Pretty Boy started walking again, moving towards the far entrance as the lorry's tailgate disappeared from view. Both cast quick but penetrating glances between the cluster of outbuildings as they strode casually past and continued up the lane. Neither spoke for nearly a minute, until they were out in open countryside again.

Suddenly Winston stopped, on the pretext of retying his boot laces. Kneeling down, he cast a wary eye back towards the farm to check everything before rising to his feet again and glancing questioningly at Pretty Boy.

'Well? What do you think?'

Pretty Boy looked at him dubiously. 'I think we could have a problem,' he said. 'That lorry was empty.'

'You sure?' Winston asked.

Pretty Boy nodded emphatically. 'I checked the underframe and the wheel clearance as she went by. She was riding high. That truck was unladen, I'd swear it.'

'Shit.' Winston vented his frustration in the single, explosive curse. The implications were obvious. Lorries served one of two purposes. They either delivered things, or they carried them away. And if it was arriving empty, it was a pretty sure bet that it wouldn't be leaving in the same condition.

'Looks like they're getting ready to ship a consignment out,' Pretty Boy observed. 'Guess we're going to have to change our plans, eh, boss?'

Winston nodded. 'And bloody fast,' he added. 'We'd better get back to the RV pronto.'

'At a standard rambler's pace?' Pretty Boy asked sarcastically.

Winston glared at him. 'What do you think? We backtrack until we're out of sight of that farmhouse and then we run like fuck.'

Which is exactly what they did.

The rendezvous point and main base had been set up in a small copse on the blind side of a hill which overlooked the farm. Offering good cover for the men and supplies, it was an excellent vantage-point, and would have been ideal for a sneak attack at night. In broad daylight, however, it was next to useless. Having left the cover of the trees, anyone trying to approach the farm down the side of the bare, grassy hill would be in clear view all the way.

Inside the operations-control lorry, Major Anderson listened to Winston's report, accepting the unwelcome news with a worried frown. Besides screwing his plans up, it also gave him a tough decision to make. It was all a question of timing. How soon would the drug manufacturers make their move? he wondered.

It was a question Winston had already considered. 'Well, can we afford to wait for nightfall as we'd planned?' he asked.

Anderson shrugged. 'Who the hell knows?' He was silent for a long time, pondering over the problem and trying to weigh up all the possibilities and their consequences. It was a complex issue, and one he really wished he didn't have to decide upon so hastily. His original plan, to insert his men under cover of darkness and achieve a quick surprise attack, had been basically simple.

More for his own benefit than anything else, he voiced the alternatives. 'If we wait, then we run the risk of them getting that lorry loaded and out. Then there'll be another batch of this stuff hitting the streets. If we go in too early, we lose any element of surprise and we risk taking losses.' Anderson paused, looking at Winston. 'Any suggestions?'

'Only one,' Winston murmured. 'Suppose we just back off and wait to intercept the lorry well away from the farm? Then we can attack the HQ later, as per the original plan.'

Anderson shook his head. 'Two main problems. Firstly, there's still the chance that the green slime have this all wrong and there's really nothing particularly sinister going on at that farm. We shoot up a vehicle and perhaps kill a couple of civilians doing nothing more than shipping a few sacks of horse shit and we'll have really blown it for ourselves. Number two, even if they are what we think they are, there's a strong possibility they'll have some sort of radio link between the lorry and the base. First sign of trouble and all the birds will have flown the nest. We'd have no chance of rounding them all up in open countryside like this.'

'So what it boils down to is either we play safe and risk letting them get the drugs out, or we go in early and risk ourselves?'

Major Anderson nodded, a wry smile on his face. 'No choice at all really, is it?' he said. He looked up at Winston. 'How soon can you have your unit ready to go?'

The question didn't really need any consideration. The two Tweedles were currently manning the observation post less than a quarter of a mile away. A simple recall over the radio and they could be on their way back to base. Then it would be simply a question of getting to the armoury lorry and tooling up.

'Twenty minutes,' Winston said confidently. 'Fifteen if you're in a hurry.'

Anderson smiled. 'Oh, I think we might stretch to half an hour,' he said generously.

He pulled out the aerial reconnaissance map and spread it out. 'Our best chance is to split into two forces and RV again here,' he said, jabbing his finger down at the spot Winston and Pretty Boy had just left. 'I'll take Captain Feeney and his men and skirt around the far side of this hill to approach the farm from the opposite direction. You'll join up with Butch Blake and make the most discreet approach you can along that lane.' He looked up questioningly. 'What sort of cover are you going to have?'

'There's a flood ditch which seems to run all along the side,' Winston told him. 'We can use that.'

'Good,' Anderson said, looking relieved. 'That means we should all be able to get at least as far as the farm outbuildings without being bumped. After that it's anyone's guess.' He paused, studying Winston and Pretty Boy intently. 'I don't need to stress to either of you that we are dealing with civilians here, and we're in a very sticky and unusual situation. We do not open fire unless fired upon. However, if and when that happens, then strict CRW rules apply. All targets are to be neutralized unless they surrender unambiguously.'

'Got you, boss,' Winston muttered. 'It'll be as clean as our friends down there want it to be.'

Anderson nodded. 'Right.' He traced his finger over the map and into the cluster of outbuildings, finally locating the main farmhouse. 'Once we break cover of these buildings we'll be totally exposed and only a direct frontal attack will be open to us. One unit apiece will take the front, back and sides of the farmhouse and we'll go in together, after achieving our priority aim of disabling that lorry. I'm taking in an M72 anti-tank weapon. If we are under fire at that point I'll blow out the front wall of the building to facilitate entry.' He looked up from the map. 'All clear?'

'As a virgin's piss, boss,' Pretty Boy said, grinning. 'Not that I ever met one, of course.'

Anderson seemed as satisfied as he could be with the hastily changed plans. 'Right,' he said, checking his watch before looking at Winston. 'Recall your men, get kitted up and join up with Captain Blake. We'll RV at exactly 1730 hours.'

Winston grinned. 'Just when they'll be having their tea,' he said sarcastically. 'Won't that be a pleasant surprise for them?'

He turned to leave, ushering Pretty Boy ahead of him.

'Oh, by the way,' Anderson called after them, having an afterthought. 'You two *will* get changed into something a bit more suitable, won't you? You look like a couple of pooftahs dressed like that.'

Pretty Boy turned on him, a sheepish grin on his face. 'We'll be dressed in our Sunday best, boss,' he promised.

Anderson smiled back. 'No you won't,' he insisted. 'You'll be wearing Noddy suits and respirators. If that *is* a drug factory down there we don't know what kinds of chemicals and stuff are likely to be floating around if the bullets start to fly.'

10

Paul Carney heard the faint sound of music coming from the inside of his flat as he reached the top of the stairs, and was instantly on the alert. He crept up to the door and slipped the key into the lock as silently as he could. Taking a deep breath, he flung the door open and threw himself into the room, tensed for potential trouble.

Linda sat on the sofa, sipping at a gin and tonic and listening to the stereo unit. She looked up quickly as he burst in, at first in alarm and then in relieved amusement.

'Who were you expecting? The Mafia?'

Carney sighed. 'What are you doing here?' he demanded.

Linda shrugged. 'Well, I must admit that I hadn't expected a rapturous welcome,' she observed. 'But I am still your wife, and I still have a key.' She paused, forcing a thin smile. 'I thought it was time we talked, Paul.'

Carney sighed again. 'We *did* talk,' he reminded her. 'And we decided it was best if you left for a while. Gave me the time I needed to think things over.'

'It's already been nearly seven months,' Linda pointed out. 'And where the hell have you been for the past three weeks? You've left your job, you've not been answering the phone and all Harry Manners would tell me is that you'd had some sort of transfer and couldn't go into details.'

'I've been away,' Carney said simply. There wasn't much else he could tell her, under the restrictions of his security oath.

Linda accepted it at face value, given no other choice. 'Well, are you ready to talk about us yet? See if there's any chance of patching up our marriage?' She looked like a helpless child. 'For Christ's sake, Paul, I still love you. I made a stupid mistake, and I'm sorry. It was a one-night stand and I'll never do it again. I know now what I could lose – what I may already have lost.'

Carney's face was an agony of indecision. Part of him wanted to rush towards her, sweep her up in his arms and kiss her, tell her that he forgave her. But the other part, the deep, inner part which was still hurting, fought against the impulse, reminding him that he just did not have the capacity to forgive. It was more than wounded male ego, more than stupid pride. It was a fundamental part of his being, so powerful and inflexible that it was one of his greatest strengths – and his greatest weakness.

He stared at his wife hopelessly. 'I still need time, Linda. You have to give me some space.'

'For what? Meditation on a mountain top?' Linda demanded, her desperation lending a shrill edge to her voice. 'Do you have to purify yourself before you can even consider forgiving me? For God's sake, Paul, you're forty-three years of age and you haven't yet learned to forgive the world for not being perfect.'

Carney looked defensive. 'It's not like that,' he muttered.

'So what is it like? Are you afraid that some of my dirt is going to rub off on to that nice shiny suit of armour you wear?'

Carney spread his hands in a gesture of impotence. 'Look, I've got a lot of other things on my mind right now. My new job – it's important.'

Linda nodded sadly, reading the implicit message between the lines. 'And I'm not, I suppose?' She finished her drink, rose to her feet and set the empty glass down on the mantelpiece. She looked at him miserably for several moments, waiting for him to say something to stop her leaving. But he was silent.

Finally, Linda gave in, accepting the inevitable. 'All right, love, you go and saddle up Rosinante and ride off to the windmills. But Sancho Panza quits. I'll see a solicitor next week.' She took a key from her handbag and placed it next to the empty glass before walking to the door. 'Goodbye, Paul.'

Carney stood mutely, watching her go. He wanted to say something to her, but nothing would come. Linda closed the door behind her and he was alone. He heard her soft footsteps fade away down the stairs. In sheer frustration, he crossed the lounge and slammed his fist against the wall. It didn't make him feel any better.

He picked up the telephone and dialled Harry Manners's number. 'Harry? It's me, Paul. Listen, what's the latest on Sofrides?'

Manners was guarded. 'What's your interest, Paul?'

'Purely professional,' Carney assured him. 'Basically, is he in or out?'

Manners paused on the other end of the line, still unsure of Carney's motives. But he'd been ordered to afford the man every assistance, so he didn't have much choice in the matter. 'All right, Sofrides is still in the hospital,' he admitted finally. 'But he should be discharged in the next day or so. After that, he walks.'

'Jesus Christ!' Carney found it impossible to control his anger and sense of frustration.

There was no hint of apology in Manners's voice. 'You didn't leave us much choice, Paul. Sofrides claims that the girl turned up at his flat already stoned and just keeled over. He says he was taking the girl to hospital when you stopped him, but you never gave him a chance to explain.'

Carney snorted derisively. 'Taking her to hospital? In the bloody *boot*? Come off it, Harry. You believe that crap?'

'I don't – but a jury might,' Manners said. 'It's just not worth bringing a prosecution. A good brief, and he'll get off scot-free. The little bastard might even bung in a claim for aggra-vated assault as well.' The man paused. 'Which brings me back to my original question – what's your interest in him now? Any further contact might be construed as police harassment.'

'I just need to talk to him, that's all,' Carney said reassur-ingly. 'I won't even raise my voice at the little scumbag, I promise. It's just that Sofrides shouldn't have been handling smack in the first place. He's always been strictly a nose-candy man in the past. Which could suggest he's branching out into new areas – and if he is, he may well have heard some whis-pers on this new drug. It's a long shot, but it could be worth following up.'

It seemed like a reasonable explanation, and Manners accepted it, albeit grudgingly. 'OK, I'll grant you clearance to see him,' he conceded. 'But just watch yourself, that's all.'

'Yeah. I'll be a regular boy scout,' Carney promised, and hung up.

Tony Sofrides looked up from his hospital bed apprehensively as Carney strolled into the ward. He reached hurriedly for the emergency button dangling above his bandaged head.

Carney strode across the room and snatched it out of the youth's hand before he had a chance to use it. 'You won't need that, Tony,' he said, grinning savagely. 'Just a nice friendly little chat.'

The look of fright on Sofrides's face faded away, to be replaced with one of arrogance. He realized that Carney had probably been warned not to even touch him. 'Yeah? Brought me some grapes then, have you, copper?'

Carney smiled. 'Better than that, Tony. I'm bringing you a chance of staying alive – at a price.'

Sofrides looked alarmed again. 'What are you bloody talking about?'

Carney shrugged and spread his hands. 'Oh, it's quite simple really. You offered me a deal – remember? To set up someone like Jack Mottram for me?'

'Get stuffed, Carney,' Sofrides blustered. 'All deals are off. My brief says I walk this one, no sweat. You fucking blew it.'

Carney refused to be rattled, keeping a chilling smile on his face. 'You might find it rather difficult to walk – with both your kneecaps missing,' he pointed out. 'Jack's a bad lad. He doesn't like grasses very much.'

Sofrides grinned defiantly. 'Yeah, well, I ain't gonna grass, am I? There's no bloody percentage in it for me now, is there?'

Carney sighed heavily. It was obvious that the dealer didn't quite get the picture, so he decided to spell it out for him. 'Now, *you* know that . . . and *I* know that. But Jack Mottram doesn't know it. And when a heavy hand descends on his collar, and a friendly little voice informs him that a certain little Greek put the word out, you're not going to be a very good life-insurance prospect, Tony.'

The brief flicker of fear which crossed Sofrides's face was quickly snuffed out by a look of bravado. Coppers – even undercover drugs coppers – didn't do certain things. There was a certain amount of understanding between the police and the criminal fraternity. A code of practice.

Sofrides sneered. 'You wouldn't fit up someone like Jack Mottram, and we both know it,' he said confidently.

Carney flashed his cool smile again. He had an ace up his sleeve now. He was no longer bound by his previous limitations. 'Oh, did I forget to tell you, Tony? We just changed the rules,' he said in a quiet but utterly menacing tone. 'Like you said earlier, all deals are off, and so are the gloves.'

'You're bluffing, you bastard,' Sofrides said, but he didn't sound quite so convinced.

'So call it,' Carney suggested casually, turning as if to leave. 'Get smart for the first time in your miserable little life, Tony. I'm offering you the best deal you're likely to get.'

It seemed to swing the balance. Sofrides called after him as Carney moved towards the door. 'OK, so what do you want to know?'

Carney smiled to himself before turning round again. When he did so, his face was composed and serious. 'Nirvana, Tony? Ever heard of it?'

A slightly puzzled look flitted across the Greek's face. 'Yeah, I've heard about it,' he admitted. 'Ain't never come across it yet, though. It's pretty new.'

Carney took this at face value. 'But if you *did* want to get hold of it, where would you go?' he asked.

The puzzled look returned. 'What's the big deal with that stuff? It's only pill-poppers' rubbish, from the whispers I've heard. I mean, like it ain't heavy shit or anything. Wouldn't have thought it was even in your league, Carney.'

It was interesting information, Carney thought. 'So that's the word out on the streets, is it?' he queried. 'That Nirvana is just a low-grade buzz?'

Sofrides shrugged. 'Something like that. Club stuff – know what I mean? Not the sort of gear any serious dealer gets involved with.'

'But there must be some sort of distribution network,' Carney pointed out. 'Somebody's got to be handling it in bulk.'

Sofrides shook his head. 'Well, if there is, then I don't know anything about it – and that's the truth.'

Knowing Sofrides for a lying little toerag, Carney was quite surprised to find that in this case he believed him. He tried another tack. 'You said it's on the club scene. Give me the name of a couple.'

A crafty look spread over Sofrides's face. Something told him he was going to get off light. 'And if I do, you'll back off?' he asked.

Carney nodded. 'That's the deal,' he confirmed.

Sofrides thought about it for a second, before giving a faint shrug. 'OK, but there's only one place I've heard of. Norma Jean's, down Kilburn way.' He looked up at Carney, a flash of his old arrogance returning. 'Now, how about you fucking off and leaving me in peace?'

Carney grinned, turning towards the door. 'Sure, Tony. And I'll give your love to Jack Mottram when I see him.'

He walked out of the ward without turning round to see the look of fear that had returned to the young man's face.

11

Two hundred yards from the farm's outbuildings, Winston lay on his belly in the mud of the culvert, for once in his life actually glad to be wearing the protective NBC suit. Immediately behind him, Pretty Boy and the two Tweedles had also come to a halt, waiting for Major Anderson and Captain Feeney to complete the longer journey around the far side of the farmhouse.

Winston checked his watch, then wriggled over on to his side, holding his Heckler & Koch MP5 sub-machine-gun clear of the mud. He raised his head just enough to see over the prone figure of Pretty Boy and identify Butch Blake and his men, some fifty yards behind them. He held up three fingers, receiving a brief thumbs up from Butch in return. Three more minutes and they would complete their approach, hopefully just as Anderson reached his own destination.

Pretty Boy pulled himself up over Winston's legs, lifting his S-6 respirator away from his face and grinning. 'We're going to look pretty stupid if there's nothing but a bunch of carrot-crunchers in there, aren't we?' he whispered.

Beneath his own mask, Winston smiled to himself, knowing exactly what the man meant. Suited up and armed to the teeth as they were, they represented a lethal, full-scale attack force which would strike terror into the hearts of even the most hardened terrorist group. If the green slime had got it wrong, and they burst in on a group of perfectly innocent yokels, there were likely to be deaths from heart attacks without a single shot being fired.

And an attack force they most certainly were. In addition to guns and knives, each man carried six grenades clipped to his belt webbing. Three 'flash-bang' stun grenades and three of the conventional fragmentation type. Their sheer fire-power was awesome; in addition to the standard Browning HP hand-guns in their belt pouches, every trooper carried a devastating MP5, with the single exception of Tweedledum, who had chosen to arm himself with a Remington 870 pump-action shotgun.

Winston checked his watch again, as the seconds to RV time ticked away. Finally he rolled back on to his belly and began to wriggle along the culvert in the direction of the farm buildings once more. If Major Anderson's estimation had been correct, the combined assault should start exactly on schedule. A few moments later, he had the satisfaction of seeing a faint flash of something dark moving against the green of the open countryside on the far side of the farm entrance. It could only be Anderson and the rest of the force. Using the contours of the land, he had managed to get the main body of his men to within fifty yards of the outbuildings. They were almost ready to attack.

Winston strained his eyes, picking out individual troopers and the deployment of the two units. One man – it looked like Jumbo Jackson – had dropped behind to set up a heavy machine-gun to provide rear covering fire. The rest were making their way stealthily towards the farm entrance, using the massive bulk of one of the disused barns to hide their approach from the farmhouse itself. Provided there were no lookouts in the outbuildings, the trap should be sprung in a matter of moments.

It proved to be a vain hope. As Anderson led his men clear of their last ground cover, Winston heard the sharp, staccato bark of an Uzi machine-pistol. He saw one of the troopers throw his MP5 into the air as he was hit. He fell, rolled over, and lay still.

'Fuck it!' Winston growled under his breath. Their chance of a surprise attack was gone, and there was no longer any doubt that they were facing an armed and dangerous enemy. The sound of the Uzi had now been supplemented by the individual crack of at least two handguns, and Anderson and his men were caught in a very open and vulnerable position. The only choice now left open to them was a frontal rush assault, counting on Winston and Butch to come in behind them. Winston jumped to his feet, clambering out of the ditch into the lane. 'Shake out,' he yelled at the top of his voice, and broke into a zigzagging run towards the outbuildings.

Anderson had bolted straight for the protection of the old barn at the first sound of gunfire. Now, pressed against its reassuringly thick wall, he and the rest of the men who had made it had at least temporary protection, although they were effectively pinned down. Glancing back over his tracks, he counted two black, unmoving shapes lying in the grass. Quickly checking his companions sheltering against the barn wall, he identified them as Trooper Eddie Mentieth and Captain Feeney. Both good men, he thought, bitterly – although they were all good men. Anderson looked back again over the fields to where Jumbo had finished setting up the general-purpose machine-gun behind the partial cover of a small, grassy hummock. Knowing exactly what his comrades needed, he began to lay down a blanket of short-burst fire over their heads towards the farmhouse.

It was time to move, Anderson thought. Butch and Winston could only be a matter of a few seconds behind them now, and the longer they stayed where they were, the more vulnerable their position would become. It was impossible at that point to get an accurate fix on the position of the Uzi, and if the gunman chose to move his vantage-point, it was possible that he could get a direct line of fire upon them. Pinned against the walls of the barn, they'd be like little tin ducks on a fairground shooting range. Anderson edged his way along to the end of the barn wall and took a lightning glance around the corner. Beyond a rectangular block of concrete pigsties, there was a clear view to the farmhouse, some two hundred yards away down a slight slope.

Anderson pressed himself back against the wall, gesturing to the other men to bunch up behind him. He began to unstrap the M72 anti-tank weapon from his back as he barked out orders.

'Right, on my signal you'll make a direct assault on the farmhouse. Winston and Butch will be coming in behind you. Move in fast, zigzagging as much as possible. When you're down low enough to be clear of the rocket trail, I'll blast out the front wall and come down after you.'

Anderson spoke with a little more assurance than he actually felt. The M72 was essentially a fairly close-range weapon. Although a skilled operator could hope to hit a static target up to 300 metres away, there was no guarantee of success, and no second chance. It was a strictly one-shot weapon, firing a single 66mm rocket by conventional optical sight. Once fired, the entire system was thrown away – burned out and useless.

He pulled off the protective caps at either end of the launcher tube, extending it into firing readiness and causing the pop-up sights to click into place. Hauling it on to his right shoulder like a bazooka, Anderson wrapped his finger gently around the trigger switch. He was ready.

'OK, go!' he barked out, flattening himself against the wall as the rest of the men rushed past him and out into the open. He counted slowly to five, giving them time to get lower down the sloping approach to the farmhouse before throwing himself round the corner of the barn.

Just one shot. He had to make it good! Anderson squinted down the M72's sights, fixing them on a spot between the front door of the farmhouse and a small ground-floor window. It seemed the logical target point, since the wall would be structurally weakest around the door frame, and the window was the most likely position of any gunmen inside the building. Holding his breath, he steadied the firing tube against the corner of the wall and squeezed the trigger.

He had already tossed the spent launcher aside and pulled his MP5 up into a businesslike position before the streaming rocket trail completed its slightly erratic smoke-trail course towards the farmhouse. After setting the weapon for three-round bursts, he launched himself in pursuit of his men.

The rocket exploded with a dull roar which echoed off the surrounding hills, drowning out the sounds of gunfire for a few seconds. When the dust and falling debris had cleared, a hole the size of a small saloon car had been blown in the front wall of the farmhouse. Anderson bounded down the slope towards the rest of his men, who had taken tempo-rary cover behind the low concrete walls of the derelict pigsties. He dropped to his stomach beside the Lethal Leek, straining to identify the continuing sounds of gunfire. Up on the hill, Jumbo was still laying down a blanket of five-second bursts with the GPMG, more for psychological effect than with any chance of doing real damage. Aiming as he was over the heads of his own colleagues, Jumbo was taking no chances and deliberately firing high, most of the heavy 7.62mm slugs merely stripping slates off the roof of the farmhouse. In the lulls between the bursts, there was only the sporadic crack of perhaps three or four handguns, one of which seemed to be coming from an upstairs window of the farmhouse. The crackle of the Uzi could not be heard. Perhaps the gunman was already dead, Anderson thought. If not, he was either changing the clip or had run out of ammunition completely.

Seconds later, the machine-pistol opened up again, slugs stripping off small chips of concrete above his head.

'The bastard's moved,' the Lethal Leek observed. 'My guess is that he's over there.' He jerked the barrel of his Heckler & Koch MP5 in the direction of an old stable block to the right of the farmhouse.

Anderson accepted this assessment moodily. If the Welshman was right, it was bad news for all of them. Not only were he and his men pinned down, but the gunman would have a direct line of fire into the open courtyard between the farmhouse and the outbuilding through which Winston and Butch's units would have to make their approach. It gave the man a tactical advantage out of all proportion to his true fire-power.

But for now, Anderson had his own problems. Basically, he was stuck in a fairly safe but useless position from which he could neither advance nor retreat without snatching the initiative. He nudged the Lethal Leek in the ribs, nodding up towards the left upstairs window of the farmhouse.

'Let's take these bastards out one at a time,' he suggested. 'I'll draw his fire and you give him everything you've got.'

The Lethal Leek nodded. 'Got you, boss.' Setting his MP5 on full automatic fire, he waited for Anderson's move.

It was not long in coming. Anderson tensed himself, then rolled out of the cover of the pigsties, firing his own weapon towards the upstairs window as he did so.

The ploy worked. Three bullets smacked into the ground in his wake, as the gunman behind the window went for his first clear target. It was a calculated gamble, Anderson counting on the assumption that a handgun would be fairly inaccurate at that range. Two more shots followed, and Anderson heard the slugs whistle harmlessly over his head.

'Take him,' he hissed over at the Welshman, as he continued to draw fire from the window by spraying the top left-hand corner of the farmhouse until his magazine was empty.

The Lethal Leek sprang to his feet from behind the cover of the pigsties, his own MP5 bucking in his hands as he loosed off another full clip of thirty 9mm slugs. What was left of the glass in the window exploded into a crystalline shower of tiny shards, the surrounding frame shattering into a splintered mess. There was no returning fire. The Lethal Leek grinned over at Anderson as he rolled back into cover.

'I reckon we taught him the error of his ways, boss,' he observed, discarding the empty magazine and slotting in another.

Anderson nodded, looking around to identify the positions of his remaining men. Ted Brennon and the big Cornishman, Miles Tremathon, were crouched together some fifteen feet to his left. Only the muzzle of an MP5 poking over the concrete lip of the sties identified Pete Delaney on the adjacent side of the rectangular structure. To join them, he would have to make a skirting run around the back, but his cover was good.

Again Anderson listened to the sounds of gunfire. Just two automatic pistols remaining, he gauged – one of them on the ground floor of the farmhouse and the other coming from somewhere outside, judging by the sharper, echoless report. The Uzi was still firing in staccato bursts, but no bullets were flying their way. Anderson could only assume that the gunman had now turned his attention to the second attack force of Winston and Butch and their men.

The Uzi would have to be their problem, Anderson realized. Right now he probably had his best chance to make the final assault on the farmhouse. Two handguns would be no match for five MP5s. He glanced aside at the Lethal Leek, and then at Miles and Ted. 'OK, let's shake out,' he yelled. 'We're going in.'

Leaping to his feet, he began to run down the slope towards the farmhouse, firing three-round bursts into the gaping hole in the building's wall.

Winston, the two Tweedles and Pretty Boy remained crouched behind the cover of the outbuilding furthest from the farmhouse, where they had gone to ground immediately on bursting through the farm entrance. On the opposite side of the entrance drive, Butch, Mike Peters, Aberdeen Angus and Jimmy Phelan were similarly placed behind an old and rusting baling machine, waiting for Anderson to make his main assault. It had seemed the only sensible course of action, given their single choice of a closer approach and the defensive position of the farmhouse itself. Even though their enemy appeared to have strictly limited fire-power, the SAS men's only access to the farmhouse was across a wide, open courtyard in which they would all be sitting targets. The lorry, parked in the middle of it and facing them, might offer a safe halfway house, but only after Anderson had neutralized any threat from the farmhouse itself. By staying put, they were at least effectively blocking off any escape route and were poised to sweep in behind Anderson in a quick and clean mopping-up operation.

A renewed burst of firing from the quintet of MP5s announced that this final assault was in fact at last under way. Winston glanced over to Butch, who nodded back at him. As Anderson and his men broke from the cover of the sties and started their final run towards the farmhouse, the eight troopers launched themselves out into the drive and began a zigzagging run towards the lorry.

The Uzi chattered angrily at them. From the corner of his eye, Winston saw Jimmy Phelan twist awkwardly in mid stride, give a little yell of pain and go down, blood gushing from a thigh wound. Acting instinctively, Winston dropped on to his belly and rolled sideways to the fallen trooper as his companions continued their run towards the lorry and drew away the fire from the Uzi. He rolled Jimmy on to his back, then hastily stripped off the man's belt webbing and tightened it around his thigh above the wound to create a makeshift tourniquet. There was little else he could do. Rolling Jimmy gently back on to his belly again, Winston thrust his MP5 into his hands and patted him on the back. 'You can still give us covering fire,' he muttered to the injured trooper, preparing to scramble back to his feet and make a run for the lorry.

He held himself in check, suddenly realizing that he had given himself an unexpected tactical advantage. In the few seconds it had taken him to see to Jimmy, not a single shot had been fired in their direction. The gunman was now totally obsessed with the nearer threat of the main body of the men, now almost at the lorry. Winston's mind raced, plotting through the implications with computer-like efficiency.

The Uzi had to be positioned somewhere ahead of him, covering the vehicle. Somewhere high, Winston figured. He raised his eyes, scanning the buildings surrounding the courtyard and using his keen ears at the same time to pinpoint the source of the chattering machine-pistol.

In the old stable block to the right of the farmhouse, a small, square hole looked down over the rest of the farm buildings. It had probably once been a hayloft, Winston thought. Now it was a handy little nest for a gunman. He dropped his eyes back to the rest of the men, who had all made it to the comparative safety of the lorry. He watched Tweedledum blast out the nearside tyres with a couple of shells from the Remington, then put another couple of rounds through the radiator for good measure before joining his companions in a huddle behind the sagging vehicle.

They were now all almost directly below the hayloft, and although they were protected from its direct line of fire, their presence rather ruled out Winston's initial thought of lobbing a hand-grenade into it. The square baling hatch presented a small target, and should the grenade fail to find it, it could easily bounce off the wall and roll towards the lorry. There had to be another way to take out the Uzi, Winston thought frantically.

A slow, delicious grin spread over his black face as it came to him. An old hayloft would probably still have a fair amount of hay inside it. Even if it was empty, the wooden structure would be as dry as a tinder-box. Such a scenario offered distinct possibilities.

Still lying prone, and moving very slowly and cautiously, he released the magazine catch on his Heckler & Koch and slipped out the empty box.

They had originally all been prepared for an attack in the dark, and their armoury had reflected this probability with typical SAS efficiency and attention to detail. Winston reached down to his spare ammunition belt and, having selected a fresh thirty-round box magazine, locked it into position.

Sometimes, when making an attack in pitch darkness, it became imperative to let your fellow-troopers know your exact position. Equally, it was often extremely helpful to pinpoint a blind target, or gain a quick visual signal as to your accuracy. A short burst of tracer achieved both these objects, speedily and efficiently. And a fresh magazine of one-in-five tracer was exactly what Winston had just loaded into his MP5. Each white-hot magnesium flare would serve equally well as an incendiary device, he knew.

Jumping to his feet, Winston aimed the MP5 at the hayloft and emptied the entire magazine into it before dropping to the ground again. As he changed back to regular ammunition, he had the satisfaction of seeing the first wisps of light-coloured smoke begin to drift out of the small hatchway. Even as he watched, the smoke darkened and turned into a small but thickening cloud. It was already billowing out as the first licking flames appeared around the edges of the hatch.

The Uzi ceased firing as the flames built up quickly, reinforcing Winston's supposition that the hayloft still contained a large amount of hay or other highly combustible material. Winston climbed to his feet again and began running towards the lorry, still keeping a watchful eye on the hayloft and his finger on the trigger.

The gunman appeared, framed in the square hatchway and illuminated by the growing inferno behind him. He had little choice but to jump for his life. Given the thirty-foot drop, he might just have survived as a permanent cripple, but Aberdeen Angus saved him the pain and inconvenience. A five-second burst took the man as he fell, ensuring that he was dead before he hit the ground.

Winston completed his run to the lorry. Butch clapped him on the shoulder as he arrived. 'Smart idea,' he said warmly.

Winston grinned. 'I have a burning desire to succeed in life,' he retorted. Then, his face clouding, he glanced across at Tweedledee. 'Listen, Jimmy's been hit back there. Go and do what you can for him, will you?'

'Sure, boss.' Tweedledee didn't hesitate, setting out for the injured trooper at a loping run and pulling emergency field-dressings from his belt pouches as he moved.

'Right, let's join the boss,' Butch suggested, nodding his head towards the farmhouse. Anderson and his men had surrounded it now, and the last automatic pistol had ceased firing, its owner either dead, dispirited or out of ammo. It didn't really matter either way. From now on, it looked like a simple clean-up operation.

Anderson himself was edging along the front wall of the farmhouse, a stun grenade ready in his hand with its pin already pulled. Reaching the jagged edge of the gaping hole left by the M72 rocket, he lobbed it almost casually into the interior of the building.

Before the rolling echoes of the explosion had finished bouncing off the surrounding hills, Anderson was in through the gap, closely followed by the Lethal Leek and the rest of his men. Winston, Butch, Pretty Boy and Tweedledum were only seconds behind them, leaving Mike Peters and Aberdeen Angus to guard the crippled lorry and cut off any escape bids.

The ground floor of the farmhouse had been almost completely gutted, with interior walls knocked down, and ceiling joists inserted, to make way for a small-scale manufacturing set-up. Vats of chemical compounds, mixing drums and a pill-making machine took up most of what must have been the kitchen and living-room. The place appeared to be deserted, apart from the dead body of a single gunman slumped under a window.

Anderson pointed towards the stairs with the barrel of his MP5. 'Go and secure upstairs,' he snapped at Miles and the Lethal Leek. He looked over at Winston. 'We'll cover this floor. You sweep the storage area.'

Nodding a brief acknowledgement, Winston moved towards a clutter of crates and cardboard boxes on the far side of the makeshift laboratory. As he approached, there was the slightest sign of movement from one of the piles of boxes. Winston's finger flexed against the trigger of his Heckler & Koch. The piled boxes jumped into the air, flying apart to reveal a flash of white clothing as someone dived sideways for safety.

'Surrender now,' Winston screamed. 'You have one chance and five seconds.' He held the MP5 trained on the last estimated position of the hiding figure.

It was an offer not to be refused. A man, wearing a white laboratory coat, rose slowly from behind the scattered boxes. His hands were empty, but his eyes were full of hate. Regarding Winston with a cold, vicious stare, he spat something out in German.

'What did he say?' Winston barked to Pretty Boy, who was standing immediately behind him. Apart from his other talents, the trooper spoke five European languages with varying degrees of fluency.

'He called you a shit-eating nigger,' Pretty Boy informed him unemotionally. 'Not very polite, is he?'

Winston resisted the urge to make his own reply in fluent Heckler & Koch. The man was obviously a chemist who had been overseeing the drug production. He might have some rather useful information to pass on, so it made sense to keep him alive. At least, that was the idea.

The chemist tensed his body suddenly, jerking his right arm stiffly into the air. It was a serious mistake. The SAS were honed to split-second precision in terrorist or hostage situations. The rules were clear and unequivocal. Surrender had to be total and unambiguous. Any sudden or violent movement could only be interpreted as a potential threat, and immediately neutralized.

The Remington in Tweedledum's hands boomed out, the full charge of shot taking the chemist full in the chest at less than twelve feet. The man's immaculate white coat flowered into a wild, abstract crimson pattern, and the force of the close-range blast lifted him several inches into the air and threw his body across the jumble of boxes. Afterwards there was a sudden and complete silence.

Finally Tweedledum spoke. 'Sorry, did I do the wrong thing?' he asked.

Winston turned on him slowly, a rueful smile on his face. It was impossible to criticize the young trooper in any way. The death of their apparently sole surviving witness was regrettable, but Tweedledum had followed orders to the letter. Winston told him so, putting the soldier's mind at ease.

'What the fuck was he *doing*?' Tweedledum demanded, after a slight pause.

Winston smiled thinly again. 'He was about to give us an old-fashioned Nazi salute,' he murmured. 'You're too young to remember.'

Tweedledum gave a short, nervous laugh. 'Jesus, Sarge, what are we taking on here?'

Winston shrugged. 'I haven't got the faintest idea, Trooper,' he admitted. 'Nobody tells us a fucking thing.'

12

Norma Jean's nightclub was in a basement, directly under a large block of semi-derelict warehouses. Advertised only by a street-level entrance and a neon representation of the young Marilyn Monroe, the place had a scruffy, almost sordid look about it. From deep in its bowels, the pounding, repetitive beat of techno music echoed up into the darkened streets.

It was difficult to see the club's appeal, Carney thought, yet it was obvious that it was a highly popular venue. From a concealed position across the street, he'd been watching the place for over an hour, noting the steady stream of customers, some of them dressed in party finery as though they were going to the Lord Mayor's banquet. The clientele appeared to be predominantly white, and exclusively young.

What Carney failed to appreciate was that it was the generally unsavoury appearance of the place that gave it its greatest appeal – the direct result of a calculated approach to both design and marketing. It was geared almost exclusively to the 'rave' crowd. The deliberately planned down-beat image created the illusion of spontaneity, an almost temporary, makeshift meeting place in which the thrill of a somehow illicit party could be savoured. The incessant mind-numbing music, along with alcohol and designer drugs, did the rest.

Carney moved out from his hiding place and crossed the street for a closer look.

'What you think you're hanging about for, grandad?' said a coarse, aggressive voice from the doorway of the club.

Carney looked up into the cold, disdainful eyes of the burly bouncer who had just stepped provocatively into his path. He made a tentative move as if to sidestep the man, but the bouncer shifted his position, adopting a direct challenge.

'You deaf, grandad?' he said.

Carney stood his ground, eyeing the bouncer up and down carefully. He was young – no more than twenty-two, Carney estimated – and powerfully built, with a barrel-like chest, broad shoulders and a thick, bull-like neck which supported a stubble-covered blonde head. The standard doorman's outfit of dinner jacket, white dress shirt and black bow tie looked totally incongruous on the man, who might have looked more appropriately dressed in a rancid bearskin. He stood just over six feet tall, and probably weighed in around fifteen stone. Most likely a boxer, Carney reflected – and probably not a very good one either. The sort who was too slow and too stupid for defensive manoeuvring and relied purely on his bulk and a heavy punch. All the same, not someone to be easily pushed out of the way, and Carney didn't try. He didn't much care for the epithet 'grandad', but he kept his cool.

Carney nodded towards the club entrance. 'Thought I might take a look-see,' he said. 'I'm a music-lover,' he added sarcastically.

The bouncer snarled contemptuously. 'Fuck off. You some sort of pervert or something?'

He took a step back and pushed up the right sleeve of his tuxedo a few inches. In the faint glow of the neon lights Carney noted with a vague sense of unease the ugly symbol of the swastika tattooed on his wrist. It was there again – the connection between Nirvana and right-wing extremism – and it threw him for a few seconds. Recovering himself, he ran through a hastily improvised plan of action and decided it might just work.

Forcing an easy smile, Carney nodded at the tattoo. 'Well, at least you've got sense enough to be a member of the Brotherhood,' he said in a friendly tone. 'And here was I thinking you were just an ugly, dumb ape with nothing but highly compressed pig shit between your ears.'

This took several seconds to sink in. When it finally did so, the burly bouncer let out a strangled bellow of rage and drew back his ham-like fist.

Carney was ready for him. His few weeks of training with the SAS had added a few extra tricks to his repertoire. He avoided the pile-driving punch easily, pivoting on the balls of his feet and stepping neatly around the bouncer's side. He drove a short, stabbing knuckle punch into the area of one kidney, then spun round and delivered a toe kick to the other. Balancing himself again, Carney slammed his knee into the base of the man's spinal column.

The bouncer let out a bestial grunt, his huge frame arching backwards in agony. Carney's left arm coiled around his neck and windpipe from behind, choking off his air supply. A rabbit punch to the back of the thick neck delivered the *coup de grâce*. The man went limp in Carney's grip, and began to crumple to the pavement.

He was stunned and winded – but not unconscious. He stared up at his conqueror with dumb incomprehension in his dull eyes. Carney merely grinned at him. 'I really ought to kick your teeth in,' he said casually. 'But I'll let you off as you're one of us – even if you are in need of some serious combat training. Any one of my boys could take you apart and reassemble you as a woman in five seconds flat.'

'Your boys?' the bouncer croaked helplessly, taking the bait.

Carney nodded. 'Sons of the Swastika,' he said, picking the first name that popped into his head. He could only hope it sounded sufficiently fanatical and outrageous to be plausible. 'We take our politics seriously.'

He was acutely aware that he was on borrowed time. Several revellers arriving at the club had already witnessed the brief battle and had run inside to raise the alarm. It could only be a matter of seconds before other heavies started to pour out on to the street. Carney had time for just one parting shot.

'Maybe I'll bring a few of my lads round one night, just to suss out the recruitment prospects,' he told the still-helpless youth. 'Only next time you see me, I'll be expecting a little more respect.'

It was time to make a discreet exit. Carney managed to stroll in what he imagined to be a casual and unhurried manner as far as the first street corner, then turned into it and began to run for his life. He had already disappeared into the shadows by the time a twelve-strong gang of louts had raced out of the club and reached the corner.

Finally deciding that he was safe from pursuit, Carney slowed to a walk again and began to retrace his steps to where he had parked his car. He had one more call to make.

The Tunnel Club was more geared to Carney's age-group, if not his moral outlook on life. The late-night drinking den was predominantly frequented by the criminal fraternity, with a smattering of resting actors – although it was not unknown to a few undercover cops, Carney among them.

This time the doorman greeted Carney guardedly but with grudging respect. 'Evening, Mr Carney. Official, is it?'

Carney shook his head. 'Relax, Danny. Just a purely social call. Frankie Conran in tonight?'

Danny grinned. 'Does a pigeon shit?'

Carney took this, correctly, as an affirmation. He slid past Danny and through the tiny reception area to the long, dimly lit bar beyond.

Conran was propped up on a tall stool at the far end of the bar, chatting up a blonde former starlet who was now past her ascendancy. Carney had seen her most recently in a TV commercial for toothpaste. Tellingly, she had just started playing the mother in ads.

'Evening, Frankie,' Carney said in a friendly enough tone, seating himself beside the man. 'Drink?'

Conran looked up without smiling. His greeting was neither friendly nor wary. It was merely one of acceptance. They were not friends, yet not enemies, even though they were technically on opposite sides of the fence. Conran was basically a crook, and Carney knew it, even if the man did hide many of his more nefarious activities under the cover of a legitimate computer information service. But he hated drugs, and in this respect if nothing else he had been Carney's ally in the past. His own daughter had got caught up in the heavy drugs scene some three years earlier, and it had been primarily Carney's influence which had got her off a major charge and on to a methadone treatment scheme which eventually cured her addiction. It was a favour owed. Conran's relationship with Carney was now a strange and fragile one, walking a tightrope across the uneasy hinterland between crime and the law. Yet it was a liaison which was not all that uncommon between the two worlds. In many ways, it sometimes served both sides.

'Slumming it, are you, Carney?' Conran asked. He jerked his head towards the blonde. 'This is Pauline Ferris, the actress.'

Carney nodded. 'Yeah. Hello. Great teeth.'

Turning to the barman, Carney ordered himself a beer.

'I take it this is not a chance encounter?' Conran queried.

Carney smiled. 'You're uncommonly sharp tonight, Frankie. A word in your shell-like would be appreciated. Could we have a minute in private?'

Conran didn't look too upset about being torn away from his potential conquest. He hadn't really entertained great hopes of scoring anyway. He turned towards the actress, draping his arm briefly about her shoulders in a gesture of ownership. 'Look, sweetheart, I'll be back in about five minutes. OK?'

The woman shrugged. 'Don't hurry on my account.'

Conran stood up, picked up his drink from the bar and carried it across to an empty table at the back of the smoky room. Carney stayed at the bar for long enough to order himself an expensive beer and strolled across to join him.

'So, what are you after?' Conran asked as he sat down. 'I'm not in the grassing business, as well you know.'

'Sure,' Carney agreed. He took a sip of his beer. 'How's Dorothy, by the way?'

Conran brightened visibly at the mention of his daughter's name. 'She's fine,' he said enthusiastically. 'Still on the straight and narrow, thank God. She's got a new job with a travel firm now. Doing pretty well.'

'I'm glad to hear it,' Carney told him. The sentiment was genuine, even if he had brought the subject up as a rather unsubtle reminder.

104

Conran had not missed the point. He sighed heavily. 'All right, Carney – I still owe you. Now what is it you want to know?'

Carney paused to take another swig of beer. 'Have you still got that Eurolink computer set-up?' he asked.

Conran nodded. 'Too right,' he replied. 'Best little idea I had in years, that was. Instead of just supplying info on British companies, I now cover almost the entire commercial and industrial network of the EU. Punters are queuing up on both sides of the Channel to use the facility.'

Carney smiled knowingly. 'And no doubt it comes in useful for the odd bit of industrial espionage?'

Conran shot him a reproving stare. 'Information technology, Carney,' he corrected. 'The business of the future – and all perfectly legit.'

Carney was unconvinced, but he shrugged it off. 'Yeah, well, right now I could do with a bit of information technology myself.'

'You got it,' Conran said generously. 'Give me some details of what you want.'

Carney paused for a few moments, refining his earlier vague thoughts on the subject. He wasn't sure how much he ought to reveal, and eventually decided on the bare minimum. 'All right, there's a new drug hitting the streets, originates from Germany,' he said. 'From what we know so far, it's probably hallucinogenic and possibly a derivative of LSD. If that's so, then it's almost certainly based on ergotamine tartrate and was probably developed as a side-product of legitimate pharmaceutical research. What I need is a scan of European pharmaceutical companies known to have conducted any such research during the past two to three years. Obviously Germany's the place to concentrate on, but it wouldn't do any harm to take in Switzerland, Austria and possibly Italy. Also, it would be handy to know of any companies or organizations currently importing sizeable quantities of ergotamine tartrate into this country.' He stared Conran in the eye. 'Well? Do you think you can help me?'

Conran was thoughtful. 'This new drug,' he said eventually. 'Bad shit, is it?'

Carney nodded emphatically. 'Real bad shit,' he confirmed.

It was enough to swing the balance. 'I'll see what I can do,' Conran promised him. 'It might take a day or two.'

'Thanks, Frankie,' Carney said gratefully. 'Give me a buzz if you get anything, will you? On my home number. I'm not at the office any more.'

Conran raised one eyebrow quizzically. 'Don't tell me Mr Straight has finally fallen out with the boys in blue?'

Carney grinned secretively. 'No, I'm still firmly on the side of law and order, Frankie. Let's just say I'm running more with the boys in brown these days.' He did not elaborate, and Conran didn't push it. Their relationship had certain limits, which neither of them would ever exceed.

Carney glanced over towards the bar. The actress was just getting to her feet and preparing to leave with a muscular, good-looking young blond man who looked as though he had just come from a work-out at the local health club.

'Sorry, Frankie,' Carney said. 'But it looks as though the tooth fairy just scored herself a toy boy.'

Conran shrugged. 'What the hell,' he muttered philosophically. 'The wife wouldn't have liked her, anyway.' He glanced down at Carney's almost finished pint. 'Fancy a bit of serious drinking?'

Carney thought about it for just a moment. After the unpleasantness with Linda earlier in the day, any company was better than none, he decided.

'My round, I think,' he said, before picking up his glass and draining it.

13

It was post-mortem time in the Kremlin briefing room. A chance for the men to discuss the success or failure of the previous day's operation and to hold a Chinese Parliament about their next moves.

Making a realistic assessment of the farmhouse raid was a tricky call, Major Anderson had already decided. It could be deemed a success in one respect only – they had seized nearly a hundred kilos of the finished drug and destroyed the remaining chemical stocks along with all the manufacturing equipment. Other than that, they had achieved virtually nothing. They had no leads to follow, and virtually no idea of where to look next; or indeed who or what to look for. In effect, they were still at square one.

It was a bit like catching a lizard by the tail, Anderson reflected. The reptile's defence systems simply snapped off the trapped appendage and sealed the damaged area, and the creature scuttled away to grow a new one. It was more than just frustrating, he thought bitterly. What made it particularly galling was the fact that they had lost men – apparently pointlessly. Thanks largely to Winston's emergency medical treatment, Trooper Phelan would make it to fight another day, but Captain Feeney and Trooper Eddie Mentieth had failed to beat the clock. That made it personal, raised the stakes. It was no longer just a mission, could no longer be viewed with professional detachment. The men of 22 SAS were at war now – but where was the bloody enemy?

That Anderson's pessimistic views were shared by most of his colleagues was evident from the subdued atmosphere in the room. There was none of the usual bluster and bravado, the macabre but understandable boasts of a clean kill or a particularly close brush with death. No sick jokes, no good-natured piss-taking, no sense of elation among the survivors of yet another encounter with danger. It was as if every man present somehow sensed that he was out of his natural element, thrown into a strange and confusing situation in which the usual rules simply didn't apply.

It was probably because most of them were so young and so recently badged, Anderson decided. The requirements of their mission, and the nature of the personnel needed had forced that limitation upon them, and it had its drawbacks. Virtually none of the men had the faintest idea what it was like to face a hidden, civilian enemy. Besides himself, there were only two other troopers who had seen a tour of duty in Northern Ireland.

Anderson understood, of course – only too well. Two years of nights and days on the streets of Belfast had taught him to come to terms with the fears and uncertainties of not knowing, minute to minute, who and where your enemy actually was.

The fifteen-year-old kid on the street corner. Was it a packet of cigarettes he was just pulling from his bomber-jacket pocket – or was it a hand-grenade? The pretty girl with the smiling green eyes and the soft, lilting voice. Was she inviting you into her bed – or to an ambush where you'd be forced to your knees and shot through the back of the head?

The next car coming down the road towards the security checkpoint. Friend or foe? Was it carrying joyriding kids or armed killers?

That little glint of silver in the green country lanes of Derry. Was it the sunlight glinting off a stretch of cattle fencing – or was it a trip-wire connected up to the land-mine now only yards ahead?

So many unknowns, so many life-or-death decisions. Every day. Every hour. Every minute. The youngsters couldn't be expected to know the answers. They didn't even know the questions.

Sergeant Andrew Winston had his own set of questions to occupy his mind, and the possible answers were terrifying. Paul Carney had called him first thing that morning, passing on his discovery of yet another direct connection between the extreme right and the drug Nirvana. So soon after his own experience with the German scientist at the farmhouse, Winston found it all infinitely depressing.

How could it all start to happen again? he asked himself with a sense of disbelief. Just half a century after the holocaust which had ravaged the world and extinguished the lives of at least fifty million human beings, the madness was abroad once more. A student of modern history, and a humanitarian despite his profession, Winston carried the figures in his head. Twenty million Russians, twelve million Germans, six million Poles, six million Jews, half a million French, six hundred thousand Americans, four hundred and fifty thousand British had perished in Europe alone – all because of a single insane belief that some races were inferior to others.

How could it happen again? The question repeated itself in his brain. Was it just that people had short memories, or was the need to hate programmed into the human psyche?

As ever, there were no answers, or none that made any kind of sense. And more than anyone else, a man with black skin needed those answers.

Winston's concentration was jolted suddenly back to the present, as Major Anderson rose to his feet to open the meeting.

'It goes without saying that every trooper did his job and I'm proud of you all,' Anderson announced, starting on a positive note even though he had nothing encouraging to back it up with. 'But for the moment, at least, it's now going to be a question of waiting to see what the green slime, or our own OPI, can come up with next.' Anderson paused, looking hopefully out over the heads of the seated men. 'Unless, that is, any one of you has any useful suggestions.'

Captain Butch Blake rose to his feet. 'I assume that someone is checking out the lorry's registration?' he put in.

Anderson nodded. 'The police are running checks,' he confirmed. 'But the general feeling is that it'll turn out to be stolen, or at least fitted with false plates.'

It was time for Winston to pass on his information. He stood up, clearing his throat. 'Actually, boss, we don't all have to sit around twiddling our thumbs altogether,' he said. 'Paul Carney called me this morning with a possible new lead. He's found a London club where the drug is rumoured to be available – and, once again, there are strong indications of a link with ultra-right-wing organizations.'

It sounded promising. Anderson accepted the information gratefully. 'So what's your suggestion?' he asked.

'Carney's, actually,' Winston admitted. 'He thought we ought to send a few of our younger lads in to make contact – see what they could dig up.'

Anderson nodded thoughtfully, considering the suggestion. 'Good idea,' he admitted. 'Can I leave it to you to set something up?'

'Sure thing, boss,' Winston agreed. He paused briefly, then added: 'I also have one idea of my own. It might be a good idea to compile a list of all the known right-wing organizations and splinter groups currently in existence. It would give us another line of enquiry to be working on.'

Anderson smiled without condescension. 'OPI are already way ahead of you on that one,' he told Winston. He produced a sheet of paper from his pocket and unfolded it. 'Take your pick from this little lot. National Front Party, National Rights Movement, Britain First, National Socialist Alliance, Freedom from European Federalism, Aryan Association, White Tigers, Socialist Union Group.' Anderson broke off to draw a breath. 'Oh yes, and something called the Thule Society, whatever that is.'

Winston frowned heavily. 'I might be able to shed a little light on that one, if you're interested,' he offered.

Anderson nodded. 'Go ahead. All information is useful information,' he said.

Winston shrugged. 'Well, I'm not sure about that,' he admitted. 'But it might give you a clearer idea of the sort of nutters we could be dealing with.' He paused, putting the facts together in his head before launching into a brief history of the Thule Society.

'The original legend of Thule goes back to the mists of Nordic mythology. It was supposed to be the island centre of a vastly superior race of super-beings, which was destroyed in some great natural disaster – much like the Atlantis legend.

111

However, around 1920, an Austrian named Dietrich Eckhardt dredged this legend up from the past and took it one stage further. Tying it in with a few other conveniently similar myths, he came up with the theory that not all the supermen of Thule had actually perished with the destruction of their island home. Some, he claimed, had survived to disguise themselves as ordinary, mortal men, and had remained hidden through thousands of years, biding their time and waiting for a mysterious new messiah figure who would lead them to greatness again. At that point, they would conquer the world, exterminate the false and inferior species of mankind and bring about a new super-race.

'Eckhardt formed a secret society, which he called the Thule Society, and gathered a few fanatical followers around him who dedicated themselves to magical ceremonies, blood sacrifices and other mumbo-jumbo which was supposed to call this messiah into being.'

Winston paused for breath, and Anderson took advantage of the break to interrupt. 'This is all very interesting,' he muttered. 'But what does a nutcase and a load of mystical claptrap have to do with a bunch of neo-Nazis?'

Winston smiled bitterly. 'Only that one of the Thule Society's earliest converts was a young army corporal named Adolf Hitler,' he announced. 'Eckhardt took it upon himself to groom Hitler as his natural successor. He was initiated into secret rituals and blood oaths which apparently involved human sacrifice on quite a large scale. By the time Eckhardt died in 1923, he had left behind a nucleus of believers who included Hitler, Hess and a man called Karl Haushofer. It was Haushofer who took an ancient magical symbol for the sun – the swastika – turned it on its side and created the emblem for the National Socialist Party. The rest, as they say, is history. Several quite level-headed historians have suggested that Hitler's extermination of six million Jews and three-quarters of a million gypsies was no more than his own continuing blood sacrifice to the supermen of Thule.'

Winston finished his little speech. There was a slightly uncomfortable silence for a while. Finally Pretty Boy spoke up, a note of awe in his voice.

'Jeezus, Sarge, I didn't know you were into all this mythology stuff.'

Winston smiled faintly, tapping the side of his nose. 'Know your enemy,' he answered. The smile broadened into a grin. 'Anyway, back to more important matters. Fancy a spot of London nightclubbing?'

Pretty Boy did not look over-enthusiastic. 'Depends on who my dancing partner's going to be,' he said dubiously.

'I thought you might take Mike Peters along for the ride,' Winston told him. 'He's young, and another Londoner. You should both blend in fairly well. With a bit of luck, you might both even get your leg over.'

Pretty Boy still wasn't quite convinced. 'What's the deal?'

Winston shrugged. 'Decent hotel room for a couple of nights . . . hundred and fifty quid spending money.'

Pretty Boy considered it. 'Separate hotel rooms?' he queried. 'That bastard snores.'

Winston nodded. 'Separate rooms,' he confirmed.

Pretty Boy's face brightened. 'Throw in an extra issue of condoms and you've got yourself a volunteer,' he said.

Winston laughed sardonically. 'Sometimes, Trooper Parrit, your unselfish and unswerving dedication to duty makes me weep with pride.'

14

Over the next two days Paul Carney received three phone calls. The first was from Winston, telling him that he, Pretty Boy and Mike Peters would be in London for the Wednesday evening.

That was the good news.

The bad news came from David Grieves. 'We appear to have stirred up the shit,' were his opening words. He proceeded to fill Carney in on the unpleasant details.

Less than forty-eight hours after the SAS raid on the farmhouse, there had been an instinctive, knee-jerk and violent reaction from the people behind the drugs factory – in the form of a message telephoned direct to the newsroom of the BBC. The enemy had announced themselves.

'As we suspected, it's ultra-right-wing radicals,' Grieves explained. 'This particular bunch of nasties call themselves Second Holocaust. They're threatening violent retribution for our interference in their little operation. My guess is that we hurt them, and now they're going to hit back.'

Carney digested the information gloomily. 'What's the threat?' he asked Grieves.

'They plan to bomb a pub,' the man from military intelligence said flatly. 'It will be a place belonging to the Consolidated

Breweries group, and it will only be a warning. More pubs in the same chain will continue to be attacked until they cough up a ransom of £300,000.'

Carney sucked in his breath. 'Jesus Christ,' he sighed heavily. 'Any chance it's just a bluff?'

Grieves did not sound too hopeful. 'They never bluffed in mainland Europe,' he pointed out. 'Anyway, we should know soon enough.'

Carney's brain was racing. 'How many pubs in the Consolidated group?' he asked.

'One hundred and eighty in the Greater London area, another seventy-three in the Home Counties. A total of well over a thousand nationwide,' Grieves informed him. 'Absolutely no chance of any effective preventative measures, I'm afraid. We'd need the entire bloody army.' He paused briefly. 'I've passed the information to Hereford, of course, but there's not much any of us can do except sit and wait. The bastards appear to have us by the balls.'

It was a sobering, and probably quite accurate, assessment, Carney thought. 'Why the sudden change of tactic?' he asked.

'Again, only a personal guess,' Grieves replied. 'But the way I see it, they were probably counting on the street value of that drug consignment to keep the wheels oiled. Deprived of it, they've got to find a source of emergency funding – and quick. That's probably why they've picked a large company and gone for a comparatively small ransom demand. Chances are they'll want to pay up quickly, and under the counter, no matter what the authorities advise them, or order them, to do. Company blackmail like this isn't without precedent. It's been going on for years, and it doesn't always get made public.'

It wasn't a point Carney was prepared to argue with. He'd heard of enough comparable cases to know that Grieves was right. All sorts of scams had been pulled, with varying degrees of success, over the years. Poisoned food in supermarket chains, factory-floor sabotage, computer frauds. Often it was cheaper for the companies to pay up quietly and discreetly than to risk loss of both business and standing. Even the banks deliberately hushed up the true extent of credit-card fraud, simply writing it off in the loss column of their accounts each year.

Grieves appeared to have said his piece. 'Anyway, I just thought I'd bring you up to date,' he finished, somewhat lamely. 'I'll be in touch again if there are any new developments.'

'Yeah, thanks,' Carney said, and hung up. As Grieves had already said, there was nothing left to do except sit and wait.

He did not have to wait very long. The first pub bombing was the lead story on the BBC's *Nine O'Clock News*. It was an early report, but it seemed that they had got off comparatively lightly, with only one death and seven minor injuries.

Carney wondered if the Miller's Arms, on the fringes of Notting Hill, had been a deliberate rather than a random choice. Situated where it was, the pub had a high proportion of West Indian customers. The actual bombing was a crude and simple operation, although devastatingly effective. A standard hand-grenade, fixed to the inside of the toilet door with some sticky parcel tape, a few drawing-pins and a piece of string. As the door was pushed open, the pin of the grenade was pulled – and the simple mechanics of the crude booby-trap were activated inexorably. The poor bastard who had picked the wrong moment to go for a piss never stood a chance.

The rest of the crowded pub's clientele were luckier. The toilets were situated well away from the main bar, and an outer door shielded the interior of the pub from the force of the blast. The majority of the minor injuries were from flying glass.

The brief news item ended. Carney noted that there had been no mention of the ransom demand, or the threat to bomb other pubs. He wondered if Grieves had managed to arrange a hasty D-notice on that particular aspect of the business. It was more than probable. Media censorship was not quite as dead as many people fondly imagined.

The telephone shrilled. Carney thumbed the remote control, switching off the television, and walked across the lounge to answer his third call.

It was Frankie Conran. As promised, he was calling Carney with an update on his computer scan.

'So, what have you got for me, Frankie?' Carney asked hopefully.

'Not a great deal, I'm afraid,' Conran admitted. 'In fact, almost nothing on the drugs research front. It appears there has been virtually no new commercial research into new hallucinogens going on anywhere in Europe over the past five years.'

'I don't believe it,' Carney said flatly.

Conran was in full agreement. 'I don't believe it either,' he said. 'That's why I said it *appears* that way. Or perhaps is meant to appear.'

'Security clamp-down?' Carney asked.

'Looks like it,' Conran replied. 'The very lack of information available suggests a fairly widespread security net over the whole subject. The other possibility, of course, is that whatever research *has* been going on has been under government rather than private control.'

Carney sighed, unable to conceal his disappointment. 'Well, thanks for trying, anyway.' He was about to put the phone down when Conran spoke again.

'Hey, hold on a minute. I said I didn't have much. I didn't say I had nothing at all.' He paused for a while. 'Like I said, nothing showed up about recent research, or on official data-bases, so I decided to dig back a bit and hack into a few places I probably shouldn't.'

'And?' Carney pushed, ignoring the illegality of the act Conran had just admitted to.

'Something turned up which you might find interesting,' Conran went on. 'It sort of spun off from my suspicion of government-funded research and gave me a name. So I did a bit of checking back and found what might be a minor can of worms. Also, it's more than possible that this "new" drug of yours isn't so new after all.'

Carney was intrigued, and suddenly enthusiastic again. 'Hold on while I get a pen and paper.' Returning to the phone, he said: 'Right, so what have you got?'

'You want everything?' Conran asked. 'There's a load of details and stuff in here which might not even be relevant.'

Carney nodded. 'Give me the lot,' he confirmed. 'I can sort out what is or isn't important later.'

There was a faint hiss of indrawn breath at the other end of the phone as Conran prepared himself. After a moment, he began to read from the notes he had prepared.

'The name is Dietrich Kleiner. Born in Munich in 1918. Entered the University of Bonn in 1936 to study organic chemistry and apparently got heavily involved with campus politics almost immediately. He joined the Hitler Youth in the same year, and was a fully active Nazi Party member by late 1939. By this time he had already published a couple of scientific papers about the effects of chemical contamination on the human system, and was reckoned to be something of a whizz-kid by his contemporaries. During the war years, he was almost certainly working for the Nazis – probably on potential chemical or biological warfare projects. His name popped up again at the Nuremberg war crimes trials; he was accused of conducting experiments on Jewish internees in Buchenwald. He was found guilty and sentenced to ten years' imprisonment. He was released early, in 1951, and settled in Austria. It seems he lectured at the University of Vienna during the period 1953–57 in what was then the new science of biochemistry. In 1959 he returned to Germany, where he took up a research position with a major pharmaceutical company and stayed with them for ten years. Most of his work at that time was with LSD and the new synthetic offshoot MDA.'

Conran paused. 'That's alphamethyl-3, 4-methylene, by the way. See what I mean about a load of extraneous details?'

Carney brushed the digression aside impatiently. 'I told you – just give me everything you've got.'

'OK.' Conran paused only to draw another deep breath. 'So, that takes Kleiner up to the early 1970s,' he continued. 'He then moved to a smaller company, called Fleisch-Müller Pharmaceuticals, where he was probably involved in similar work. And here's where it starts to get interesting. In 1973 Fleisch-Müller attracted the interest of the East German authorities with the development of some new drug which apparently had distinct military potential. But that's where the trail seems to come to an end. A pretty solid security curtain drops down after that.'

It was starting to come together, Carney thought. A drug which raised natural aggression levels would have fairly obvious warfare applications. The East Germans would probably have been acting purely as brokers for their puppetmasters, the Soviets. At that time the Cold War was still very much a reality.

'Anything at all on Kleiner after that?' he asked.

'Nothing at all,' Conran replied. 'He just disappears from the face of the earth. The assumption, of course, must be that he went over the Wall.'

That was the one bit which refused to make any kind of sense, Carney realized. Why would a dyed-in-the-wool fascist want to go to work for a left-wing regime? Unless, of course, he had been given no choice in the matter.

'Anyway, that's it as far as Kleiner is concerned,' Conran continued. 'He could well be dead by now. But there's just one little postscript to the story which might interest you. Three years ago, Fleisch-Müller Pharmaceuticals ran into some financial troubles. They were bought up and asset-stripped – including the purchase of all the patents they held at the time – by a financial consortium. The actual purchasing company was German, but the parent concern is British – Trans-Europe Holdings PLC, the chairman of which is none other than Cecil Hargreaves.'

The name rang vague bells in Carney's head, but he had to think about it for a while.

'Hargreaves – wasn't he the guy who launched that "British or Bust" campaign back in the mid-eighties?' he said finally.

Conran chuckled. 'The very same. A real nationalist nutcase. Right-wing as they come. Interesting, eh?'

It was indeed. Very interesting, Carney reflected. The saga seemed to have come full circle, and the timing was just about right. It coincided perfectly with the first outbreaks of violence in Europe, and it placed Dietrich Kleiner's formula in the hands of a rich, powerful man known to have extreme right-wing sympathies.

Whether or not it would lead anywhere from there was something else again.

15

By the time Winston, Pretty Boy and Mike Peters arrived at Carney's flat on Wednesday evening, the second pub bombing had taken place as threatened. Another Consolidated Breweries outlet, the Prince Albert, situated in the heart of the City, just off Bishopsgate, was frequented mostly by business executives, office workers and secretaries. The attack had taken place at six o'clock in the evening, in broad daylight, and when the pub was filled to capacity with people having a quick drink after work.

It was cold-blooded carnage. At least a dozen commuters would not catch their evening trains home to the suburbs that night, or ever again.

Again, an ordinary hand-grenade had been used – but there was a difference. No crude booby-trap this time, the bomb had been fired directly from a launcher through the pub's street window from a passing car. It was another chilling reminder of what sophisticated modern weaponry these people seemed to be able to get their hands on.

And the ransom demand had gone up – from three hundred to four hundred thousand. Another message to the BBC newsroom warned that it would rise a further hundred thousand each day until the ransom was paid in full.

Winston sprawled out on Carney's sofa as Pretty Boy and Peters carried a succession of large cardboard boxes up from the Range Rover they had driven from Hereford. Carney viewed the mounting pile of boxes dubiously. His flat was rapidly beginning to look like a storage depot.

'Travelling light, I see,' he said to Winston.

The big Barbadian shrugged. 'We needed an equipment cache in London,' he explained casually. 'Didn't think you'd mind.'

'Equipment?' Carney raised one eyebrow querulously. To confirm his sudden suspicion, he walked over to the nearest box and opened it, peering in at its contents. His first impression had been wrong, he realized. His flat was not being turned into a storage depot – it was being turned into an arsenal. He took a quick look at the contents of a couple more boxes, hardly believing the sheer amount of weaponry the SAS men had brought with them. Guns, grenades, spare ammunition. There was even what looked to Carney's untrained eye like some sort of rocket-launcher.

He looked over at Winston in disbelief. 'Jesus Christ! Are you expecting a bloody siege or something?'

Winston looked a bit more serious now. 'We need a place where we can tool up quickly, and on the spot,' he explained. 'As this isn't exactly the sort of luggage you can leave in a locker at Waterloo Station, and we can't all walk round the streets of London looking like extras from a Rambo movie, we thought your place was ideal.'

Carney conceded the point grudgingly. 'It's gonna give me a hell of a lot of explaining to do when the vicar pops in for tea,' he muttered, smiling ruefully.

Pretty Boy had just carried in the last box. He glanced at Winston. 'Where do you want the plastic explosive, boss?' he asked casually.

Winston was equally laid-back. 'Just dump it down anywhere for the time being,' he said.

Pretty Boy took the command at face value, doing exactly that. He dropped the heavy box to the floor with a thump which brought Carney's heart up into the back of his throat. 'Relax,' he said, grinning, seeing the man's obvious discomfort. 'This stuff's safe as houses until you stick a detonator into it.'

Carney remained unconvinced. He took another incredulous look at the armoury which had been deposited on his living-room floor. 'What do you need all this stuff for?' he demanded. 'There's only three of you, for Christ's sake.'

Winston gave a friendly laugh. 'Hell, man, it's not just for us – it's for the whole unit,' he said. 'Sorry, didn't I make that clear?'

Carney suddenly felt rather stupid. 'No, I don't think you mentioned it,' he said sheepishly, shaking his head.

Winston's face took on a serious look. 'Anyway, from the way things are shaping up, we might need it,' he pointed out. 'We don't know what sort of stuff we're going to come up against. I suppose you've heard that the bastards used a grenade-launcher in the latest attack?'

Carney nodded grimly. 'Yeah, I heard,' he said. 'What other nasty little tricks are they likely to have up their sleeves?'

Mike Peters shot him a reassuring grin. 'Nothing we can't match,' he boasted. 'We have a few little aces of our own.' He reached down to one of the boxes, drawing out a short, squat sub-machine-gun which looked as efficient and deadly as it was compact. 'These little beauties, for starters. Ain't they gorgeous?'

It was hardly an adjective which Carney would have used. The gun was a coldly efficient killing machine, nothing more.

'What the hell is it?' he asked, not recognizing the gun.

'Specially modified Heckler & Koch MP5K,' Peters told him. 'Designed expressly for counter-terrorist work. So short you can hide it in the glove compartment of a car – or even under your arm, if need be. Basically, you can take one of these little babies anywhere.'

'But not into a bloody disco, I hope,' Carney said warily. He had just had an apocalyptic vision of the two young men strolling into Norma Jean's looking like Delta Force Three.

'No, unfortunately not,' Peters agreed. He looked, and sounded, quite disappointed. A second later, his face brightened. Peeling back his jacket, he exposed the Browning 9mm High Power handgun tucked neatly into a specially designed armpit holster. 'Just gonna have to rely on the old peashooter instead.'

Winston, who up to this point had seemed completely laid-back, showed the first sign of authority. 'No bloody way, Trooper,' he said in a quiet but firm voice. 'You can forget any ideas about taking hardware into a crowded public place. This is supposed to be just a recce mission – remember?'

Peters's look of dismay was immediately echoed by Pretty Boy, who went one stage further by vocalizing his concern. 'Jeezus, boss, you ain't gonna strip us clean?'

The look on the young man's face was almost one of anguish, Carney thought, failing to understand the reluctance of all SAS troopers to go into any situation without some sort of a weapon, even if it was only a knife. It was a regimental tradition which had become almost a superstition.

But tradition or superstition, in this case Winston was adamant. 'No guns,' he repeated flatly. He uncoiled himself from Carney's sofa and crossed to another of the unopened boxes. 'However, you won't be quite as innocent as a pair

126

of choirboys,' he added, drawing out from the box a pair of oblong black plastic devices slightly larger than a TV remote control. 'You'll be carrying Scorpion electronic stunners, for emergency use only.'

Carney was fascinated. He held out his hand to Winston, hoping for a closer look at one of the gadgets. Winston handed him one, and Carney studied it closely. It did indeed look like a remote control, except that the numbered buttons were missing. There were only three main touch controls, plus a small rocker switch mounted on the side. There was also a translucent, ridged plastic panel at one end, which reminded Carney of the electronic flash unit of a camera. But the most distinctive feature of the otherwise bland black box was the pair of pointed, shiny metal prongs which protruded from its end like horns.

'What is it, exactly?' Carney asked.

Winston grinned. 'It's basically an upgraded version of an anti-mugging device they've been marketing in the United States for some time. Illegal in this country, of course, although there has been some talk of issuing them to the police. Actually, we've been waiting for a chance to field-test them.'

Carney had heard of such devices, although he had never actually seen one before. 'Do they work?' he asked.

Winston nodded emphatically. 'Oh, they work all right. Fully charged up, this little beast will deliver an electric jolt of between forty and fifty thousand volts. That's enough to stun, or partially paralyse, the average person for at least forty-five seconds.'

'Can they kill?' Carney wanted to know.

Winston shrugged. 'Under certain circumstances, yes,' he admitted. 'That's one of the main reasons why they're still banned in this country. Anyone with a weak heart, for instance, or an epileptic, would be at risk. And of course they'd be absolutely lethal to anyone wearing a pacemaker.'

Carney hefted the Scorpion in his hand experimentally. 'I suppose the general idea is, you stab your victim with the metal prongs and then zap him?'

Winston nodded. 'That's the basic procedure,' he agreed. 'Although this particular model has a couple of rather handy little extra features. For a start, it'll fire a pressurized-gas-powered metal dart on a wire, up to a distance of five metres. So you can disable an attacker before he actually gets close enough to touch you.' He pointed out the plastic panel. 'And there's also a high-intensity flash unit as an alternative defence mechanism. It'll give either a single bright flash or a pulsing strobe effect. Either will effectively blind anyone for several seconds if it goes off directly in their eyes. Particularly effective in the dark, of course.'

Winston paused. 'Here, I'll show you.' He thumbed the rocker switch on the side. The gadget began to emit a faint electrical hum as its capacitors charged up. Suddenly, without warning, Winston thrust the machine towards Carney's face and discharged it.

The world suddenly exploded into an incandescent white fireball, turning quickly to pitch-darkness in which a negative image of Winston stood like a life-sized snowman. Then the black faded too, to be replaced by a red, swirling haze in which dark blotches danced like a swarm of demented butterflies.

Carney was completely and utterly disoriented. He felt off balance, frightened and vulnerable. The sound of Winston talking to him came through like a voice from the other side of the grave. 'Right now you're totally helpless,' Winston was saying. 'I could do just about anything to you that I wanted.'

Not in a mood to argue, Carney screwed his eyes shut and shook his head, trying to clear his brain and his vision. The first took no more than a few seconds. It was almost a full minute before he could see normally once more. He glared at Winston. 'I asked you how the bloody thing worked, for Christ's sake. I wasn't expecting a personal demonstration.'

Winston was unrepentant. 'Count that as your first instruction lesson,' he said. 'If you ever have to use one of these things, make sure you blink or look the other way.' He paused, grinning. 'Now, anything else you'd like to know?'

Carney grinned. 'I suddenly seem to have lost all sense of curiosity,' he said. His eyesight had recovered sufficiently to allow him to glance at his watch. It was nearly ten p.m. 'Probably time to make a move,' he suggested.

Winston nodded, and jerked his thumb down at the boxes of hardware on the floor. 'Let's just get this little lot stowed away somewhere and we'll get moving.' He looked up at Carney. 'Got any suggestions?'

Carney could only shrug. 'Put it anywhere you can find room for it,' he said, becoming almost as blasé about the armaments as his colleagues. 'Only I'd probably sleep a bit better if you didn't stash it under my bed.'

16

Following Carney's instructions, Winston pulled the Range Rover into the kerb about two hundred yards short of the entrance to Norma Jean's. He switched off the engine and lights, then turned to Peters and Pretty Boy in the back seats.

'Right, you've each got your brief. Go in with a high profile, put yourselves about a bit. You're a couple of likely lads who like to live high and aren't averse to a spot of bother. Find out what you can, do your jobs and don't enjoy yourselves too much.' He paused, allowing a faint grin to creep over his face. 'Oh, and if either of you should find yourselves waking up in a strange bedroom in the morning, remember we RV at Carney's flat at exactly 1000 hours.'

'And what are you going to be doing while we're struggling not to enjoy ourselves, boss?' Pretty Boy asked.

Winston smiled. 'Oh, the usual high-society hobnobbing and social whirl. Carney and I are going to pay an unscheduled visit to the rich and powerful Mr Hargreaves.'

'Well, give him our love, boss,' Peters said, reaching for the door handle. He jumped down to the pavement, quickly followed by Pretty Boy. They began to walk up the street towards the nightclub.

Winston did not start the Range Rover again immediately. He fished under his seat, eventually pulling out a Browning HP and a shoulder holster, which he dropped in Carney's lap. 'Here, put this on before I forget.'

Carney looked at the gun, and then up at Winston's serious face, in surprise. 'I thought you said no hardware?'

Winston nodded thoughtfully, his face still serious. 'Yeah. But *we're* not going dancing, are we?'

Winston eased the Range Rover down the long, tree-lined drive which led to Cecil Hargreaves's private estate in an exclusive area of Borehamwood.

'Impressive, huh?' he said to Carney, with a brief sideways glance.

Carney said nothing, studying the mansion-like building beyond the high metal gates at the end of the drive. It looked like some latter-day fortress, the house itself standing some hundred yards behind a sturdy ten-foot wall, topped by a further eighteen inches of razor wire, probably electrified. Hargreaves was obviously a man who did not care for unexpected vistors.

Winston slowed down, pulling up just short of the gates. 'What now?' he asked.

It was a good question. Carney thought about it, as he took a good look around at the other security devices protecting the house and grounds. The place was sealed off as tightly as any high-security facility. That their approach to the gates had already been monitored was in little doubt. Carney had noted the rows of partially concealed floodlights between the trees all the way up the drive, and was sure he had also spotted at least four video scanners mounted high up in their branches. The presence of two wide-angle TV cameras set on top of the massive gatepost supports seemed to confirm this. Studying them more carefully, Carney figured they were probably part of a highly sophisticated, multi-function security system set for full-colour visual and infra-red scanning. They were fully motorized for a 180-degree sweep and vertical tracking, and their field of vision left no blind areas. Tiny red LED indicators showed that they were active. It would be impossible to approach the gates without coming under close surveillance.

Turning to Winston, Carney finally answered his question. 'The way I see it, we really don't have much choice,' he pointed out. 'Basically, we knock on the door and ask if Cecil can come out to play.'

He opened the Range Rover door and stepped out. Almost immediately, a bright spotlight snapped on, bathing him in its illumination. Probably activated by body temperature, Carney thought. Hargreaves had obviously cut no corners with his security arrangements. He waited for Winston to climb out and join him before walking cautiously up to the gates.

There was no need to ring the bell set into the right-hand gatepost. A gruff voice grated out from a small speaker mounted just above it.

'Who are you, and what do you want? Unexpected visitors aren't welcome here.'

Carney drew his ID card from his pocket, holding it up towards the video scanner above his head. 'Police. We'd like to speak to Mr Hargreaves.'

There was a moment's hesitation before the speaker grille squawked again. 'Got a warrant? If not, fuck off and come back when you have.' The intercom system gave a loud click and fell silent.

'Well, I guess that gives us our answer,' Winston observed laconically. 'Our Cecil isn't the fun-loving type.'

'Yeah.' Carney shrugged carelessly and turned back towards the Range Rover. 'Well, I suppose we might as well go home.' He began to walk back towards the car.

Winston ran after him, catching up and about to say something. Carney silenced him with a warning flash of his eyes. He climbed back into the Range Rover and closed the doors before speaking in a low whisper. 'I thought the gate area might be bugged for sound as well as visual.'

'So, what are you thinking?' Winston whispered back.

Carney sucked at his teeth. 'I'm thinking that if Hargreaves won't come out, then we're going to have to go in,' he said. 'The question is – how? That place is sewn up tighter than Fort Knox.'

Winston grinned roguishly. 'There's always a weak spot,' he said. 'We've just got to find it. If we can't, we'll just have to make one.' He started the engine and did a three-point turn in the drive, which was suddenly plunged into darkness again behind them as the security floodlights cut out.

It was almost like a signal for the furtive whispering to stop. Carney relaxed visibly, adopting his normal voice. 'Seems to me that all we have to do is get in there,' he pointed out. 'Once we're in, what the hell can the man do? Whoever is on guard duty already thinks we're cops, and he'll probably report straight to Hargreaves. No matter what he's actually mixed up in, to all intents and purposes he's a respectable and fairly public figure. He couldn't risk any violence on his own home patch.'

It made sense, Winston realized. Slipping the Range Rover into gear, he set off back down the drive, glancing at Carney. 'Let's take a little scenic tour of the rest of the estate, shall we?'

Pretty Boy nodded at the pint glass in Peters's hand, a slightly scornful look on his face. 'The boss said high living,' he pointed out, shouting above the din of the disco music. 'And you're slurping down pints of bitter like a bloody navvy.' He waved his own can of expensive Japanese lager in the air. 'You got to have a bit of class these days.'

Peters was unimpressed. 'All these fancy designer beers taste weak as virgin's piss to me.'

Pretty Boy looked smug and superior. 'You're just not with it, mate. Out of touch.'

Peters shrugged and took another long draught of his beer. 'Who the fuck cares?' He jerked his head towards Pretty Boy's drink. 'Anyway, what does it taste like?'

Pretty Boy grinned. 'Like a virgin's bloody piss,' he admitted. 'And these plonkers pay the equivalent of about four quid a pint for it.'

The bar area was on a mezzanine level mounted above the crowded dance floor. Pretty Boy looked down over the twitching and jerking mass, screwing up his eyes against the glare of the flashing disco lights and pulsing laser beams. 'Anyway, we were told to make contact,' he reminded Peters. 'See anything you fancy making contact with?'

Peters swept his eyes over the floor, finally picking out a willowy blonde girl dancing with a slightly plump redhead. 'How about those two?' he suggested. 'Don't think much of yours, though.'

Pretty Boy gave the two girls a cursory glance, finally shrugging philosophically. 'The blonde looks fine to me, my old son. Let's go for it.' Leaving the half-finished can of beer on the bar, he began to stride purposefully towards the stairs leading down to the dance floor. Peters followed him, grinning awkwardly. He'd been conned again. But what the hell? It was only a job, after all.

* * *

Winston was wrong about the weak spot in Hargreaves's security system, and he was man enough to admit it. After a third futile sweep of the estate's perimeter walls, he was about ready to concede defeat. 'Short of parachuting in, I'd say we were buggered,' he said flatly. 'And as we're a bit short on air support right now, I don't have much to offer in the suggestions department.'

But Carney wasn't really listening. He was thinking. The germ of a wildly improbable idea was just beginning to sprout in his mind. A faint, almost secretive smile began to spread across his face. It was just so bloody crazy, it might just work, for Christ's sake!

Winston couldn't help but notice the expression on Carney's face. 'You got a plan,' he asked, in surprise.

Carney nodded thoughtfully. 'Maybe "plan" is rather too strong a word,' he admitted. 'But I do have an idea, which is a start.'

Winston was intrigued. 'Well, are you planning to share it?'

Carney did not answer him directly. 'You know the old saying – that a chain is only as strong as its weakest link?' he said. 'Well, maybe that works the other way round, as well.'

Winston was totally confused, and it showed on his face.

Carney grinned. 'Perhaps the best place to create a weakness is at the strongest point,' he went on. 'Use the very strength of the system against itself.'

Winston was now completely lost, and admitted it. 'I haven't the faintest idea what you're talking about,' he told Carney.

It was time for an explanation, Carney realized, the final scheme only just having come together fully in his head.

'The main gate,' he said. 'It's where they must think their system is absolutely foolproof. All we have to do is convince them that it isn't.'

Slowly and carefully, Carney began to spell out his idea in greater detail. Dubious at first, Winston nevertheless found himself increasingly impressed. He wasn't a man who gave his respect easily – especially to a civvy. But Paul Carney was earning it – and quickly.

The blonde and the redhead had turned out to be a double disaster, on all fronts. Close up, the blonde had about as much sexual allure as the bouncers and the plump redhead's face sprouted acne like midnight in a mushroom patch.

More importantly, neither of them wanted to talk. All attempts to start a conversation were met with the same blank, glassy-eyed stare and the cow-like cud-chewing of gum. It was fairly clear that all the two girls wanted to do was to dance – or at least continue to move, zombie-like, to the non-stop pounding bass. After ten minutes in which both Peters and Pretty Boy had failed to elicit the first names of their new companions, it had become glaringly obvious that their value as an information source was absolute zero.

Exchanging a quick and meaningful glance, the two troopers cut out in mid-number, leaving the two girls still gyrating on the dance floor. Two other young men stepped in to take their place without a break in the beat.

Pretty Boy headed back to the bar.

'Well, that was a bloody waste of time,' he said irritably, then ordered himself another can of lager.

Peters nodded in agreement. 'Maybe we're going about this the wrong way,' he said. 'Trying to pick up a pair of birds together ain't gonna get us anywhere.'

'So what do you reckon?' Pretty Boy asked.

Peters grinned wickedly, nodding over to a table overlooking the dance floor where a reasonably attractive brunette sat with a rough-looking man, looking slightly bored. 'How about stirring the shit up a bit?' he suggested. 'I'll be here for backup if you get into any bother.'

Pretty Boy flashed him a contemptuous but good-natured sneer. 'You patronizing little bastard.' He took another deep swig of his beer.

'Dutch courage?' Peters taunted him. 'Or are you just waiting for me to make the first move?'

Pretty Boy's eyes glittered. 'No, I was waiting for you to place your bet,' he said. 'Fifty quid says I can pull it off in one.'

Peters rose to the challenge. 'You're on.'

Pretty Boy grinned triumphantly. 'Right, now watch a master in action – and eat your fuckin' heart out,' he declared, striding off towards the couple at the table.

The young man eyed Pretty Boy with guarded hostility as he hovered provocatively above the table, openly ogling the brunette. 'What the hell do you want?' he rasped.

Pretty Boy smiled disarmingly. 'I want to finish my beer,' he said casually. 'Then I can ask this gorgeous young lady to dance with me.' He was watching the girl's green eyes like a hawk, reading her reactions. For the moment, they showed just the faintest flicker of amusement. It was enough!

The young man's face registered only incredulity at the brazenness of Pretty Boy's challenge – for challenge it most certainly was. At once, primal, instinctive forces came into play.

The girl's companion glared up at Pretty Boy. 'She's with me,' he growled. 'And she stays that way. Now fuck off – unless you're looking for trouble.'

It was crunch time. Pretty Boy knew the rules of the game, and stuck to them. With casual, deliberate menace, he drained the last drop of lager from his can and proceeded to crush it slowly in his fist into a mangled ball of metal before setting it down on the table top. It was one of Pretty Boy's favourite party pieces, and rarely failed to impress – even though it involved technique as much as brute strength.

'Trouble?' he enquired innocently, with a quiet, confident smile on his face. 'No, I don't want any trouble, man. I've already got all the trouble I can handle.'

He looked into the girl's eyes again, finding the glitter of excitement and admiration he had been seeking. 'Now, how about that dance?' he said softly, reaching out to take the girl's hand as she rose from her chair.

Peters watched the little scene play out to its conclusion, a grudging smile on his face. Confident that the girl's former companion was not going to make a move, he turned back towards the bar, mentally shrugging off his fifty quid. There were usually compensations in life, he thought to himself philosophically, as his eyes fell on the pert little table waitress who had just approached the bar beside him.

'This place is pretty deadly, ain't it?' he murmured, with a knowing grin. 'How does a guy get a bit of a buzz around here?'

The waitress looked at him with a slightly mocking smile. 'Depends what you're looking for,' she said, a trifle warily.

Peters shook his head, still grinning. 'Nah. It depends on what's available,' he corrected her.

The girl smiled more openly. They understood one another.

17

Everything hinged on the field and range of the body-heat scanner. Carney was counting on the fact that it was a ninety-degree fixed beam, covering the area of the drive directly in front of the gates. If he was right, they should be able to approach the gates by creeping round the outside of the perimeter walls without triggering off the floodlights. If he was wrong, then the plan ground to an abrupt halt right there.

The theory was about to be put to the test. His back flattened against the wall, Carney was no more than two feet from the high brick pillar of the left-hand gatepost, the charging Scorpion stunner humming faintly in his hand. He edged a few inches nearer and froze, his eyes fixed on the tiny red eye of the video scanner as it slowly panned from side to side, monitoring and recording everything in its wide field of vision. It was a field of vision which ended with the massive bulk of the gatepost itself! And since that protruded out a good eight inches from the main wall, that left a small blind area which was protected from the camera's prying eye.

Carney smiled to himself, realizing that Winston had been right after all. There *was* always a weak spot – or at least a tiny flaw which could be exploited. Still with a watchful eye on the camera, he slid further along the wall until he was safely tucked into the safety zone. On the other side of the driveway, Winston had taken up a similar position, and so far the floodlights had not come on. It was looking hopeful.

He glanced down at the Scorpion in his hand, checking that it was in single-flash mode. Satisfied that it was, and that it was fully charged, he raised the device above his head at arm's length in preparation.

Timing was crucial. Carney bided his time, allowing the video camera to make two complete sweeps and gauging the time it took to complete its full 180-degree pan. The entire cycle took exactly twenty-five seconds. Tensing himself, he watched the camera complete its scan in his direction, stop for a fraction of a second and then begin to swing back towards the centre of the drive.

He moved quickly out of the protective lee behind the gate-post, pointing the flash unit directly at the camera lens and firing it off. In the momentary glare, he could just pick out the bulky shape of Winston, copying his move with utter precision. A second flash exploded into the lens of the right-hand camera.

The plan was essentially simple. Somehow they had to convince whoever was monitoring the security scanners that the system was malfunctioning. The glaring discharge of the light guns would appear on the monitor screens inside the mansion house as a sudden and inexplicable burst of static – first one camera, then the other. One or two such occurrences might be dismissed as nothing more than a temporary fault. A continuing series could well suggest a complete system breakdown.

The camera, still on remote control, began to swing back in Carney's direction. The Scorpion units had a recharge time of at least twenty seconds, which left very little leeway. Holding his breath and muttering a silent prayer, he pressed the firing button as the camera completed its return traverse. Their luck was holding; the Scorpion fired again, exactly on cue.

Winston set off his second discharge seconds later. Carney glanced up at the nearest camera hopefully. The red operating light was still on, the smooth traversing motion unbroken. He initiated the sequence twice more.

Carney's heart jumped as the panning camera stopped suddenly, in mid-sweep. The tiny red light flickered out. As he had hoped, whoever was monitoring the scanning system was shutting it down temporarily, perhaps hoping that it would reset itself automatically.

It was time to move. There was no way of knowing how long the camera would remain switched off. Carney could only assume that the entire security system was linked together, and there was no independent backup. Ducking out from behind the cover of the gatepost, he dashed into the centre of the drive in front of the tall wrought-iron gates as Winston ran out to meet him.

Swiftly Winston uncoiled the length of nylon rope he had brought from the back of the Range Rover. With a heavy tyre lever tied to one end, it was a hastily improvised grapple. Swinging it in his hands, Winston threw it up over the gate, where it lodged securely in position behind a couple of the ornamental spikes on top. Giving it one quick tug by way of a test, Winston began to shin up the front of the gate, flipping himself over the top to slide down the vertical bars on the inside. Carney was a matter of a few seconds behind him. They were inside the grounds.

'Come on, this way,' Winston hissed. Breaking into a loping run, he headed across the large lawn towards the side of the house. The silence was suddenly shattered by a loud bark, which echoed through the darkness towards them. Carney felt his heart sink. He hadn't even thought about guard dogs. Straining his eyes towards the house, and the sound of the barking animal, he was just able to pick out the vague shape of a huge German shepherd bounding across the grass towards them.

'Leave this to me,' Winston hissed, pushing Carney out of the way behind him. He bent to a crouch, directly confronting the charging dog. Just as the animal reached the end of its attack run, and launched itself into the air at his face, Winston flexed his knees, springing up to his full height. His arms snaked out, grasping the dog's front legs and wrenching them savagely apart with all his strength. There was a horrible sound of splintering bone and tearing sinew. The dog let out a single brief and bloodcurdling yelp of agony and dropped dead at Winston's feet, bright fresh blood frothing from its mouth.

Winston backed away, his huge frame shaking with anger and revulsion. 'Shit,' he cursed under his breath, with real feeling. 'I love dogs.'

Carney looked down aghast at the dead animal. 'What the hell did you do?' he whispered.

Winston regarded him glumly. 'Design fault,' he muttered. 'They've been bred for shape – long, lean body and big chest. It's caused a certain degree of malformation in the internal skeletal structure. Ribcage is set too far forward. Put sudden and heavy strain on the front shoulders and it splinters inwards, puncturing the heart.' He looked up at Carney, giving a thin, bitter smile. 'It works on Dobermanns, too. It's Rottweilers that are the tricky ones – you have to punch them directly under the snout before they get their teeth into you.'

Carney wrinkled his nose in distaste. 'Thanks for the crash course in advanced dog handling,' he murmured. 'Now let's get the hell out of the open before they send an RSPCA hit man after us.'

It was a savage joke, but underlined a very real danger. The dog's frantic barking must have alerted someone, and it could only be a matter of moments now before its sudden disappearance, coupled with the apparent failure of the security cameras, caused that someone to put two and two together. Judging from the scope of Hargreaves's security measures so far, it was a pretty fair bet that he would also have armed bodyguards as a backup. Carney's original hypothesis – that Hargreaves would not want to risk violence in his own grounds – was no longer quite so secure. The unavoidable killing of the dog had changed things. The security guards now had an excuse for direct retaliation, and if they were feeling jumpy, they might well shoot first and ask questions later. Standing out there in the middle of the lawn, they presented a tempting target.

Similar thoughts had already occurred to Winston.

Poised on the balls of his feet, he shot Carney a brief, querulous glance. 'Where?' he hissed.

Carney shrugged, realizing that they had little choice other than to revert to the original plan. They had to make contact with Hargreaves direct, trusting that he would react as Carney had assumed. He nodded towards the house, where lights had begun to snap on in several of the ground-floor rooms. 'I guess we go for the front door,' he suggested. 'I think someone's expecting us.'

Breaking into a run, both men headed for the front of the house. The massive door was already opening.

Standard heavy, Carney thought, as he eyed the formidable bulk of the man framed in the stone porch. All brawn and very little brain, and trained to follow very specific orders. Without such orders, he was not a threat.

The man looked at Carney and Winston with a surly expression. 'Persistent bastards, aren't you?' He jabbed a thick finger in Carney's chest. 'I told you once to fuck off. Now I'm telling you again – and take the razor with you.'

The racial slur brought a frown to Winston's face. He recognized the criminal rhyming slang – razor-blade, spade. 'Now that's not very polite,' he said sombrely. 'And I get very angry when people aren't polite. Now you just trot back indoors like you've been trained to do and give your boss a message that we want to see him.'

The heavy's countenance darkened. He turned on Winston, his ugly face creasing up into a snarl. 'Uppity bastard,' he spat out. 'Maybe I'd better teach you a lesson.'

His right hand dived behind the lapel of his jacket, reaching for the Mauser holstered under his shoulder. His movements were fast – but no match for the highly tuned reactions of an SAS trooper. Winston's own hand snaked to his right-hand pocket, flashing out again with the Scorpion stunner firmly in his grip. In one smooth movement, he jabbed the pointed prongs of the device through the thin material of the man's shirt and pressed the discharge button.

The big man stiffened. Almost simultaneously there was a muffled explosion and the smell of cordite. The heavy crumpled to the floor.

Winston cursed for the second time that night. 'Fuck it,' he said wearily. 'That wasn't supposed to happen.'

Carney understood only too well what had gone wrong. The man must have reached the butt of his gun at the very second Winston had used the stunner. With his finger already wrapped around the trigger, he had been ready to draw as the charge hit him. Muscular reflex had done the rest. The jolt had travelled down his arm to his hand, contracting the muscles.

Still trapped inside the confines of the holster, and at point-blank range, an exploding .32 slug carried a hell of a punch. The heavy had a hole the size of a fist blown in his side.

The echoes of the gunshot had hardly died away before Carney and Winston heard the click of two revolver hammers being cocked immediately behind them.

'Freeze right there, or you're both dead,' came a harsh voice, utterly chilling in its sincerity.

Carney spread his hands out slowly from his side, palms upward. Winston dropped the stunner, adopting a similar stance. Carney winced slightly as a gun barrel was jammed viciously into his ribs. A well-trained hand frisked him quickly and efficiently, drawing the Browning HP from its hiding place. The rest of the contents of his pockets quickly followed. Winston was not treated so leniently. A vicious kick in the back of his knee sent him sprawling to the ground with a dull groan of pain. A heavy boot slammed down on the back of his neck, pinning him there.

It was a strange and unbelievably tense little tableau which seemed to last for ever. Frozen like a dummy, Carney fully expected to feel the searing pain of a bullet tearing through his back at any second. Finally, through the half-open front door, he saw the figure of a man step out into the hallway of the house.

It had to be Hargreaves, Carney figured. The man was in his late fifties, but in superb physical condition for his age. His face, sun-tanned and healthy-looking, was surmounted by a leonine mane of silvery-grey hair, immaculately styled. Clad in a scarlet and gold Japanese robe of pure silk, he looked like the living epitome of wealth and power. Incongruously, there was a thin smile on his face, although it was possible to detect a seething anger just behind it.

147

'Bring them in,' the man snapped.

Carney lurched forward as the gun jabbed painfully into his ribcage again. The second bodyguard removed his foot from Winston's neck, urging him back to his feet with a couple of kicks in the side.

The party stepped forward over the body of the doorman and entered the house. The man was not yet dead, but no one made any move to help him. It was only a matter of a few moments, and he was well beyond any miracle of medicine or surgery.

'You do seem uncommonly anxious to see me,' the man said to Carney, confirming that he was indeed Hargreaves. 'Although telephoning for an appointment would have been so much less messy.' He paused to glance dispassionately at the dying man sprawled over his front porch. 'And good help is *so* difficult to find these days.'

For just a second, a look of concern showed through the mask of the fixed smile. 'I take it you've killed the dog as well?'

Winston nodded. 'I'm sorry about the dog,' he said quietly, meaning it.

Hargreaves ignored him, still directing himself to Carney. 'I shall quite miss the vicious beast,' he murmured, sounding almost affectionate for the merest fraction of a second. As though embarrassed by any sign of human weakness, his mood changed abruptly. 'Bring them to my study,' he snapped curtly to the two bodyguards, turning away and walking down the long hallway towards the rear of the house.

Once in his study, Hargreaves seated himself behind a huge, green-leather-topped desk. 'Make sure they're both completely clean,' he told his bodyguards. 'And then leave us. One of you had better wait outside the door, just in case.'

Carney and Winston had no choice but to submit to a second and completely thorough frisking, during which the

148

contents of their pockets were dumped unceremoniously on Hargreaves's desk. Their two Brownings, with the ammunition clips removed, were laid down last of all.

Hargreaves seemed satisfied. He dismissed the two body-guards with a curt nod of his head. As they left the room, he picked up Carney's ID card and glanced at it briefly before looking up at him curiously.

'An official police warrant card,' he mused, also picking up one of the handguns and studying it. 'But this is hardly standard police issue.' He paused, thoughtfully. 'Exactly who are you working for, Mr Carney?'

Carney said nothing. It seemed to be an answer in itself for Hargreaves, who nodded knowingly. 'Ah,' he murmured, as if everything had suddenly been made clear to him. 'Quite obviously there's no point in my picking up the phone and making a top-level complaint about the pair of you breaking into my home.' He sat back in his swivel chair, the fixed smile returning to his face. 'So what can I do for you?' he asked.

'Nirvana,' Carney said abruptly, seeing no reason to beat about the bush. 'Know anything about it?' He was watching the man's eyes like a hawk, searching for the faintest trace of a reaction, but there was nothing. The man was as cool as ice.

Hargreaves merely smiled wistfully. 'Yes, a state of inner peace,' he mused. 'Alas, not something that a businessman finds much of these days.'

'Cut the crap, Hargreaves,' Winston snapped testily. 'You know exactly what we're talking about.'

The Barbadian provoked a reaction where Carney had failed. For the briefest instant a look of vicious loathing blazed in Hargreaves's eyes.

Carney noted it with a faint sense of satisfaction. The man's racial hatred was strong enough to make it a weakness. It might be possible to play upon it.

But not for the moment. Hargreaves recovered his icy composure, looking at Winston with the innocence of a child. 'I haven't the faintest idea what you mean.'

They were getting nowhere, Carney realized. The verbal fencing could go on all night unless they established a position of strength. Perhaps it was time to throw a few cards on the table and see how they fell.

'Then let me spell it out for you,' Carney said quietly. 'Nirvana – the street name for a new drug which gives the user a sense of well-being and at the same time increases aggression. A drug very similar in fact to one developed by a certain Dietrich Kleiner while he was working for Fleisch-Müller Pharmaceuticals in Germany. A drug for which one of your subsidiary companies bought up the patent and formula just three years ago. And now that drug is on the streets, and people are getting killed.' Carney took a long, meaningful pause. 'I'd say that puts you in a rather vulnerable position – as an accessory to murder – wouldn't you?'

Hargreaves was silent for a long time. His eyes, although betraying little, were thoughtful as his mind raced through all the implications and possibilities.

Finally he smiled. 'An extremely tenuous connection, I'm sure you'll agree,' he pointed out. 'I control dozens of companies, but I don't have – couldn't possibly have – a day-to-day say in what they do, or what they buy and sell. No, I think you'll have to do a lot better than that, Mr Carney.'

It was the answer Carney had expected, and he conceded the point. 'All right. Let's look for some other connections then, shall we? Dietrich Kleiner was a Nazi. The drug has now fallen into the hands of a new bunch of neo-fascists. Your own personal links with the extreme right might not stand too close a scrutiny – if someone took the trouble to dig deep enough.'

Hargreaves didn't look quite so sure of himself any more. He was beginning to get a little rattled, Carney thought. He pushed his advantage.

'If we know this much already, you can bet your life we can find out more,' he stressed. 'And, as I think you've already worked out for yourself, we're not restricted to conventional procedures. If we dug up a connection between you and a militant neo-Nazi group, the picture might look a little different, don't you think?' Carney paused for effect. 'Second Holocaust, for instance?'

He was rewarded by a momentary flash of fear in Hargreaves's eyes.

'So you've heard of them?' he asked, seizing on it.

Hargreaves nodded faintly. 'Yes, I've heard of them. They're nasty – and they're dangerous.' All the man's bravado and confidence was melting away fast now. He looked up at Carney with a slightly helpless expression which was almost a plea. 'Look, they're absolutely nothing to do with me, you've got to believe me.'

'Then what are you afraid of?' Carney challenged him. That the man was afraid of something was no longer in doubt.

Hargreaves took a deep breath. 'Look, I've never made any great secret of my political beliefs,' he said finally. 'But I'm merely a nationalist. I'm not a Nazi.'

'There's a difference?' Winston put in sarcastically.

Hargreaves ignored him, continuing to direct himself to Carney. 'Look, you're a policeman, you must see what's happening to our society. We've allowed the very fabric of this nation to go rotten, its people trodden down and demoralized. Our very sovereignty is threatened by an increasingly federalistic Europe. Criminals freely roam the streets and get suspended sentences if they are caught at all. Children commit the most brutal murders. We have three million native Britons out of work, yet immigrants continue to pour into this small and overcrowded island home of ours . . .'

Winston cut the party political broadcast short with a bitter laugh. 'I wondered how long it would take to get round to that,' he observed. 'Repatriation's the answer, right? Pack us all into banana boats and ship us back to the coconut groves?'

For the first time, Hargreaves confronted him directly, an ingratiating smile on his face. 'Believe me, I have nothing personal against you people,' he whined. 'It's not your fault. It was our own spineless left-wing liberals who brought you into the country after the war to do all the dirty, low-paid jobs that nobody else wanted. It was a mistake. No one had taken into account your breeding capacity.'

For his own sake, as well as Winston's, Carney did not want to hear any more. He felt sickened. Hargreaves's 'you people' had said it all. He slammed his fist down on the man's desk. 'I'll repeat my earlier question,' he barked. 'What are you afraid of? Second Holocaust worries you – why?'

Hargreaves's eyes flickered nervously. He let out a long, deep sigh. 'I made the drug formula available to certain parties without knowing the connection,' he admitted finally, in a small, weak voice. 'It was a mistake, an error of judgement, and I regret it now.' The pleading look crept into his eyes again. 'But that's the sum total of my involvement, believe me. As I said, these people are dangerous – as I now know to my own cost.'

'Your cost? How?' Carney demanded, seizing on the admission.

The businessman managed a thin, bitter smile. 'You surprise me, Carney,' he muttered. 'If you could dig out Dietrich Kleiner's name, I would have thought you would have done your other homework more carefully.' He paused briefly, before dropping his final bombshell. 'Didn't you realize that Consolidated Breweries was one of the companies in the Trans-Europe Holdings group?'

There was a long, stunned silence, broken finally by the sound of Winston whistling through his teeth. 'Talk about biting the hand that feeds you,' he observed sardonically.

Hargreaves looked at the two men warily, his eyes glittering with a mixture of hope and cunning. 'So it occurs to me that we might be able to make some sort of a deal,' he suggested. 'Perhaps we are in a position to help one another.'

Winston's face was a picture of revulsion. 'Jesus Christ, I'd as soon hand-feed a fucking rattlesnake,' he muttered, even though the realization that they didn't have much choice had already dawned on him.

Carney was rather more philosophical. 'What do you suggest?' he asked calmly.

Hargreaves looked relieved. Rather *too* relieved, Carney thought. As though he had expected more opposition. The man clearly had more to hide than he was letting on.

'There are a couple of things which might help you,' Hargreaves said eventually. 'First of all, there's a big rally coming off in the very near future. It will ostensibly be the official National Rights Party, but members of all the fringe organizations are bound to be there, including Second Holocaust. I can give you names, contacts.'

'And the second thing?' Carney prompted.

Hargreaves looked nervous again. 'I've already decided to pay the ransom,' he muttered after a moment's hesitation.

'Moves to make contact and arrange the details have already been initiated. Suppose I were to arrange for you to make the delivery?'

Carney thought about the offer at some length. 'So what do you get out of all this?' he asked gravely.

Hargreaves shrugged. 'I stay clean,' he said simply. 'You make no more enquiries into my political affiliations or business connections. I would also need your reassurance that the ransom money would be handed over straight and with no tricks. The money will be genuine, and I want the transaction to go smoothly. Consolidated Breweries cannot afford a prolonged siege.'

Winston was shaking his head. 'No way,' he said flatly. 'We're out to stop these bastards, not help finance them.' He paused, staring Hargreaves in the eyes. 'Now here's the deal as I see it. You help us, and we'll back off from you personally. But we handle the ransom hand-over our way, or not at all.'

Fear flashed in Hargreaves's eyes. 'But they'll kill me if they think I've double-crossed them,' he pleaded.

There was no trace of pity on Winston's face. 'Then you'll just have to keep your head down until we've done our job, won't you?'

Hargreaves's face revealed an agony of indecision as he contemplated all the frightening possibilities. Finally he caved in with a hopeless sigh.

'All right, we'll do it your way. I'll get out of the country for a while, move to one of our operations in Germany. I have friends there.'

Winston's face creased into a scornful grin. 'Yeah, I bet you fucking have.'

18

The morning meeting had been convened in Carney's flat, as planned. It was time for the group to pool their knowledge thus far and to plan future moves.

Winston looked at the two young troopers expectantly. 'Well? Get anything?'

Pretty Boy grinned ruefully. 'Only a quick wank,' he volunteered. 'It was the wrong time of the month for a deep-penetration mission.'

Winston glared at him, letting him know that he was out of order. There were times to let bullshit and banter go unchallenged, but this was not one of them. 'Any more cracks like that and I'll deep-penetrate your arse with the business end of an M16,' he threatened.

'You're all promises, boss,' Pretty Boy shot back at him, but then fell silent, suitably chastened.

Winston glanced at Peters. 'Well? Anything we can use?'

Peters nodded. 'Maybe,' he said. 'I managed to get chatting with a bird who works at the place regularly, and I picked up a few pieces of information that could be useful.'

'Such as?' Winston prompted.

'Nirvana's usually available, at about fifteen quid a throw,'

Peters told him. 'Only the word is that it happens to be in rather short supply at the moment and the two guys that deal regularly haven't been around for a couple of days.'

Winston smiled to himself. 'Surprise, surprise,' he murmured. 'So we did manage to throw a spanner in the works.'

Peters didn't look too enthusiastic. 'Yeah, well, don't get too carried away, boss. The girl seemed pretty confident there would be another batch on the streets in a day or so.' He paused, to shrug briefly. 'It could be that we only dented their distribution network a little bit.'

It was more or less what Carney had anticipated, so he wasn't too disappointed. It was unrealistic to expect them to keep all their eggs in one basket. 'No idea of the source of this new supply, I suppose?' he wanted to know.

Peters shook his head. 'Nothing, sorry. It seemed to be pushing my luck to ask too many questions on first contact. But I think she trusts me, if I ever need to get back to her.'

Carney could only nod in agreement. The young trooper seemed to have an instinctive understanding of the situation. Undercover contacts could only be built up slowly, through mutual trust.

Winston had returned his attention to Pretty Boy. 'What about the bully-boy brigade? Anything on that front?'

Pretty Boy looked vaguely optimistic. 'Could be,' he said guardedly. 'Cheryl, the bird I scored, seems to go for the hard-man type. I think it turns her on. Anyway, I sort of gave her the impression I was a bit of a Jack-the-Lad and enjoyed the odd bit of Paki-bashing for kicks. She didn't give me anything definite, but she did drop a few vague hints that some of the guys who use the club make a few quid on the side hiring out their fists from time to time. It sounded like some sort of rent-a-riot set-up.'

Winston glanced across at Carney. 'Sound like anything you've come across before?' he asked.

Carney nodded grimly. 'All too bloody familiar,' he said. 'Amateur yobbos come a lot cheaper than professional thugs. It's not unusual for some of the more militant groups to go recruiting round the pubs before a big street rally or a demo.'

'Actually, boss,' Pretty Boy cut in, 'it occurred to me that we might set up a little demo of our own – with your help, of course.'

It was obvious that the young trooper had some kind of idea. As ever, Winston was willing to listen to it. 'Explain,' he said.

'I've arranged to meet this bird again tonight,' Pretty Boy told him. 'Like I said, she seems to be heavily into the aggro bit. I thought we might be able to put on a little show for her benefit.' He paused, looking at Winston with an awkward, rather sheepish grin.

It was this look, rather than what had already been said, that put Winston on his guard. 'What exactly did you have in mind?' he asked warily.

Pretty Boy adopted a more serious expression. 'I thought it might be possible to set up some sort of confrontation – between you and me,' he explained. 'I do you over, proving to Cheryl what an evil, nigger-hating bastard I am.'

Peters, who had been listening to all this with increasing amusement, could not resist putting in his two pennyworth. 'Christ Almighty, Pretty Boy,' he said dismissively. 'This has got to be your richest stroke yet. You get to beat the shit out of poor old Sarge so you can impress some shit-brained bird?'

Winston, however, was giving the idea serious consideration. He finally nodded his head thoughtfully. 'Yes, it might work,' he mused.

Pretty Boy looked awkward again. 'The only real problem is that it would be hard to fake,' he pointed out. 'In order to make it look totally convincing, I'd have to come in really hard. You could get hurt.'

Winston smiled knowingly. 'Yes, that thought had already occurred to me,' he said. He was thoughtful for a few more seconds. 'I could always wear a certain amount of hidden body protection, and we can rehearse a few stunts which will look convincing,' he added at last. 'Just as long as you're bloody careful where you put the boot in.' He considered it for a few seconds more, then finally made up his mind. 'OK, let's pencil that one in for a go – as long as we get time.'

The matter was decided. It was time to move on to more important business. Winston brought the two troopers up to date with their encounter with Cecil Hargreaves and his unexpected willingness to co-operate with them.

'So, basically, it's now down to Second Holocaust,' he summed up, finally. 'Consolidated Breweries are going to pay the ransom once the arrangements have been made, and we play the delivery boys. Depending, of course, on getting final approval from official channels through Lieutenant-Colonel Davies and all the backup we're likely to need.'

Pretty Boy voiced the doubt which had occurred to all of them. 'How far can we trust this Hargreaves bastard?' he wanted to know.

Winston was brutally frank. 'About as far as I'd trust you with a teenage virgin,' he admitted. 'But then it wouldn't appear to be in the man's best interest to dump on us. He's got too much to lose.' He paused, and shrugged philosophically. 'On the face of it, this could give us our best chance yet of tackling these bastards face to face, putting them under some real pressure.'

'How do you see it?' Carney asked.

Winston smiled grimly. 'If we can hit them on two fronts – choke off their drugs and extortion funds as we move in closer to their actual membership structure – something's got to give. We've got a couple of new angles now – maybe it's time to pull out all the stops and really put the squeeze on. Let the bastards know we're coming.'

'And then what?' Carney asked bluntly. 'We don't really know exactly how desperate, or ruthless, these jokers are likely to get.'

Winston nodded glumly. 'That's why I'm going to have to talk to Barney Davies,' he admitted. 'Basically, I think it's high time the bright sparks who dreamt up this little caper in the first place decide exactly how far they want, or are prepared, to go.'

19

The answer, when it finally came, was the unequivocal 'All the way'. On Lieutenant-Colonel Davies's direct orders, the entire force had been put on a state of alert and was ready to move at a moment's notice. The men of 22 SAS were ready to go to war and more than spoiling for a fight. Everyone had been expecting a quick and early breakthrough with the raid on the farmhouse drug factory. When that had turned into a non-event, it had left behind a deep sense of frustration. Now, at last, there was a sense of purpose again. Two new names had been added to the plaque on the base of the regimental clock at Stirling Lines and the legendary camaraderie of the SAS demanded vengeance – just as soon as the enemy chose to show itself.

Winston's London unit had been supplemented by Ted Brennon, Miles Tremathon and Hugh Thomas, the Lethal Leek. The transfer of personnel served two purposes, strengthening Winston's ability to cover any possible leads arising from their current contacts and giving the three troopers a new boss following the death of Captain Feeney. Perhaps more importantly, it also ensured that there was a reasonably sized strike force ready and on the spot should the rumoured fascist rally take place at short notice. It left Major Anderson and the main force free to respond to any new information from intelligence sources as well as primed to back up the ransom hand-over, once the details had been finalized.

Carney's little flat had now become a temporary barracks room as well as an arsenal, with Carney himself feeling increasingly out of place. He had been able to relate to Winston, and had managed to get along fairly well with Pretty Boy and Peters. Outnumbered six to one, and acutely aware of the age gap between himself and the young troopers, he was beginning to feel like the proverbial spare prick at a wedding.

He managed to convey these vague feelings of uneasiness in a rare quiet moment alone with Winston, as the troopers took over his bedroom to play cards.

Winston listened patiently as Carney expressed his misgivings. Finally, his face registered a sympathetic smile. 'But that's not all, is it?' he said knowingly.

Carney shook his head, impressed by the big Barbadian's capacity for sympathy and understanding. 'No, that's not all.'

Winston was thoughtful for a while. 'Look, what you're really worried about is that you're about to be frozen out,' he said, hitting the nail squarely on the head. 'You're afraid there isn't going to be any part for you to play if things start really popping. Am I right?'

Carney nodded miserably. 'And you're not going to assure me otherwise, are you?' he said, making it a statement rather than a question. He looked Winston squarely in the eye, waiting for the man's response.

It was a look of regret, confirming Carney's worst fears. Winston shook his head slowly. 'No,' he said flatly. 'I can't tell you anything different.' He paused, racking his brains for something to say which might conceivably soften the blow. In the end there seemed little more he could say than to remind Carney of something he should have realized all along. 'You were told at the start that you'd be kept out of combat situations wherever possible,' he said gently. 'Nothing's changed from that.'

Carney let out a short, bitter laugh. 'Goddammit, a hell of a lot's changed. I got involved, for a start.'

Winston fell silent. He could only feel sorry for the man. Carney had been given a rare insight into a different world, a different way of life which was almost impossible for the average outsider to even contemplate, let alone understand. He had received a taste of what it could mean to be SAS, to be part of a uniquely close, almost mystical brotherhood who lived and shared danger and companionship on a completely different level from most other men. To have been that close and yet so far, Winston reflected. Yes, he could only feel sorry for Carney, with his sense of impotence and frustration.

He offered him the only comfort he could. 'Look at it this way, Paul,' he said, using Carney's first name for the first time since they had met. 'This thing isn't over yet – not by a long way.'

As if right on cue to confirm this statement, Carney's telephone shrilled. He jumped up, crossing the lounge to snatch it up. It was Hargreaves, and he sounded edgy. Carney flipped on the tape recorder Winston had wired into his telephone.

'Is everything arranged?' Carney asked.

There was a faint catch in the other man's voice as he answered. 'They're prepared to go ahead – but there's a problem,' he said shakily.

'What sort of problem?' Carney demanded, trying to hide his sudden concern.

'They've taken out a little insurance policy,' Hargreaves told him. 'There's another bomb, in another pub. But this one's different – it's already in place, and fitted with a timing device. We'll only get the exact location and instructions for defusing it if the ransom hand-over goes without a hitch.'

'Damn.' Carney's mind raced, trying to see ways round the unexpected complication. 'When and where is the money due to be handed over?' he demanded.

'That's the only part we don't know yet,' Hargreaves told him. 'The method of transfer has already been arranged. The money is packed in a red Samsonite suitcase which is ready and waiting for collection at the reception desk of the Courtland Hotel in Knightsbridge. The actual hand-over will be tomorrow. Details will be announced in the personal columns of the *Evening Standard* this evening. It will take the form of a message to Gloria from Stanley, giving a time and meeting place.'

Carney ran the plans through his head quickly, looking for anything which didn't sound right, or could possibly go wrong. There were a dozen such things, he realized – but the basic scheme seemed workable enough.

'All right, so how do we collect the money?' he asked.

'The hotel manager is expecting someone by the name of Gilmour,' Hargreaves told him. 'He will hand over the case on request at exactly nine o'clock this evening.'

Faint warning bells rang in Carney's head. He didn't like the idea of being pinned down to a precise time. 'Why not until nine?' he asked suspiciously.

'Because that's when he comes on duty,' Hargreaves said. 'And only he can authorize the handing over of the suitcase. That's *my* little insurance policy – against someone making a sneak pick-up.'

'And what else?' Carney asked brusquely. There was something the man hadn't told him, he was sure.

There was a short pause as Hargreaves thought about things. 'All right, there is one more little detail,' he admitted at last. 'By nine o'clock I'll be on a flight to Bonn. I need to feel sure that I am safe and out of here if anything goes wrong.'

It all made sense, Carney decided, although his suspicions were far from allayed. But there was not much more he could do about it. For the moment at least, Hargreaves was calling the shots. He dropped the receiver back into its cradle and rewound the tape recorder for Winston to check the conversation.

'Well?' he asked, after Winston had played the tape through a couple of times.

The Barbadian looked dubious. 'I don't trust that bastard,' he said candidly. 'And something smells.'

Carney shared his sentiments exactly. 'Seems to me we're the only ones without a safety net here,' he observed. 'The point is, what the hell can we do about it?'

Winston was thoughtful for a while. 'I think we need to modify our plans slightly,' he said at last.

As promised, the brief coded message in the personal columns of the *Evening Standard* gave precise instructions:

'Gloria – See you by the bandstand in Green Park at midday – Stanley.'

Later editions of the paper, and the evening television news, carried no stories of further bombings. On the face of it, Second Holocaust appeared to be keeping their word.

20

'Well, how do I look?' Winston asked, parading himself like a model on a catwalk.

Pretty Boy, Carney and the Lethal Leek scrutinized him from all angles, taking in his general appearance. There was no doubt that he looked slightly odd to those who knew him well and were used to his huge, muscular but lean frame. Now, with several rolls of crêpe bandage bound around his ribcage, a bulletproof vest under his shirt and a padded, heavy-duty sports jockstrap protecting his groin area, he looked strangely swollen and misshapen.

Pretty Boy delivered the consensus of opinion. 'Well, you look a bit like a sumo wrestler who's been on a diet, boss, but I guess you'll do.'

Winston glanced at Carney, inviting a second, more critical assessment. Carney shrugged faintly. 'What the hell?' he said. 'You're not going to be under a spotlight and no one's going to be looking at you that closely. I don't see any problem.' He paused, giving Winston a reassuring grin. 'Besides, this is showbusiness.'

Winston seemed satisfied. He turned to Pretty Boy. 'Right, now remember those moves we rehearsed, and don't throw anything unexpected at me.'

Pretty Boy nodded, now completely serious. 'By the book, boss,' he vowed.

Winston checked his watch. It was nearly eight o'clock. They had exactly half an hour to get Pretty Boy to his date and set up the fake fight and a further half an hour's leeway to arrange the pick-up of the ransom money. There was just enough time for one last run-through of the arrangements.

'OK, let's just make sure that everyone knows his job,' Winston said. 'Trooper Peters goes directly to the nightclub to follow up his own contacts and wait for Pretty Boy and his girlfriend. That gives us a homing pigeon if Pretty Boy has any info by the time he gets to the club.' Winston nodded at Hugh Thomas. 'The Leek stays here with Carney. They're our relay station and emergency backup unit. Anyone with any information can pass it back here for forwarding to Major Anderson at Stirling Lines if deemed necessary. That also goes for anyone hitting unexpected trouble.'

Winston paused to take a breath, then turned to Ted Brennon and Miles Tremathon. 'You two will shadow me discreetly until the fight is over. Just in case any other young thugs decide to join in the attack, you'll be around in the background to make sure I don't get seriously hurt. As soon as it's over, and you know I'm safe, you make the pick-up at the Courtland Hotel and bring the money straight back here.' Winston finished his little speech and eyed each man in turn. 'Any questions?'

There were none. Winston had spelled everything out in clear, logical terms. Each of them had his specific orders to follow.

'Right, let's do it,' he said firmly. 'It's showtime.'

Winston was already installed in the pub as Pretty Boy walked in with the girl. He sat alone at a table near the door, sipping at his beer and ignoring the rest of the customers, especially the big Cornishman Tremathon and the wiry little Scouser Brennon, sitting up at the bar on stools.

He did not, however, ignore Pretty Boy's date, casting a frankly admiring gaze over her shapely young body as her escort ushered her through the door. It was a prearranged move, but Winston enjoyed it anyway. Cheryl Taylor was quite a looker, he had to admit. Perhaps just a shade top-heavy in the tit department for his personal taste, and a bit too wide in the hips – but a body definitely designed for comfort rather than speed. Her face was pretty enough, and shown off to its best advantage by a curly mass of naturally blonde hair. It was only the corners of her generous mouth, turned down in an apparently permanent pout, and the cold precision in her blue eyes, which lent her a hard, almost sluttish appearance.

But certainly not a woman any man would want to kick out of his bed, Winston decided. The delicious irony of the situation brought a smile to his face. He was going to get beaten up to improve Pretty Boy's chances of getting the girl into bed in the first place. Ogling her as he was, his smile passed for a lecherous leer, which did not go unnoticed.

Cheryl was used to the hungry looks of men – black or white. As usual, she took it as a compliment. Not so Pretty Boy, responding as programmed.

'Is that black bastard blimping you?' he growled.

Cheryl shrugged it off. 'Let the bastard dream,' she murmured casually. 'Before he goes home to his big fat momma.' She looked away from Winston, casting her eyes around the uncrowded pub for more sops to her vanity. Brennon and Tremathon obliged, both running approving eyes up and down the girl's shapely legs and body.

Pretty Boy led her to the bar and ordered drinks. When they arrived he paid and they made their way to an empty

169

table at the rear of the pub, Pretty Boy all the while casting baleful looks in Winston's direction.

'Why so jumpy?' Cheryl asked, aware that Pretty Boy seemed upset by the black man's presence. 'You're not the jealous type, are you?'

'Bloody right I am,' Pretty Boy said vehemently. 'And I don't like the way that nigger looked at you.'

Discreetly, he scanned the girl's eyes, noting the faint glimmer of excitement which crossed them momentarily. She liked being a catalyst, he told himself. She'd encourage, even welcome violent jealousy, though she wouldn't push it.

'Did you hear about the surfer who found a drowned nigger on the beach?' he asked the girl in a loud voice. 'He skinned the fucker and made a new wetsuit.'

Winston deliberately ignored the vicious joke. It was sicker than most and just happened to be one that he hadn't heard before. He found himself wondering idly whether it had already done the rounds back at Stirling Lines. Or whether Pretty Boy had ever told it before under other circumstances. For personal reasons, he preferred to think not.

Cheryl giggled nervously, reaching across the table to clutch at Pretty Boy's arm. 'Shush – he'll hear you,' she hissed under her breath.

He shrugged with affected bravado. 'I don't give a shit if he does,' he boasted loudly. 'Gutless bastard won't have the bottle to do anything about it. Only time they'll fight at all is when they're at least three to one.'

Cheryl was suddenly aware that the focus of attention had shifted from herself. 'Anyway, forget about him,' she said, clutching Pretty Boy's arm again possessively. 'Where are you going to take me tonight?'

Pretty Boy shrugged. 'I thought we'd have a couple of drinks and go on to the club,' he suggested. 'Maybe score a little buzz – you know?'

Cheryl pouted sexily, eyeing him over the top of her glass of Diamond White. 'And I thought you might be wanting to score something else tonight,' she teased him, openly provocative. 'My little problem – it's finished now.'

Pretty Boy grinned widely. 'Even better, darling,' he said as he laid his hand over hers and squeezed it.

Winston glanced at his watch. They were running short of time. He made a big show of finishing his drink, finally pushing himself to his feet. He allowed his eyes to linger on Cheryl's body again, a slightly mocking smile on his face, before moving towards the door.

Pretty Boy's face was taut with anger. 'He did it again, the cheeky bastard,' he spat out. 'That black shit gave you the eye.'

Cheryl could sense something was about to break, and she wasn't sure that it suited her purpose for the moment. The time for trouble was later, when her date had had a chance to spend a bit of money on her, show her a good time. She most definitely did not fancy going round with some dishevelled and possibly beaten-up wreck of a guy for the rest of the evening. She smiled disarmingly. 'I didn't see anything,' she lied. 'Maybe you were just imagining it.'

'No bloody way,' Pretty Boy told her angrily. 'That bastard looked you over as if you were something hanging up in a butcher's window – and I'm not going to let him get away with it. That's one jumped-up nigger who needs teaching a lesson.'

Pretty Boy threw the rest of his drink down his throat, glaring over at the door through which Winston had just exited. He jumped to his feet, looking down at Cheryl. 'I'm going after that sonofabitch,' he told her. 'He needs a bloody good kicking. You want to wait here until I come back?'

171

Cheryl sighed resignedly, thinking it through quickly. It was obvious that she wasn't going to get the attention she demanded until this little game was over. In the meantime, she might as well get a little vicarious excitement, she thought. Just in case the evening was going to turn out a complete washout on other fronts. She ran through various worst-case scenarios in her calculating little brain. If Pretty Boy came out the worse for wear from the encounter, she could always dump him. That still left her choices. She could go to the club on her own, confident that there would be another man with money in his pocket and a prick in his pants. There always was. On the other hand, she could come back to the bar and finish her drink. She had already noticed the two hunky guys propped up at the bar as she came in with Pretty Boy. So what if one of them sounded like a yokel and the other spoke with a Liverpool accent you could cut with a knife? They were both beefy men – and both interested. Cheryl had seen the looks they had given her earlier. They were interested all right.

She pushed her half-finished drink to the centre of the table, standing up to join Pretty Boy, who was clearly itching to get after the departed black man.

'I'll come with you,' she told him. 'But just watch yourself, OK?'

Pretty Boy sneered at her. 'I can take that bastard with one hand tied behind my back,' he said with total confidence.

Pulling the girl by the hand, he headed for the door, looking out on to the darkened street. Winston had crossed the road, and was just about to turn down a narrow alley between some shops. It was all part of the plan, and Winston's insurance. The fight would look more convincing in the dark, and the more private it was, the better.

'Come on,' Pretty Boy said, dragging the girl across the

road. Reaching the far pavement, he paused, rooted around in his pocket and pulled out a bicycle chain.

Cheryl looked at the weapon with a certain awe, her eyes glinting. 'You really come prepared for bother, don't you?' she said, unaware that all the props for the little charade had been bought only that afternoon.

Pretty Boy shook his head. 'Not prepared – looking,' he said thickly. 'I fucking hate those black bastards.' He coiled the chain around his hand, leaving a loop of eight or nine inches hanging loose. Telling Cheryl to stay behind, he ran into the dark alley in pursuit of his quarry.

Winston was walking unhurriedly past rows of dustbins and empty cardboard boxes. He stopped suddenly, turning round warily at the sound of running footsteps. For a moment it seemed that he would turn again and run, but he stood his ground.

Pretty Boy stopped and sized up the situation. Cheryl stood at the end of the alley, watching Pretty Boy as he started to move forward again cautiously until he was within six feet of the big man. He swung the chain menacingly from his wrist.

'I want a word with you, nigger,' he hissed.

Winston's white teeth flashed in the dim light as he grinned back defiantly. 'You'd better run on home, white boy,' he sneered. 'Before you get more than you bargained for.'

Pretty Boy flexed the chain in his hand, edging a few steps nearer. 'I didn't like the way you looked at my girl,' he growled.

Winston grinned again, but moved back cautiously against the partial protection of the wall. 'Maybe you'd better ask her how she feels about it,' he challenged. 'Looked to me like she was the sort of bitch who liked her meat on the dark side.'

'Bastard,' Pretty Boy roared, apparently stung by the slur. He ran forward, wielding the chain above his head and swinging it in a vicious arc at the black man's head. For a horrible second he thought he had misjudged the distance and was going to catch Winston's face with the end of the chain – a mistake which would almost certainly have smashed the man's jawbone. He needn't have worried. With lightning-fast reactions, Winston ducked, twisting his body away so that the heavy chain merely smashed into the wall, sending chips of broken brick flying in all directions. Jumping back, Winston's hand flashed under his jacket, emerging with a wicked-looking eight-inch commando knife in his grip.

It was Pretty Boy's turn to jump backwards, assuming a more defensive position. He poised himself on the balls of his feet, facing his opponent and allowing the chain to uncoil from his wrist to its full length. Knowing that Cheryl couldn't see his face, he flashed Winston a quick, knowing smile. They were now in a position they had shared a dozen times before – albeit under the controlled conditions of the close-quarter combat gym back at Stirling Lines. Two superbly trained warriors, with both fighting and defensive skills honed to a degree of precision which was almost an art form. From here on, it was pure choreography.

Winston leapt forward, his knife arm fully extended. With a vicious slicing motion, he made a feinting stab at Pretty Boy's belly. As though he had springs built into his feet, Pretty Boy jumped backwards a good three feet, landing on his toes. Extending his own arm, he began to whirl the chain in front of him like a propeller.

The next moves had been painstakingly rehearsed for much of the afternoon. Appearing to make an error of judgement, Winston tried another feinting lunge at Pretty Boy's guts, holding the knife at arm's length. The whirling chain connected solidly with the heavy metal blade, sending it spinning away out of his grasp. It clattered to the floor of the alley several yards away in the darkness.

'Got you now, you nigger bastard,' Pretty Boy screamed, for Cheryl's benefit. He moved in towards his now defence-less victim, slashing the chain in a criss-cross pattern at Winston's padded chest and drawing a series of convincing grunts of pain from the black man's lips.

It was time to go down, Winston realized. He backed away from Pretty Boy's attack, losing his footing on the rough cobbled ground and falling backwards. He collapsed on to his back, absorbing some of the shock by rolling sideways.

Pretty Boy moved in for the kill. Make it look good, Winston had urged him when they had plotted out the fight. Caught up in his role, although hardly enjoying it, Pretty Boy stepped towards his fallen opponent and swung his right foot viciously towards the man's ribs, only turning his foot at the last moment so that the side rather than the point of his boot made contact.

With all the flair of a professional actor, Winston screamed in agony, writhing on the ground as though badly hurt. Pretty Boy continued to rain kicks into his chest, grunting with the sheer exertion of his efforts.

Satisfied that her man now had the situation firmly under control, Cheryl began to walk down the alley towards them, as they knew she would.

'She's coming. Time for the big scene,' Winston hissed.

Sneaking his hand quickly into his jacket pocket, he pulled out the two capsules of imitation blood which he had purchased in Soho earlier that day. He sliced them open with his thumbnail and squirted the red over his head and face. In the dim light, it looked more than convincing. Winston lay still now, apparently unconscious. Pretty Boy stepped back from his battered, blood-stained victim as Cheryl approached. She looked down at the black man's crumpled body without compassion.

It was time for the *coup de grâce*, Pretty Boy decided. He

stepped forward again, drawing back his right leg and aiming one final, vicious kick at Winston's ribs. Inch-perfect, the heavy front of Pretty Boy's boot slammed against the two thin slats of wood which Winston had carefully taped against his ribcage. Muffled by the layers of crepe bandage and his jacket, the sharp crack which they gave out provided a more than passable imitation of snapping bone.

Pretty Boy stepped back, glancing aside at the girl with a look of savage joy on his face. 'That taught the bastard,' he said, triumphantly, between heavy gasps for breath.

Cheryl's eyes were dancing with fire. Her face was flushed, her red lips slack and slightly apart. She too was breathing heavily, erratically. She looked like a woman on the point of orgasm, Pretty Boy thought – and the realization both excited him and repulsed him at the same time. For the merest fraction of a second, he felt like taking her right then, against the wall of the alley. He fought the momentary impulse, instead marshalling his thoughts. There was a job to do, and it wasn't over yet. The entire, violent charade had been for a greater purpose than just a quick and animal-like knee-trembler.

Controlling himself, Pretty Boy moved away from Winston's prone form, pushing the girl ahead of him. 'Come on, we'd better get out of here,' he grunted, whirling the bicycle chain above his head and flinging it away into the darkness.

Cheryl pressed herself against him, wrapping her arm around his waist. Pretty Boy could feel her body heat surging into his flesh in pulsing, orgasmic waves. Temptation rose in him again, stronger this time.

But the girl's next words were as effective a passion-killer as any icy shower. 'You really showed that piece of black trash,' she told him, her tone at the same time cold and appreciative. 'You should have killed the bastard.'

21

The Lethal Leek was bored. He rummaged through Carney's tape and CD selection for the fourth time that night, still failing to find anything that appealed to him. Unusually for a Welshman, his tastes did not run to opera or classical music, and what few pop albums Carney did possess were years out of date.

He picked up the TV remote control and flicked through the channels without finding anything which took his interest. 'You should have satellite,' he complained to Carney rather peevishly. 'There'd be some sport on, then.'

Carney said nothing. He'd given up trying to converse with the Welshman at least an hour earlier, when it became apparent that there was absolutely no point of contact between them. Hugh Thomas had joined the army straight from school, serving three years with the Welsh Guards before transferring to the SAS. It was the only world he had ever known, and it seriously limited both his field of experience and conversation. Rugby Union, and the many different ways of killing a person with one's bare hands, were just about it.

The Welshman stared morosely at his watch. 'Reckon the boss should be limping his way back home about now,' he said. 'Looks like patching him up will be about the only excitement we're going to get tonight.'

It was not what Carney wanted to hear. He was still in a state of mild depression following his earlier talk with Winston, and the last thing he needed was more gloom and despondency. Reminded by the Lethal Leek's reference to the time, he wondered idly how Ted Brennon and Miles Tremathon were getting on with the pick-up and how it must feel to cart nearly half a million pounds in banknotes halfway across London.

There was a knock on the door. Caught in a daydream, Carney wasn't concentrating. His usual sense of caution went to the winds. Without thinking, he crossed the room and opened the door, half expecting to see Winston's black face grinning at him.

He was wrong – on all counts. The face which greeted him was white – deathly white – and it belonged to Cecil Hargreaves. And he most certainly wasn't grinning. Carney had only a fraction of a second to recognize the look of fear on the man's features before two other, even more disconcerting factors registered. One was the pair of nasty-looking heavies who stood immediately behind him, and the second was that both were wielding sawn-off shotguns. After that, everything happened in a blur.

The two gunmen burst into the flat, pushing Hargreaves ahead of them. As the nearest one covered Carney, his companion leapt across the room towards the Lethal Leek, who was already clawing inside his jacket for his shoulder-holstered Browning.

'Don't even think about it,' the second heavy barked warningly. In the split second in which the Welshman froze with indecision, he had stepped forward and smashed the twin barrels of the shotgun against the side of his head. The SAS man collapsed soundlessly, out cold. Even as he fell to the floor, the gunman was rushing past him to search the other rooms of the flat. He returned quickly, nodding reassuringly at his companion. 'It's clean,' he called out, in what seemed an unnecessarily loud voice.

From outside in the hallway, a fourth man stepped into the flat and closed the door quietly behind him.

Carney appraised this new visitor carefully. He was different from his companions, physically tall but lacking the brutish bulk of the professional bodyguard or thug. His clothes were well cut and chosen with some taste, and his cool grey eyes were alert and analytical, betraying a keen intelligence. There was also something about the way the two gunmen acted almost deferentially towards him which told Carney he was a man of some authority, if not a leader.

The two thugs were merely true to type. The first, the one who had so efficiently disposed of the Lethal Leek, was muscular and powerful, with a square-jawed, bullet-shaped head atop a thick, stubby neck. His companion was shorter and heavier, and seemed ill at ease, even nervous.

Hargreaves was starting to blubber apologetically, his former composure completely shattered by obvious terror. 'They picked me up at the airport . . . I had no choice but to tell them,' he blurted out. 'They'd have killed me.'

Carney regarded the man with a contemptuous, pitying sneer. 'You bloody fool,' he said coldly. 'They're going to have to kill you anyway.'

The grey-eyed man turned to Carney, a faint but chilling smile on his face. 'Ah, you're a realist, Mr Carney,' he murmured. 'I do so admire a man who can see things in a pragmatic light. Perhaps that means that you'll be sensible enough to co-operate with us.'

Carney glared at him. 'Who the hell are you?'

The man's eyes narrowed thoughtfully for a moment, then he shrugged his shoulders in a careless gesture. 'Since it really isn't going to matter too much to you, I don't see why I shouldn't tell you,' he said quietly. 'My name is David Scott. But perhaps more to the point, who – or what – are you?'

Carney held the man in an eyeball-to-eyeball confrontation. 'You appear to already know my name,' he pointed out.

Scott allowed himself a thin smile. 'Oh yes, I know your name, Mr Carney,' he conceded. 'Our mutual friend Mr Hargreaves was most helpful with what limited information he had at his disposal. However, he was less forthcoming on specifics. He apparently seems to imagine that you're part of some special unit, or task force of some kind.' Scott paused, to emphasize what he was about to say. 'The thing is, Carney, I don't care a great deal for mere speculation. I like to *know* things.'

Carney grinned defiantly. 'Life must get terribly frustrating for you,' he said, with mock sympathy.

Scott was not amused. He clucked his teeth irritably. 'Oh dear, I do hope you're not going to be tiresome, Mr Carney,' he chided. 'It gets so messy.'

He nodded over at the shorter of the gunmen. 'Roger, please show Mr Carney what we do with people who cause us problems.'

Carney tensed as the thug turned towards him, giggling inanely. Seeing the mad gleam in the man's eyes, he was forced to revise his earlier opinion. He had taken his excitable and awkward manner for nervousness. But he'd been wrong. Roger suffered not from insecurity but from serious mental instability. The man was a nutcase, probably a psychopath.

Scott rolled his grey eyes heavenwards. It was the look of an employer seriously considering dismissing an underling for total incompetence. 'No, Roger, don't damage Mr Carney just yet. He may still be useful to us.' He glanced sideways at Hargreaves, who had sunk down on to the sofa. 'I think Mr Hargreaves will suffice as a demonstration model for the moment. I don't believe we've yet pointed out to him the penalties for trying to double-cross us.'

As the heavy stepped towards the quaking businessman, Scott flashed Carney a chilling smile. 'Observe the artistry of a craftsman at his work, Mr Carney,' he cooed.

Repulsed and yet fascinated, Carney watched the thug launch into a savage and ferocious attack on the defenceless man, using the butt and barrels of the shotgun on every part of his head and body. In seconds, Hargreaves's face was a mask of blood and his body reduced to a crumpled, quivering heap. The beating continued with sadistic precision until finally he passed into merciful unconsciousness.

Scott had watched it all with cold detachment. His face was devoid of expression when he finally looked back at Carney. 'Now, back to business,' he said calmly. 'I need to know exactly what sort of unit you are working with, its approximate strength and the full scope of its brief.'

Despite what had happened to Hargreaves, Carney dared to be defiant. Some little inner voice told him that compliance with Scott would not save him from a beating – or worse. On the contrary, it might even hasten it. The best he could do was to play for time, and Scott himself was the key to that. The man was basically an educated bully. He revelled in showing off his power and he enjoyed the sensation of engendering fear. He was also an egotist, Carney figured, inordinately proud of himself and boastful to the point of vanity.

'Who we are is not really important to you,' Carney said firmly. 'What matters is that we're strong enough to stop you.'

He tensed himself, waiting for the signal which would set Scott's gorilla upon him, but it didn't come. Instead, Scott merely chuckled, as though he found Carney an amusing diversion to be savoured.

'Stop us, Mr Carney? Oh no, you won't do that. At best you might slow down, even slightly hamper, the growth of our operation in this country. But our strength in mainland Europe is already something too powerful to be stopped. We can only grow, spread – control. The time is right, you see, Mr Carney. History is on our side. The world has been waiting for us.'

Carney could only stare at the man in blank incomprehension. That an apparently educated and civilized man could still believe in such an old and insane dream was incredible in itself. What made it totally lunatic was the fact that the man appeared to regard himself as some sort of a messiah. He resisted the impulse to laugh openly in Scott's face. For the moment he was winning precious extra minutes of life. It would be stupid to throw that small advantage away by openly antagonizing him.

He nodded down at Hargreaves. 'Your former colleague already outlined what he thought was wrong with society,' he pointed out. 'So what's your prescription for the malady?'

Scott's eyes searched Carney's warily, seeking the faintest trace of derision. 'Are you being flippant, Mr Carney? I do hope not.'

Carney was straight-faced. 'Actually I'm quite serious. I'm a copper, after all. There are a few things about the System I'd like to change myself.'

Scott nodded thoughtfully. 'Yes, I'm sure there are,' he said. 'But somehow I don't quite see you as a potential convert.' He paused. 'However, my "prescription", as you put it, is basically quite simple. We tear a rotten society apart from the inside and then reshape it into a new order. With the help of our drug, we have the ability to turn the dregs of the younger generation into a ragged, undisciplined yet reasonably effective army of destruction. And what they destroy, we shall be in a position to rebuild, using all the hidden wealth and power which has been buried in Europe and this country for over half a century.'

Carney was unable to resist a note of sarcasm creeping into his voice. 'So the revolution starts tomorrow, does it?' he asked.

Scott smiled thinly. 'There's no great hurry, Mr Carney. The tide of history has taught us patience, and now that tide is flowing in our favour. You have only to look at the trend of European politics over the last few years. A new kind of radical federalism is already with us.'

Suddenly Carney did not feel quite so confident. It was easy to dismiss a madman with a mad dream, comforting to believe that the forces of rationality and right would always prevail. But there was a frightening plausibility in Scott's argument – a germ of truth. With a sickening feeling in his gut, Carney realized that the man was in part right.

Perhaps Carney's face betrayed the fact that Scott had got through to him. For whatever reason, it seemed the man had tired of talking. The Lethal Leek was recovering consciousness. Groggily, he began to pull himself to his feet. Bullet-head let him rise, eventually prodding him with the business end of his shotgun until he collapsed on to the sofa beside the still-unconscious Hargreaves.

Scott eyed the latter dispassionately for a few seconds before turning back to Carney. 'Now, the answer to my question,' he snapped. He reached into his coat pocket, drew out a 9mm Beretta pistol and methodically screwed a fresh silencer on to the end of the barrel. He flashed Carney one of his ice-cold smiles. 'In the interests of saving time, I have decided not to have you beaten up, Mr Carney,' he announced. 'It occurs to me that you are probably the sort of man who would take a lot of unnecessary punishment before talking, and we are starting to run behind schedule. We have a rendezvous with some of your colleagues at the Courtland Hotel, I believe.'

Carney sneaked a quick glance at the clock on the mantel-piece. It was nearly ten to nine. 'I think you're going to be too late,' he pointed out. 'You've just cost yourselves four hundred thousand quid.'

Scott seemed unperturbed as he cocked the Beretta and aimed it deliberately at the Lethal Leek's head. 'As a matter of fact, it is your friends who will be too late,' he said calmly. 'And you now have exactly ten seconds to tell me the precise nature of your special task force before your companion here dies.'

The Lethal Leek glared up at Scott defiantly. 'Don't tell 'em a fucking thing,' he hissed. 'Let the bastards find out the hard way.'

Carney's eyes were hypnotized by Scott's finger, flexed against the trigger of the pistol. His mind raced as the precious seconds ticked away. It was not just the Welshman's life at stake here, he realized. He now knew that Tremathon and Brennon were walking straight into a trap. There was also the terrifying possibility that Scott and his cronies would search the flat after they had killed the Welshman and himself. It was unthinkable that the cache of sophisticated weaponry concealed there should fall into the hands of such fanatics. Out of panic, and sheer desperation, a wild bluff was born.

'All right, I'll tell you,' Carney blurted out. 'Seeing as how you'll be finding out in another couple of minutes anyway.'

The Beretta wavered, momentarily, in Scott's hand. Carney dared to hope that he had at least cast doubts into the man's mind. Finally, Scott lowered the gun. 'Explain yourself, Mr Carney.'

Carney faced him squarely. 'As you have worked out for yourselves, we are part of a special SWAT team,' he lied. 'And of course we have more than adequate backup.' Carney paused, forcing a look of confidence on to his face which he didn't really feel. 'Did it not occur to you that we would have some sort of fail-safe procedure?' he said calmly. He nodded over towards the telephone. 'My orders are to call in to base every thirty minutes as long as the situation is green. Your unexpected arrival postponed one of those calls.' Carney feigned a triumphant smirk. 'So you see we are in a much stronger position than you imagined. At this very minute this building is being surrounded by trained snipers. You'll never get out alive.'

Doubt flickered across Scott's face. His eyes bored into Carney's, seeking the faintest sign of weakness and finding none.

'You're bluffing,' he hissed, but there was uncertainty in his tone.

Carney grinned – genuinely this time. He had the man rattled, and it was time to press the advantage. 'You're not a stupid man, Scott,' he said quietly. 'Misguided, perhaps, but not stupid. You *know* I'm not bluffing. Why else do you think I was so eager to hear you talk about your insane little plans? Did you really imagine I wanted to hear all the drivel from your sick and twisted little mind? I needed time, Scott – time that you and your pet animals just ran out of.'

Carney was chancing his luck now, and he knew it. He had no idea how far the man could be pushed, especially in front of his thugs, but it was essential that he made his play as convincing as possible. And insulting a man holding a gun seemed as good a way as any of reinforcing a bluff, even if it was highly dangerous.

The Lethal Leek had caught on to Carney's little ploy now, and added his own fuel to the smouldering fire. 'Looks like we got a great chance here to check out our response times,' he muttered. 'The next couple of minutes should be interesting.'

It was the final touch which pushed Scott over the edge, from uncertainty into panic. His eyes showing open fear now, he snapped his fingers at Bullet-head. 'Check the windows and the landing outside,' he barked.

The man hastened to obey, striding across the flat to peer through the curtains into the dark street below. 'I can't see nothing,' he growled, turning away to cross the room again and check outside the door. 'It looks all clear to me.'

For a fraction of a second, the smile returned to Scott's face, but it was cosmetic, masking the worry beneath it. He stared at Carney again, an unspoken question in his eyes, but the policeman's face was bland, giving away nothing.

Finally, Scott seemed to come to a decision. 'So we both lose, Mr Carney,' he said resignedly. 'A pity.'

Scott backed away towards the door, still holding the pistol. Carney's stomach felt like an ice-pack resting on top of his bowels. A single bullet through his brain – or the blast of a twelve-bore into his guts? He wondered, momentarily and fancifully, if any one form of death was preferable to another. One popular fallacy, however, was dispelled once and for all. Facing extinction, his past life did not flash before him like a video on fast forward. On the contrary, every remaining millisecond seemed to grate past with agonizing slowness, like a series of freeze frames.

Suddenly Scott was gone, followed closely by Bullet-head. The Giggler remained – a sort of rear guard, covering the room with the shotgun as he too began to back slowly towards the door.

Carney's eyes were rooted on the two deadly circles made by the barrels of the shotgun. The Giggler was framed in the doorway now, one foot already in the passage outside. Now was the time, Carney thought, wondering if he would see or hear anything before a cone of lethal lead pellets tore his body to shreds.

Then the shotgun dipped towards the floor. The Giggler moved fully back into the outer hallway, fumbling for something in his pocket. Carney heard a faint metallic click, the sound of something heavy thudding on to the carpeted floor of the flat and the door slamming, quickly followed by running footsteps.

His eyes flashed to the floor, identifying the hand-grenade before it stopped rolling. So he'd been wrong, he thought bitterly. Death came in three choices, not two.

The Lethal Leek had seen the grenade too, and his brain raced into overdrive. Conventional Mills bomb, army issue. Probably a standard seven-second fuse, once the pin had been pulled and the spring-catch released.

Seven seconds . . .

It was not just his superb training which spurred the Welshman into lightning action. It was a fury born of desperation, an instinct for survival which went beyond normal human reaction.

'Dive,' he screamed to Carney, already springing to his feet and clawing at the inert body of Hargreaves on the sofa beside him. The man was a dead weight, and it took an almost superhuman effort to pull him from his slumped position. But pull him upright the Lethal Leek did, using the inertia of the man's moving body to throw him forwards and downwards to the floor, his belly pressed over the grenade. Swivelling on his toes, he launched himself in a long, low dive over the back of the sofa.

A split second before he hit the floor, the Lethal Leek heard the dull 'whoomph' of the exploding bomb. The pressure shock made his ears pop, and rocked the interior of the flat, but Hargreaves's soft body absorbed the main force of the blast, along with the deadly shards of flying shrapnel.

It was a full thirty seconds before the Welshman hauled himself to his feet, his head throbbing. He looked first at Carney, lying face down in the far corner of the room where he had dived for cover. The man was moving, he thought, with a sense of relief. He staggered across to Carney as he pushed himself up on to his elbows, reaching down to grasp his arm and steady him as he began to crawl groggily to his knees and then to his feet.

The Lethal Leek was too bloody ugly to be an angel, Carney thought, his mind still dazed by the blast. That meant he was still alive. He found it almost impossible to take in, and scanned his own body with disbelief. Apart from the fact that his ears felt as though they were plugged with wet concrete and a whole gang of navvies were using pneumatic drills on the inside of his skull, he appeared to be undamaged. Eventually Carney stood upright on shaky legs, propping himself up against the padded arm of the sofa.

A dim memory of the last few seconds returned. He looked across the floor to where the shattered, shapeless and bloody form of what had once been Cecil Hargreaves was completely ruining five hundred quid's worth of fitted beige carpet. He had to fight the impulse to retch, as nausea rose in his throat to join the throbbing in his head. It felt like the grand-daddy of all hangovers.

The Lethal Leek grinned at him. 'Sorry about the hasty redecoration job,' he muttered as he ran his eyes over the blood-splattered walls and ceiling. 'I hope red's one of your favourite colours.'

Some sort of thanks were called for, Carney thought. 'Christ, how did you move so bloody fast?' he asked. He nodded down at the remains of Hargreaves. 'But for you, we'd both be like him. I guess I owe you my life.'

The Welshman shrugged. 'Actually, you weren't the first person in my thoughts at the time,' he admitted with a grin.

It seemed to put things in the right perspective, somehow, Carney realized. His admiration for the men of the SAS moved one step closer to hero worship.

The Lethal Leek was already moving towards the telephone. He snatched up the receiver and held it to his ear, but it was dead, its delicate internal parts rendered useless by the explosion.

'Shit,' he growled, dropping the useless instrument to the floor. He looked across at Carney, his face taut with the sudden urgency of the situation. 'I've got to get to a bloody phone and report in to Major Anderson. From the sound of things, Ted and Miles could be walking straight into a bloody ambush.'

Carney's mind jerked back to reality. He thought quickly. 'Turn left outside . . . the next street corner,' he snapped. 'There's a payphone there.'

The Welshman dived into the bedroom, emerging again with an MP5K in his hand. He turned again towards the

189

door. 'Look, I'm going to call in and then head straight for the hotel myself. They might need all the help they can get.'

Carney managed a thin smile. 'And leave me all alone to explain this lot to the bloody neighbours?' he muttered. 'I'm coming with you.'

The Lethal Leek looked dubious. 'Aren't we supposed to keep you out of possible combat situations?'

Carney laughed openly, quickly surveying the shattered flat and the body of Hargreaves once more. 'What the fuck would you call this, then?' he asked.

The Lethal Leek did not have time to argue. And Carney did appear to have a point.

22

Winston sat in the bar of the Courtland Hotel, where he'd checked into a second-floor room some half an hour earlier. Although he didn't know it at that point, his initial mistrust of the man Hargreaves had been well founded, and the contingency plans he had initiated were about to be put to the test.

With apparent disinterest, he let his eyes rove casually around the bar and into the lobby beyond, surveying his fellow guests and customers. Two faces were more than familiar to him, but he did not acknowledge them. Together as ever, Tweedledum and Tweedledee shared a small table by the bar's front window, in a position from which they had a clear view of the hotel's double swing doors and the street. The two bulky carrier bags which nestled beneath the table ostensibly contained nothing more than the results of a day's shopping in the capital. Only they, and Winston, knew differently.

At Winston's insistence on backup, the pair had been flown down from Hereford in one of the Italian-designed Agusta A-109 helicopters maintained by the Army Air Corps' S Detachment permanently based at Stirling Lines. Landed at City Airport helipad, and quickly transferred to the hotel by taxi, they had been there by the time Winston had taken a few small but essential pieces of luggage up to his room.

Of Miles Tremathon and Ted Brennon, there was still no sign. Winston glanced anxiously at the clock on the wall of the lobby. It was seven minutes past nine. With a slight feeling of annoyance, he wondered what was holding them up.

In fact, it was the canny and close-handed nature of the Cornishman which had held the pair up. Compared with a true son of the red soil, a Scotsman was a veritable profligate, as anyone who had ever waited for someone else to buy the next round in a Penzance pub knew only too well.

Unused to what he considered to be 'fancy' city prices, Tremathon had taken it into his head to quibble about the cost of taxi fares with a cockney cabby even though they were already running three minutes behind schedule. The resultant prolonged argument had not resulted in any cash reduction but the Cornishman would forever after claim – with some justification – that it had saved his life.

For in the lobby of the Courtland Hotel, other eyes besides Winston's were watching the clock and becoming very nervous indeed.

Daniel Jefferies was good at following orders, even passing them on to others, but none too inventive when it came to making his own decisions. It was this essential character flaw, as much as anything else, that had led him to Second Holocaust in the first place. Shielded within the protective shell of an organization which cloaked itself in secret power and violence, even the weakest of men could feel an illusion of strength. Now, faced with an unexpected situation, Jefferies was helpless again. He needed instructions. Reaching for the mobile phone in his pocket, he punched out a number. The call was answered almost immediately.

'Something's wrong, boss,' Jefferies said nervously. 'No one's shown. What do we do?'

On the other end of the phone, David Scott sat suddenly upright in the rear seat of his Lexus, a look of worry on his face. He leaned forward, hissing to Bullet-head in the driving seat. 'How long before we get to the hotel?'

Bullet-head shrugged. 'Dunno, boss. With this traffic, maybe five, maybe ten minutes.'

Scott gave vent to a muffled curse. As he had told Carney earlier, he didn't care for uncertainties and he liked it even less when things went wrong. His original plans had been simple, direct – and intended to kill two birds with one stone. Jefferies and his two other henchmen planted in the Courtland Hotel had been instructed to watch out for whoever came to pick up the ransom payment, track them, kill them and snatch the case. Quick, clean and efficient, the scheme should have achieved the dual object of securing the money while neutralizing more of the opposition. The failure of that opposition to turn up was more of an irritation than a problem.

Scott ran swiftly through his immediate priorities. The money was of supreme importance. Without that, he would be forced to go cap in hand back to his superiors, who disliked abrupt changes of plan even more than he did. Even worse, any suggestion of incompetence was punished – quickly and decisively.

So the money first, Scott thought. He would have to take any other problems as they came. He returned his attention to the car phone.

'So, what do you think?' Jefferies was asking, more than a little nervous himself. The penalties for failure permeated right down through the structure of the organization. The buck always stopped at the last guy in the line.

Scott forced himself to sound calm. 'Just make the pick-up yourself and then get the hell out of there. After that, just follow instructions as planned. You shouldn't encounter any problems.'

Scott was wrong. He hadn't counted Sergeant Andrew Winston into the equation.

Winston eyed the man using the mobile phone with the faintest glimmer of suspicion. Not that there was anything unusual about the act in itself, he thought. Mobiles were everywhere – the current craze among the yuppie set, the serious business community and the poseurs. Yet a couple of things didn't seem quite right. The man was standing less than ten feet from the hotel's own bank of courtesy phones, which offered some degree of privacy and comfort with stools and a soundproof Perspex hood. Yet he chose to make his call standing in the middle of a crowded lobby. To Winston's mind, that suggested an unusual degree of urgency, even panic. His keen senses alerted, he studied the man more carefully.

There was no doubt about it – the man was nervous. Winston could tell from his body language alone, even though he was too far away for him to see his face clearly. Slowly the SAS man raised his hand to the top of his head, pretending to scratch at his wiry black thatch. It was a subtle, prearranged signal to the two Tweedles. Confident that they were now watching him, Winston made a discreet but perfectly clear gesture with his index finger, directing their attention towards Jefferies, then rose to his feet and crossed the bar towards the lobby area.

Replacing the mobile phone in his pocket, Jefferies signalled his own backup team with a faint nod in their direction. It was a gesture other men might have missed, but Winston was already looking out for it. Instinct had alerted him to the man's suspicious behaviour, but it was pure logic which told him that Jefferies was unlikely to be working alone. Following the man's eyeline, Winston rapidly identified his two cronies, who had been lurking around the hotel brochure racks, pretending to check out sightseeing trips. They were both young, and seemed somehow ill at ease in their smart suits, as though they would have been more comfortable in jeans. The same was true of the way both men clutched their black attaché cases. It was an awkward, nervous grip, not the relaxed hold of someone used to carrying such an item. Winston suspected that each case contained something far more deadly than boardroom documents.

Suddenly he no longer suspected. He *knew* – with that sixth sense for trouble which had been programmed into him by a lifetime of training. He changed direction, skirting around the edge of the lobby towards the far end of the reception desk as the two men began to move towards Jefferies.

Back in the bar, Tweedledum picked up Winston's sudden wariness. He'd worked close to the big Barbadian enough times to know every little nuance of his body language. It was something approaching telepathy. He nudged Tweedledee gently in the ribs. 'Something's about to pop,' he murmured.

His companion merely nodded silently. Moving in complete unison, like twin parts of a well-oiled machine, both men began to reach down slowly and with apparent casualness to the carrier bags secreted beneath the table.

Like the flywheel of some giant engine gradually building up power, events began to move now with increasing speed and inevitability, generating their own momentum.

Shadowed by his two colleagues, Jefferies moved towards the reception area, attracting the attention of the young girl behind the desk. She slid over with a polite smile, listening to him attentively. Seconds later, she beckoned to the manager, who stepped over to join them. After a few seconds of conversation, the man nodded, withdrawing a bunch of keys from his pocket and bending down behind the desk. Rising again, he placed a red Samsonite suitcase on the counter.

Tweedledum and Tweedledee had their respective carrier bags on their laps now, the masking pieces of fancy wrapping paper inside peeled back to reveal the ready and waiting MP5Ks. They stared intently across at the little tableau unfolding at the reception desk, and checked Winston's relative position. He was now edging his way round the far wall of the lobby, towards the front door.

'It's looking a little messy at the moment,' Tweedledee whispered anxiously.

Tweedledum nodded, knowing exactly what his partner meant. There were at least a dozen people milling about in the lobby, creating a wall of innocent potential victims between them and their target. He glanced sideways towards the front door, nudging Tweedledee to make him follow his eyes. Tweedledee nodded, attuned to his buddy's thoughts. The doorway and the vestibule were clear, giving them a safe and direct line of fire should it become necessary.

Winston had already considered the problem, and was also taking up a safe position. He unbuttoned his jacket casually, giving him immediate access to the Browning under his shoulder. He watched Jefferies like a hawk as the man picked up the suitcase from the reception desk and turned towards the door.

It was looking good, he thought, with a certain amount of relief. The vestibule was the trap area. Once Jefferies and his men were within ten feet of the door, he could take them with a minimum of dramatics. The Tweedles were there to keep things clean. It should be simple, effective, and quick enough to avoid any panic.

Jefferies walked towards the hotel entrance, feeling increasingly relaxed. His earlier fears of a trap were beginning to recede now, as it seemed the pick-up had been smooth and uncomplicated. He felt sure that any interception would have occurred the moment the suitcase appeared on the reception desk. He'd been looking out carefully, but had seen no sign of a reaction anywhere in the lobby. With increasing confidence in every step, and secure in the knowledge that Dennings and McKinley were right on his heels, he strode towards the swing doors.

These opened inwards at that precise moment, as Tremathon and Brennon chose to make their belated and exceedingly ill-timed entrance, to be confronted by the sight of a man carrying a red Samsonite suitcase hurrying towards them.

Jefferies froze in his tracks, instantly alerted by the two men's immediate reaction. The look of panic which flashed across his face was in turn a clear signal to the two troopers, triggering in them a gut response. The situation was now taking on a life of its own, heading towards a crisis with terrible inevitability.

Watching the sudden drama explode before his eyes, knowing what was about to happen and utterly powerless to do anything about it, Winston felt frustration rise like a solid lump in his throat. His eyes flashed to the two henchmen, who were both snapping open their attache cases and drawing out what Winston immediately recognized as a pair of Czech-built Skorpion machine-pistols, their folding metal stocks clipped down over the front of their stubby barrels.

They were all perhaps split seconds away from a civilian catastrophe, Winston thought. Each of the 7.65mm weapons boasted the short-burst capacity of a full sub-machine-gun. If the gunmen opened fire in the middle of the crowded lobby, it would be a slaughter.

There was nothing he could do to help Brennon and Tremathon. Their only protection lay in the fact that Jefferies was temporarily caught smack in the middle of the line of fire between them and his own men. Tweedledum and Tweedledee were equally hampered by the number of innocent bystanders clustered around the two gunmen. Winston made the only move he could.

The Browning leapt into his hand. Raising it above his head, Winston fired two shots into the ceiling. 'Everybody hit the floor,' he screamed out at the top of his voice, racing for the cover of a drinks machine positioned between the two lift doors.

There was a moment of stunned silence as Winston's pre-emptive move took effect. With superb reflexes, Brennon and Tremathon took advantage of their brief and precious respite to throw themselves back out through the heavy glass swing doors, drawing their own handguns and taking up defensive positions.

Then panic erupted. The lobby was suddenly a mob of frightened, screaming people, some throwing themselves to the floor as Winston had commanded, some turning to run for the nearest protection they could find.

Jefferies dropped the red suitcase to the floor, diving into his coat to pull out a heavy Colt automatic. He grabbed the arm of the woman standing nearest to him and pulled her to his side, wrapping his left arm around her neck. Pulling her in front of him like a human shield, he held the Colt against the side of her cheek. His eyes darted around the lobby and beyond, searching out the opposition.

Pressed against the side of the drinks machine, Winston mouthed a silent prayer to a God he only half believed in. The situation was still critical, still potentially explosive, but miraculously no shots other than his own had yet been fired. If everyone kept their heads, they might all get through the next few crucial minutes without casualties.

Jefferies' two gunmen had now begun to herd a small bunch of terrified people into a group, covering them with the Skorpions. The boss had his own hostage, and could take his chances. It was every man for himself.

'Holy shit. What the fuck do we do now?' Tweedledee hissed under his breath. He cradled the MP5K impotently on his knees under the cover of the bar table, knowing that it was useless in the present circumstances. There was no way they could open fire while the gunmen held hostages, yet the two men themselves presented clear targets. It was a nasty position to be in.

Tweedledum gazed fearfully over at Winston. 'More to the point, what about the boss?' he whispered back, realizing that Winston was in the most vulnerable position of all. His brain raced into overdrive, seeking a way out. A series of tiny, winking lights to Winston's right suddenly attracted his attention. It was the lift indicator. Someone was descending to the ground floor, or the lift was returning on automatic, he realized, and in that second a wild idea sprang into his mind.

There was only seconds to put it into operation. He kicked Tweedledee's legs under the table, getting his instant and full attention. 'The second that lift door by the boss opens, get ready to bug out and create a diversion,' he hissed.

Tweedledee's eyes flashed a question. 'Bug out where?'

His partner gave a thin smile. There's only one way out,' he said jerking his head slightly to indicate the window behind them. 'You've seen 'em do it in the movies.'

The lift indicator had sunk to the bottom light. The doors began to hiss open. Putting their faith completely in Winston's uncanny reaction time, the two Tweedles threw themselves to their feet, grabbed up their chairs and made a dive for the window. Tweedledum had just time to scream a single clue to Winston as they both crashed through the glass and into the street outside.

'Going up, boss.'

Winston had already heard the faint hiss of the lift doors, but his first thought had been only of another innocent bystander bursting unexpectedly into an already volatile situation. The sudden and unexpected commotion over in the bar, and Tweedledum's hastily shouted message, poured into his calculator of a brain like an information overload. It was only pure instinct which enabled him to process it in time.

The young girl stepping out of the lift didn't even have time to react to the sight of armed gunmen rounding up hostages. Winston's huge body crashed into her, knocking her backwards through the open mouth of the lift door. Winston threw himself in behind her, pressing against the side of the lift cage and punching the top floor and emergency-close buttons simultaneously. A single shot from Jefferies' Colt slammed harmlessly into the back wall of the lift as the doors began to slide to.

The lift began to move upwards. Winston bent to the floor and hauled the badly winded but otherwise unhurt girl to her feet. She stared at the gun in his hand in terror, her mouth dropping open in preparation for a scream.

Winston knew he had only a few precious seconds, as the Courtland Hotel was only five storeys high. He clamped his huge hand over the girl's mouth, speaking quietly but insistently.

'Listen, you've just got to believe me but I'm one of the good guys,' he told her. 'When this lift stops I want you to get out, find the first available fire alarm and set it off. Then make for the emergency fire escape as fast as you can and get out of here.' He took his hand from the girl's mouth, smiling at her. 'Now, have you got that?'

The girl nodded, uncertainly. The lift stopped with a faint jolt and the doors began to open. Winston pushed the still frightened girl gently towards the landing, flashing her another smile. 'Please trust me, and do it,' he said quickly, before ducking back into the lift and stabbing at the button for the second floor.

The shrill, insistent sound of the hotel's fire warning system was already filling the corridors as Winston reached the door of his room. He smiled to himself with grim satisfaction, reassured that at least the bulk of the residents and staff would shortly be on their way to safety. Letting himself into the room, he rushed across to the bed, reached underneath it and drew out the single holdall he had brought with him. The radiophone was tucked away beneath a small pile of spare magazines for the Heckler & Koch. He snatched it up and punched out Major Anderson's priority number. His call was answered almost immediately.

Winston's opening message was terse and to the point, covering the basics. 'Major? It's Winston. We have a hostage situation at the Courtland. Three gunmen that I know of – two Skorpions and one handgun. I'm on the inside, and I'll do what I can.'

Anderson digested the information rapidly. 'Estimate of hostages?' he asked.

'Probably around twenty,' Winston told him. 'Hopefully the majority of the guests are evacuating right now via the emergency fire escapes.'

'Situation?' Anderson's questions were the basic ones, part of the standard operating procedure for dealing with all types of siege or hostage situations. SOPs served a valuable and well-defined purpose in SAS tactics, providing a speedy and comprehensive checklist of the various factors involved. They helped commanders to collect vital information which would assist them in making an early assessment of each individual situation and planning a successful rescue.

'At the moment, the ground floor – lobby and bar areas,' Winston reported. 'But they could move. It's too open and too vulnerable. My guess is that they'll probably lock the main doors and move the hostages to a more secure area. The kitchens might be a good bet.'

Winston broke off and took a few seconds to consider his own position. 'Anyway, I'm getting set to bug out,' he told Anderson when he spoke again. 'They know I'm loose and one of them will probably come looking for me. I've got four men on the outside and I can probably be of greatest use with them.'

'I agree,' Anderson said. 'You can count on backup within the hour. I'll have Lieutenant-Colonel Davies get official clearance and set up a command cell at the local police station. Sit tight until we establish communication and see if they have any demands.'

'And if shooting starts in the meantime?' Winston asked.

'ERP,' Anderson replied curtly. It was the answer Winston had expected. Once the first hostage got killed, standard operating procedures went by the board and the emergency rescue plan swung into operation. It usually meant a direct frontal assault, in which casualties could be high. It was not a preferred option, but it usually worked, and it underpinned the basic beliefs of most government and security agencies around the world. There was no giving in to terrorism. Only swift and complete retribution.

'One last thing,' Winston said. 'My guess is that these bastards are still counting on their pub bomb as a negotiating factor. Are we in a position to neutralize that threat at this time?'

'About fifteen seconds after you sign off and get the hell out of there,' Anderson assured him. 'We finally got to use the boys in blue.'

Winston nodded with satisfaction. He cut off the transmission, tucking the instrument safely away in his belt. Returning his attention to the holdall, he began selecting his weaponry.

23

True to his last word to Winston, Major Anderson's first call was to Commissioner McMillan.

'Sir, I think it advisable that we initiate the emergency procedure that we discussed earlier at this time,' he said simply.

There was no argument. 'I'll see to it at once,' McMillan said, replacing the receiver in its cradle for just long enough to break off the connection. Lifting it again, he keyed the number for the direct line to the special operations room at Scotland Yard and passed on the order.

It was a large-scale operation, but it had been well rehearsed and carefully prepared. On McMillan's command, a standby team of twenty secretaries and switchboard operators manned a prepared bank of telephones which had been cleared of all other incoming and outgoing calls. Each operator had a typewritten list of numbers to call. The entire operation had been timed to take exactly twelve minutes. At the end of that time every Consolidated Breweries pub in the Greater London area would have been warned, evacuated and placed under police guard at a safe distance.

It was the first fully joint operation between the SAS and the police. It had taken a massive mobilization of manpower, but it would work. Consolidated Breweries might lose another pub, but there would be no loss of life.

Tremathon and Brennon were still crouched in a defensive position on the outside of the hotel doors, discreetly watching the developing situation inside the lobby through the plate glass. Most of the hostages had now been lined up in a sort of human wall between the vestibule and the three gunmen, who had now taken up position behind the reception desk, each with two hostages held at gunpoint. For the moment, it was a stand-off situation in which neither side could do anything except wait.

'Hello, what have we got here?' came a familiar voice from behind Tremathon's back. 'A couple of pervy peeping Toms, from the look of it.'

The Cornishman whirled to confront Tweedledum and Tweedledee, both grinning and still shaking splinters of glass out of their hair. Apart from a few slashes in their clothing, they both appeared undamaged.

'Where the hell did you two come from?' he asked in surprise.

Tweedledee grinned. 'We used the emergency exit,' he said. His face became more serious. 'Did the boss make it out of there OK?'

Brennon nodded. 'He suddenly made a dive for the lift and then he was gone,' he said, much to Tweedledee's obvious relief. 'So far no one's gone after him. I think they're still too busy trying to figure out what to do. Something tells me our friends in there aren't all that used to this sort of thing.' He broke off, to nod at the MP5Ks the two Tweedles were toting. 'Well, thank God somebody thought to bring some heavy artillery,' he muttered. 'All Miles and I have are our Brownings and one spare clip apiece.'

Tweedledum was taking a quick look in through the door at the line of hostages. 'Not that anything's much use to us at the moment,' he observed glumly. 'Fucking Gazza couldn't sneak a shot past that defensive wall.'

'So, what do we do?' Brennon asked. It was a good question, to which nobody had a good answer.

Tweedledum shrugged. 'I guess we can only wait,' he suggested feebly. 'It depends on what the boss is doing in there, and whatever else is going on. At a pinch, I'd say that all hell's going to break loose any time now.'

It was a pretty safe bet, since it was obvious that something had to happen soon. The hotel fire alarm was still clanging shrilly, as neither Jefferies nor his men had yet thought to shut it off. The noise had already attracted a crowd of sensation-seekers, who were congregating at a safe distance on the other side of the road. Their numbers were being swelled by evacuees from the hotel, who were pouring out of the emergency exits at the rear of the building and coming round in desperate need of information or reassurance. The emergency services must already be on their way. Tweedledum wished the boss was there to take charge of things. He was dressed in mufti, carrying no identification or papers and without any form of authorization. Trying to explain to the police what he was doing carrying a sub-machine-gun around the streets of central London was not a task he was relishing.

As if to reinforce these misgivings, the first faint sounds of approaching sirens and fire-engine bells could be heard in the distance.

The situation seemed reasonably stable for the moment, Jefferies thought. He had absolutely no idea of what was going on outside, or what steps the authorities might be taking. But for now there was no direct threat, and the large number of hostages would appear to be keeping them safe from attack. His only immediate worry was the armed black man who had escaped from the lobby. Jefferies had no doubt that it was he who had set off the fire alarm, and that he was probably still somewhere in the hotel. Who he was, and what he could possibly do, were completely unknown factors.

The initial panic of the hostages had started to subside now, as the stronger of them came to terms with their fate and the more nervous elements merely cowered into submission. Screaming had given way to quiet sobbing and a dull buzz of anxious conversation as the confused hostages hopelessly quizzed each other in half a dozen languages. In any case most of it was completely swamped by the continued noise of the fire alarm.

His own initial tendency to panic had been controlled by more direct means. At the first opportunity Jefferies had popped a small white pill into his mouth and swallowed it. As always, the drug absorbed rapidly into the bloodstream and hit the brain, producing an illusory feeling of calm and well-being. Other effects would follow later, he knew, but for the moment Nirvana made him feel rational and in control of the situation. Control was power. Power was control. The two fed on each other like a snake chewing its way up its own tail.

Jefferies dragged his female hostage in the direction of the hotel manager, waving his Colt under the man's nose. 'Can you shut this damned alarm off?' he demanded.

The man nodded. 'There's a master control underneath the desk.'

'Then do it,' Jefferies snapped. 'And no bloody tricks.'

The manager moved nervously along the desk, doing what he was told. The abrupt shut-down of the alarm also served to stun the hostages into momentary silence. A deathly hush fell over the lobby.

Jefferies took advantage of the brief respite to pull out his mobile phone. He pushed his hostage roughly aside, waving the gun at her. 'You just stay right there,' he told her. 'I'll be watching you.' Retreating to a quiet corner, he punched out David Scott's mobile number.

Scott received the unwelcome news with a sinking feeling in the pit of his stomach, his initial flare of anger at Jefferies' stupidity quickly swamped by concerns for his own highly vulnerable position.

Much of the apparent confidence he had exuded to Carney earlier in the evening had been mere bluster. In truth, Scott knew only too well that Second Holocaust's UK operation was still embryonic, still lacking the cohesive organizational structure of its European counterparts. Slow but insidious growth was the essential nature of the entire movement. Essentially a cellular development, it depended on the creation of large numbers of small, largely independent units which served mainly as recruitment centres and drug distribution networks. Given the nature of the recruits, and the effects of Nirvana, spin-offs into other forms of criminal activity were virtually inevitable, with the result that each cell was more or less self-funding. Growing dependency upon the drug ensured a loyal following and created a strong inducement to recruit further members in return for free supplies.

In the past this underground structure had been one of the movement's greatest strengths, allowing it to grow and spread almost unnoticed by the authorities. Like a fungus, it spread its filaments underground until individual groups became large enough and powerful enough to overlap, merge and become part of the greater, more unified organization. It had worked in Germany, it had worked in Italy and it was showing every sign of working in France.

But something had gone wrong in Britain. They'd been picked up and identified too early, and they'd been attacked with unusual tenacity. The loss of the drug factory in Norfolk could in itself perhaps have been written off as just a temporary set-back, but it was being followed up with a combination of intelligence and direct action which suggested a concerted and sophisticated counter-force.

It was almost as if they were being coerced into coming out into the open, Scott thought to himself. Someone, somewhere, appeared to have an instinctive knowledge of how the organization functioned, and how best to attack it.

And now this fiasco at the Courtland Hotel, Scott reflected bitterly. He should have known better than to entrust such a delicate mission to a poor fool like Jefferies. A direct confrontation on this scale was the last thing they needed, and its timing could not have been more disastrous. The massive London right-wing rally, and the invaluable propaganda and recruitment opportunities it would present, was now only days away. Representatives and delegates of a dozen political movements were already converging on the capital, along with section chiefs of many of the European chapters of Second Holocaust. It was a time to be showing strength, not weakness.

As his car approached the Courtland Hotel, Scott leaned forward to Bullet-head. 'Just drive past slowly,' he snapped. 'Then take the first turning and find somewhere quiet to park. I must think this thing through.'

Scott stared out through the tinted side windows of the Lexus as it cruised past the hotel entrance, noting the four armed troopers still crouching in the doorway. Looking ahead through the windscreen again, he saw the flashing blue lights of the first of a small fleet of police cars converging on the hotel from the opposite direction and frowned heavily. The whole area would soon be swarming with cops. It would not be a healthy place to be, especially with two sawn-off shotguns and a brace of hand-grenades in the car.

It was time for a hasty change of plan. Scott tapped Bullet-head lightly on the shoulder. 'Forget that last instruction,' he muttered. 'Keep driving for another mile before you turn off.'

He sat back in his seat as the car began to gather speed again, forcing himself to relax and try to think things through in a logical manner. The significance of the two sub-machine-guns had not escaped him. Hardly police issue, they were almost certainly army weapons, Scott realized – which tended to override his earlier theory that his persecutors were merely a special police unit of some kind. It would also help to explain the devastatingly successful raid on the farmhouse, which appeared to have been carried out with military precision.

Taking this assumption one stage further, Scott applied it to the current situation at the hotel. If some branch of the military *were* involved, then they had all the fire-power and manpower at their disposal to turn it into a completely hopeless situation in which there could only be one possible outcome. The unfortunate incident would quickly turn into a full-scale siege which would end in either total surrender or a bloodbath. Either way, it seemed depressingly obvious that Second Holocaust could only come out of it as the losers – and would be clearly seen to be so. The possible consequences were frightening.

It was the single word 'siege' which finally gave Scott the clue that brought it all together in his head in a series of vivid and dramatic mental images.

Princes Gate, the Iranian Embassy, 1980. And a group of men who had created a piece of history, a modern legend.

With a final, sickening certainty, Scott knew who his enemy was, and his shoulders slumped in resignation. A particularly cruel fate had pitched him against no less an adversary than the SAS. His despair was complete now, as a lifetime of grandiose dreams started popping away in his mind's eye like so many insignificant little puffs of smoke.

24

The first police car slewed to a halt outside the hotel entrance. This was the tricky bit, Tweedledum realized. He lowered the Heckler & Koch gently to the pavement, then stepped towards the car slowly and cautiously with his hands held above his head and smiling as reassuringly as he could.

The cop in the passenger seat was only a kid, he thought, seeing the young man's frightened face staring at him through the closed window. He was probably pissing his pants, the poor little bastard. One minute cruising along in his nice comfortable patrol car ogling the tarts and kerb-crawlers and the next confronted by a bunch of dangerous-looking nutters with sub-machine-guns. The main thing was that neither the kid nor his partner should panic. Still holding his hands up in an attitude of surrender, he stopped at the side of the car and waited for a reaction.

Apparently beginning to realize that the armed men offered no immediate threat, the young cop wound down the window and peered out nervously. In the driver's seat, his partner kept the engine running and his hand on the gear lever.

'What the hell's going on?' the cop wanted to know, in a slightly shaky voice.

It was a fair enough question, Tweedledum thought. He was about to launch into an explanation when

Winston appeared from nowhere, gently nudging him to one side and taking control of the situation. 'I'll handle this, Trooper,' he said firmly.

Tweedledum grinned with relief. 'Good to see you, boss,' he said. 'I wasn't sure you could make it.'

Winston flashed him a grateful smile. 'Thanks to you,' he replied. 'That was good thinking.' He turned his attention back to the two cops in the car, who were now looking even more confused and wary.

'Have you had any briefing from base for this operation?' he demanded.

The first policeman shook his head. 'We were pulled off routine patrol in response to a fire call,' he explained. 'It was only a couple of seconds ago they told us there was some sort of a situation developing down here. I think there's about four other units on their way.' He paused, then repeated his earlier question. 'So what the hell *is* going on?'

Winston put it as succinctly as he could. 'There is an armed terrorist situation inside this hotel. They have a large number of hostages. I'm Sergeant Andrew Winston, of 22 SAS, and these are my men. I take it neither of you are armed?'

The cop shook his head again.

'Right, then I suggest you pull out of this immediate area,' Winston told him. 'And start clearing people off the streets as fast as you can. We're going to need room to move and there could be a lot of gunplay.'

Both policemen looked unsure. Winston understood that it was difficult for them to trust him. In their position he would have felt exactly the same. Nevertheless he needed to convince them quickly.

214

The sooner the area was cleared, the better. He spoke again, this time more forcefully. 'Look, right this minute my superiors will be contacting yours,' he explained. 'Complete authorization from the very top to let us get on with our job should be approved in the next few minutes. In the meantime you could be doing a lot to make sure that no innocent people get hurt.'

The two cops were almost convinced, Winston thought, but suddenly it didn't matter any more. Three more police cars appeared from the other end of the street, escorting a pair of fire engines. One of the cars pulled up beside the first. A uniformed sergeant jumped out, hurrying over and banging on the driver's side window. 'You two get your arses out of here,' he barked. 'I want this entire area cordoned off for a quarter of a mile in every direction.' He turned his attention to Winston. 'You Winston?'

The Barbadian nodded. 'Have you been fully briefed?' he asked.

It was the police sergeant's turn to nod agreement. 'Our orders are to hand control over to you until your immediate commanding officer gets here. We're to assist you in any way we can. Just tell us what you want us to do.'

Winston glanced to one side as the first police car began to move away. 'Looks like you're already doing it,' he observed. 'Just get everybody out of the area and keep them away.' He paused, looking at the fire engines and their baffled crews. 'And get those vehicles out of here. There isn't any fire and they'll only cause additional confusion.'

'You've got it,' the sergeant said. He eyed Winston curiously, a shadow of doubt remaining on his face. 'Look, Sergeant, this is the real thing, isn't it?' he asked. 'I mean, it's not a combined forces or civil defence drill or anything like that?'

Winston's face was grim as he shook his head and said: 'No, this is the real thing, all right. Real terrorists, real guns and real hostages.'

'Shit,' the sergeant hissed. It wasn't the answer he'd really wanted to hear.

Daniel Jefferies was a frightened man. It was now nearly ten minutes since he had called Scott for instructions and he still hadn't received a reply. Had the man abandoned him, left him to sort out the mess for himself? If so, what was he supposed to do? His men were getting edgy, having received no clear instructions themselves. How were they likely to react if this stalemate continued to drag on indefinitely? And the hostages – how much longer could they be expected to remain comparatively docile?

So many questions, buzzing around inside his head like a swarm of angry flies. Questions that he didn't have answers for, problems which demanded decisions he was unable to make. And that was only inside the hotel. What the authorities might be planning or doing on the outside created a whole new set of imponderables. Jefferies had seen the flashing blue lights of several police cars through the glass swing doors, and he was uncomfortably aware that the doors themselves remained under armed guard. But what was actually *happening*?

In desperation, Jefferies popped another Nirvana pill, in the vain hope that the drug could somehow fill the cold, empty void he seemed to feel in his head and in his guts.

Scott felt a strange sort of calm descending on him. Perhaps it was resignation, yet it didn't feel like it. It was an odd sensation, which actually seemed to be filling him with a new sense of purpose and confidence.

Actually knowing who the enemy was, and realizing the total hopelessness of the situation, had at first brought nothing but despair. Yet, perversely, that realization also narrowed the choice of options, serving to focus and concentrate his attention. When there was no hope at all, worrying about it seemed both pointless and irrelevant.

And the situation at the Courtland Hotel was most definitely hopeless, Scott knew. There could be no possible doubt about that. Jefferies and his two thugs could not possibly win against the might of the SAS under any circumstances. Whether the siege lasted an hour, a day or even longer, the hotel would eventually be stormed and they would be killed or captured. So Jefferies still had a choice. He could surrender or die.

Scott had little doubt about which option the man, left to his own devices, would choose. He doubted very much if Jefferies actually had the bottle to hold out once he understood the true nature of his situation. In fact, Scott was slightly surprised that he had had the guts to take hostages in the first place.

He could only think that it had been a panic reaction rather than a planned and considered move.

The question that Scott had to deal with was which option would best serve him and the organization. Jefferies and his two gunmen didn't even enter into the equation. They were totally expendable, irrelevant, cannon-fodder – as were the rest of the street louts and bully boys which Second Holocaust used to further its ends. But even cannon-fodder had its uses, as every warmonger since Attila the Hun had known only too well. And perhaps every movement needed its martyrs, Scott reflected.

An idea was beginning to gell in his head. While he still retained a strong element of control over the outcome of the situation, perhaps he ought to be using it. Once the SAS made their move, it would be lost for ever. But just for the moment, Scott was still the puppet-master who held the strings. Jefferies and his men would still jump to his commands, and could force the next moves in the game.

To order them to surrender seemed pointless, achieving nothing except failure in the eyes of the world. They would be exposed as impotent and weak, having neither the guts nor the ability to back up their tough talk. Better a blaze of brief glory in which they could be seen to be crushed by a ruthless and vastly superior force. The spark of political freedom and thought extinguished by the mindless mechanics of authority.

There was one major flaw in this scenario, however – the essential weakness of Jefferies. Scott somehow doubted that he would have the guts required to follow orders if told to make a stand, turn the siege into a fight. He would need to be given some incentive – something even stronger than the fear of punishment for failure. A chance to believe that there was some hope, that he was not alone.

Scott smiled to himself, aware that he had exactly what was needed at his fingertips. All over the city, the gangs of thugs and rowdies were already on standby for the rally. Scott would simply call some of them out a little early. He grabbed his mobile phone and started to make a series of calls. Afterwards he got back to Jefferies. The man sounded panicky. A few more minutes and it might have been too late.

'What's happening? What's going on out there?' Jefferies asked in a tremulous voice.

Scott's tone was calm and reassuring. 'It's going to be all right,' he said. 'I've already taken steps to get you out of there safely. Now all you have to do is to sit tight, stay calm and wait for further instructions. No one's going to start shooting until they open up communications and see what demands you are going to make. We've just got to make sure that we have a few extra negotiating points.'

Scott broke off the connection before the man could start asking too many awkward questions. For the moment, just the promise of help would have to be enough to keep him quiet.

25

Seated at the bar in Norma Jean's, Pretty Boy noticed the small group of yobbos heading towards his table and tensed himself for trouble. He recognized only two of the gang, but it was enough to start warning bells ringing faintly in the back of his mind. One of the group was the young man who had been with Cheryl the previous night, before he had bluffed him off. It looked as though he had recruited a few of his mates, along with the big ape Pretty Boy recognized as the bouncer who usually stood outside the club.

'I think your boyfriend could be coming to claim you back,' Pretty Boy said to the girl sitting opposite him. 'Jealous type, is he?'

Cheryl glanced up as the gang approached. She looked back at Pretty Boy, smiling. 'Forget it,' she said. 'Johnny's OK about that. I've already squared him. Besides, Max, the bouncer, won't have any trouble inside the club.'

She seemed pretty confident, Pretty Boy thought. Even so, he remained on his guard as the group reached the table and stopped. He looked up stony-faced, eyeing the former boyfriend in a direct challenge.

There was no trace of animosity on Johnny's face. For the

moment, he simply appeared to be weighing up the SAS man.

'Cheryl here reckons you're a bit tasty in a fight,' he said matter-of-factly. 'Is that right?'

Pretty Boy maintained full eye contact as he shrugged with deliberate casualness. 'I can handle myself,' he said flatly. 'If I *have* to,' he added, with heavy emphasis. He paused for a couple of seconds to let that sink in. 'Well, do I have to?' he asked finally.

Johnny grinned, returning the shrug. 'That's up to you,' he said easily. 'Just thought you might fancy a bit of excitement, that's all. And make yourself a few quid, if you're interested.'

Pretty Boy wasn't quite sure where the conversation was headed. It seemed best to just play along for a while. 'I'm always interested,' he murmured guardedly, his face still giving nothing away. 'It depends on the deal.'

Johnny thought about this for a while and at last nodded. 'Fair enough,' he conceded. 'OK, I'll level with you. A friend of ours needs a little street demo set up real quick and we could do with all the bodies we can get hold of. Show stuff – know what I mean? Bit of rioting, bit of aggro, maybe loot a couple of shops – that sort of thing. Couple of hours, that's all. And there's fifty quid in it for you, no questions asked. A bit more if you get busted, or get hurt.' Johnny paused, looking at Pretty Boy questioningly. 'Well? What do you reckon?'

Caught on the hop, Pretty Boy was forced to do some pretty fast thinking. Nothing had been said that in any way suggested a link with either the drug distribution network or Second Holocaust. All he had actually been invited to join appeared to be a street riot, as a hired thug. He reminded himself that his orders were to infiltrate the bully-boy network and find out everything he could. Johnny's offer was surely his best chance yet of doing exactly that.

It was a tricky call, but on balance Pretty Boy was very tempted to let it pass. The immediate problem was how to extricate himself from the situation without spoiling his future chances, or appearing to chicken out. The girl seemed his best bet. Perhaps he could use her as an excuse.

He glanced across the table at Cheryl. 'Well, how do you feel about it?' he asked. 'It'd hardly be that nice quiet romantic night I had in mind, would it?'

Pretty Boy had been hoping for backup, but it wasn't forthcoming. Cheryl's eyes were sparkling. 'What the hell?' she said recklessly. 'It could be a blast.' She smiled across the table at him, a suggestive, sexy pout tugging at the corners of her lips. 'Besides, I could always lick your wounds for you afterwards.'

Johnny appeared to be getting anxious. It was obvious that there was some urgency in the situation, and it put Pretty Boy under even more unwanted pressure.

'Well?' Johnny repeated. 'You coming or not? We've got to get across to this fucking hotel in Knightsbridge.'

Pretty Boy had already more or less resigned himself to the situation, but this final piece of information was the clincher, he realized with a shock. He had no idea what the possible connection could be, but it was just too much to be pure coincidence. His eyes darted briefly towards Peters, seated some fifteen feet away at the bar. As he had expected, the man had been monitoring the situation discreetly, ever since the group had first approached Pretty Boy's table.

Pretty Boy looked up at Johnny. 'OK, I'm in,' he said decisively. 'But I've got to take a piss first.' Without giving anyone a chance to object, he rose from the table and headed off towards the toilets, counting on Peters to read the situation correctly and follow him. Out of the corner of his eye, he had the satisfaction of seeing his colleague begin to slide off his stool.

Pretty Boy was waiting for him just inside the toilets.

'What the fuck's going on?' Peters hissed, clearly concerned. 'You got trouble?'

Pretty Boy shook his head. 'Not that sort of trouble.' He explained the situation as briefly as possible. 'I haven't got the faintest idea what's actually going down,' he admitted finally. 'But you'd better make sure somebody knows about it.'

'Damn right,' Peters said. 'Leave it to me.' He clapped Pretty Boy on the shoulder. 'Look – you watch out for yourself, OK? Those bastards look like they could be mean.'

Pretty Boy grinned. 'So can I,' he said quickly.

The police had done their job with remarkable efficiency, Winston thought. The immediate environs of the Courtland Hotel had been cleared and cordoned off in a matter of minutes and the surrounding area sealed off with hastily conscripted reinforcements. The command control post had been set up at Knightsbridge police station and was now fully operational and backed up with two well-equipped mobile communications and relay vans on site. Winston now had a direct telephone link to the main switchboard of the hotel, which had itself been isolated to cut off any other incoming or outgoing calls. Also at his disposal were a PA system and a pair of broadcasting loudspeaker vehicles capable of blasting out a couple of hundred watts of sound. The idea of bombarding siege locations with ear-splitting music was currently popular in the USA, but Winston was not convinced of its effectiveness. To his way of thinking, it could have an equally debilitating effect on the hostages as well as the terrorists – and a tense, nervy hostage could be a recipe for disaster.

Besides, he and his men would also be affected, even wearing ear protection, and he preferred to work with a clear head.

Perhaps twenty minutes had now passed since his initial call to Major Anderson, and the situation inside the hotel remained stable and outwardly calm. It was time to check in again.

'So, what's the picture?' Anderson wanted to know. He sounded alert, but not worried.

Winston told him. 'Nothing much has changed. They haven't even moved from the lobby. We could go straight in through the windows at any time. Do you want a candid personal assessment?'

'Which is?' Anderson asked.

'These guys are strictly amateurs,' Winston said confidently. 'I think they just panicked and now they haven't the faintest idea what to do. My guess is that by now they're probably primed for a little friendly suggestion.'

Anderson thought it over for a few seconds, then said: 'Yes, you could well be right. I suppose there's no harm in giving it a try. I assume you have communication set up?'

'Interior and exterior,' Winston confirmed.

'All right, give it a try,' Anderson told him. 'Offer them the chance to give themselves up, or at least release some of the hostages as proof of good intent. They'll probably try to use the pub bomb as a bargaining point, but it might not be a good idea to let them know we have at least partially neutralized that threat. Feeling they still have an edge might well make them feel more secure, and we don't want them getting too edgy. If there's the faintest chance of ending this thing quickly and cleanly, we might as well go for it.'

'And if not?' Winston wanted to know.

'Captain Blake and his men are already well on their way in another Agusta,' Anderson said. 'The police have already arranged for one of their own choppers to intercept them and guide them in. They're also trying to pick up detailed plans of the hotel in case you have to storm it. They've identified the architect and they're trying to contact him. If they can get hold of the plans they'll be delivered directly to you as soon as possible.' Major Anderson paused. 'Oh yes, and the Lethal Leek's also on his way to join you, but he might have Carney with him. I want him kept well away from the action, is that clear?'

'You got it, boss,' Winston assured him.

'Right, anything else you need to know?'

Winston shook his head. 'No, I think that about covers it for now. I'll be back to you after I've spoken to our friends.' A sudden afterthought struck him. 'Oh, what's the ETA on Butch Blake and the Third Cavalry?'

'About another thirty minutes,' Anderson said. 'And then as long as it takes to find the nearest drop zone. We're not sure yet if the hotel has a flat roof or not.'

Winston tucked the radiophone back in his belt and headed for the nearest communications van. He'd try the discreet approach first, through the conventional telephone lines. It would cause less panic than having messages blaring out over the PA system, and it was more personal. If his theories were right, the three gunmen should be about ready to listen to the calm, reassuring voice of reason. With a bit of luck, they might even be ready to take up the first sensible offer of a quick and clean way to end this thing. There was only one way to find out.

26

In the oppressive silence of the lobby, the sudden and unexpected buzzing of the reception desk switchboard made everybody jump, not least Jefferies. Unable to identify the nature or the source of the sound immediately, he sprang in the direction of the manager, waving the Colt menacingly in his face.

'What's that?' he hissed, aggressive yet edgy at the same time. The overdose of Nirvana coursing through his system was already producing erratic responses, causing violent and unpredictable mood swings. Although it gave him anger as a motivating force, it could not eradicate his basic cowardice and sense of insecurity, which in turn increased his sense of rage and frustration. He was in a highly volatile state of mind.

The manager indicated the switchboard behind him with a shaking finger. 'Incoming call,' he croaked through dry lips.

Jefferies thought quickly. It could just be a routine enquiry, although it seemed far more likely that it would be the first attempt by the authorities to establish contact. He was mildly surprised that they had not attempted to communicate before now. It was certainly not from David Scott, who would undoubtedly have used his mobile. Faced with direct confrontation for the first time, Jefferies was suddenly and uncomfortably aware that he had not even the faintest idea of how to handle the unfamiliar situation. He didn't even know what he was supposed to ask for.

He toyed with the idea of simply ignoring the call. Let the bastards sweat it out for a bit, he thought. Let them come crawling when they got worried enough. But this feeling of defiance faded quickly in the cold light of reality. It all boiled down to a question of who was sweating the most. Neither Dennings nor McKinley had said anything directly to him since the siege began, but he had caught enough of their nervous, uncertain glances to know that the two gunmen were as unsure of themselves as he was. Jefferies was not at all sure how much pressure either man could take, or how far they were prepared to go. They were both thugs, and he had no doubts that each of them had killed in the past. But whether or not they would be prepared to open fire on a crowd of innocent hostages was another matter.

The switchboard was still buzzing and the frightened manager was looking at him with nervous, questioning eyes. Jefferies made a snap decision.

'Answer it,' he barked.

His hands trembling violently, the manager stepped over to flip the incoming call through the nearest desk phone and picked it up. 'Good afternoon, Courtland Hotel,' he grated out, from pure force of habit.

Winston listened to the faltering, shaky voice on the other end of the line and made his own instinctive judgement. It didn't belong to one of the gunmen, he was sure. He kept his voice deliberately low and reassuring. 'Who am I speaking to?' he asked guardedly.

'I'm the manager,' the man stuttered. 'Can I help you?'

228

Winston's voice exuded calm confidence. 'Now listen to me,' he murmured gently but insistently. 'Just relax and try to stay calm. We're going to get you all out of there safely. Now let me speak to whoever seems to be in control in there.'

It was an unfortunate choice of phrase for someone in a state of mind like that of Jefferies, who had been eavesdropping the brief conversation. Flaring up with anger again, he snatched the telephone from the manager's hand. 'Not *seems* to be in control, you bastard,' he spat aggressively into the mouthpiece. 'I *am* in fucking control – and don't any of you pigs out there forget it.'

The response was totally different from what he had expected, and it threw him.

'I'm going to terminate this conversation,' Winston told him in a calm, deliberate tone. 'I'll call back in ten minutes when you may be prepared to talk more reasonably.'

Winston hung up the phone abruptly, sitting back to reflect on the brief but highly illuminating exchange. Though little had been said, it had actually told him a great deal, and established a definite psychological advantage in his favour. He now had a much more detailed mental profile of the man holding the hostages. He was impetuous, which meant he was nervy; he was aggressive, which invariably suggested underlying fear; and he was egocentric, a stance almost certainly masking insecurity. Every one of these weaknesses could be used as a potent weapon against the man, and in fact Winston had already fired the first shot. Cutting the conversation off had been exactly the right thing to do, Winston thought confidently. Like a spoilt child throwing a violent tantrum, the very last thing Jefferies was expecting was to be ignored. Winston's reaction would confuse, hurt and ultimately weaken the man even more. It had also clearly indicated who actually held the trump card. Who controlled the communication also controlled the negotiations.

All in all, Winston felt quite satisfied with the results of his first contact. No harm had been done, and a position of strength had been established. Two other small clues had been gleaned from the man's use of the term 'pigs'. He probably hated authority figures and was obviously under the impression that he was only up against the conventional police force. Winston made a mental note not to disillusion him on that score too early in the game. As long as he was expecting normal police tactics, he would be totally unprepared for any of the peculiar little tricks the SAS kept up their sleeves. In a crisis, that could prove a very welcome advantage.

Paul Carney's keen nose for trouble was already picking up a strong whiff that all was not as it was supposed to be. The nearer the taxi got to the hotel, the stronger the feeling became. He stared out of the taxi at the growing number of young rowdies on the streets.

'Odd,' he said under his breath, more to himself than anyone else, but the Lethal Leek picked up on it.

'What's up?' he asked. He too had noticed the groups of prowling youths, but unfamiliar with the capital, had assumed it to be normal.

Carney glanced at his watch, checking his earlier supposition. 'All these kids on the streets,' he murmured. 'Something's up. It's far too early for the pubs to be turning out.'

The Welshman failed to understand Carney's concern. 'Doesn't look all that different to Cardiff on a Saturday night to me,' he replied with a faint shrug.

But Carney was unconvinced. It wasn't just the sheer numbers of kids, or the fact that they all appeared to be headed in the same general direction. There was something else – something indefinable about the way the individual groups had an almost uncanny sameness about them. Something about the swaggering, openly aggressive manner in which they walked, the odd suggestion of some common purpose. For some reason Carney found himself reminded of columns of soldier ants, or perhaps lemmings preparing to swarm.

He glanced at the Lethal Leek and shook his head. 'No, there's something in the air, something going on. I can almost taste it. Trouble's brewing, but I can't figure out why.'

The Lethal Leek didn't feel disposed to argue the point. Carney knew his patch, and he knew his job. The boss seemed to trust and respect him, and that was enough for the Welshman.

'So what do you reckon?' he asked, quite prepared to act on any suggestion Carney might make.

Carney leaned forward to the taxi driver. 'Pull in to the kerb for a minute, will you?' he asked.

The man did as he was instructed. Carney turned back to the Welshman. 'Look, you go ahead and join up with Winston at the hotel,' he suggested. 'I'm getting out to see if I can figure out what's going on.'

The Lethal Leek was slightly dubious. 'You sure you want to go out there on your own?' he asked. He had started to pick up some of Carney's bad vibes, and the faintest trace of menace in the air. Many of the smaller groups of youths had already started to form sizeable gangs, and their demeanour seemed to be hardening from mere truculence into a more open challenge. 'Maybe I ought to come with you,' he added.

Carney shook his head. 'No, Winston probably needs you more than I do. And don't worry – I'll keep my head down.' He opened the door and was stepping out when he turned back, a faint grin on his face. 'Why so concerned, anyway?

I'd have thought you'd be relieved you don't have to explain my unwanted presence to Winston.'

The Welshman smiled back. 'Shit, Carney, of course I'm concerned,' he said. 'You're almost one of us.'

Carney jumped out and slammed the cab door behind him, feeling his face warm with a flush of embarrassment.

Or perhaps it was just pride, he told himself.

At the front of a small convoy of three vehicles from the nightclub, Pretty Boy sat on the back seat of a customized Shogun, slightly crushed between Cheryl and the huge frame of Max. Up at the front, Johnny was driving, flanked by the tall, gangly Scouser they called Spider. For a yobbo, Johnny drove a pretty flash set of wheels, Pretty Boy thought. He wondered where he got his money from.

They had already started to pass several smaller groups of rowdies patrolling the streets, all converging on the Knightsbridge area. Johnny seemed heartened by the sight. He half turned towards the back of the car, grinning broadly. 'Looks like we've got a pretty good turnout,' he observed. 'Should be one hell of a night.'

It was time to ask a few questions, Pretty Boy decided. Apparently casual, he said: 'What is all this in aid of, anyway?'

Johnny shrugged evasively. 'Favour for a favour – know what I mean? And no questions asked,' he added pointedly.

Pretty Boy took the hint. Still no wiser, he fell silent as they continued to cruise towards their destination. At last Johnny brought the Shogun to a halt and switched off the engine. 'Right, this is as far as I want to take the motor,' he announced. 'No point in risking getting it all smashed up with the others.' He looked through the front windscreen up the road ahead, to where gangs appeared to be bunching up into more of a mob. Turning back to the rear of the vehicle, he grinned again. 'Besides, we'll let some of those other suckers take the initial heat from the fuzz. Time we get there, they'll have their hands full.'

He delved into his pocket, pulling out a small, flat tin and flipping it open. Picking out a small white pill, he popped it into his mouth and then offered the tin to his passengers. 'Anyone need a little hit to keep their bottle up?'

Max and Cheryl dived towards the proffered pills gratefully, helping themselves. Johnny waved the tin in Pretty Boy's direction.

'Nirvana?' Pretty Boy asked.

Johnny looked slightly surprised. 'Sure. What else?'

Pretty Boy shrugged, picking out a single pill. 'Someone told me this stuff was in short supply just now,' he said coolly.

Johnny grinned. 'Only to those who don't know the right people,' he boasted. 'You got to be one of the chosen few.' His eyes narrowed slightly as he studied Pretty Boy with the faintest trace of suspicion. 'You're a curious bastard, aren't you?'

Pretty Boy turned it into a joke, grinning stupidly. 'Yeah,' he agreed. 'It never made me any fucking smarter, through.'

Johnny smiled, apparently satisfied, but Pretty Boy had already made a mental note not to underestimate the young man again. Perhaps his boast about knowing the right people had been just bluster, but suddenly Pretty Boy doubted it. It was now more than possible that Johnny was a little higher up the organizational structure than Pretty Boy had first suspected. If so, he might well be a very useful source of information when it came to tearing it down.

Certainly it would not pay to arouse his suspicions. Pretty Boy made a great play of popping the pill into his mouth and swallowing it. Conjuring tricks had never been one of his specialities, but he did the best job he could of palming the pill and dropping it discreetly to the floor of the car, where he trapped it beneath his foot. Fairly confident that no one had noticed, he waited a few seconds before carefully pushing it out of sight under the front passenger seat.

The rest of the cars had pulled up behind the Shogun. Johnny opened the driver's door, jumped out, ran round to the second car and opened the boot. He began to pull out a selection of stout wooden batons, baseball bats and metal bars, handing them out to the other members of the gang like an official armourer.

Pretty Boy watched the scene with mounting disquiet. This was more than just a street demo, he realized grimly. This was a war party.

Bullet-head completed his second sweep around the area immediately outside the police roadblocks. He pulled the Lexus in to the side of the road and stopped, then turned to Scott. 'Seen everything you want to see, boss?'

Scott nodded. 'Yes, let's go home.' He settled back into the car's plush upholstery as it slid away again, feeling vaguely comforted by the results of his efforts. His hastily convened mob was building up nicely, perhaps even better than he had hoped. There were probably well over two hundred young thugs out on the streets already, and the smell of trouble alone would be enough to attract others. Once the rioting started in earnest, the rabble would become a wild, undisciplined but quite formidable army. The police presence he had so far observed would be totally unable to restrain them. Even if the mob achieved nothing else, they would provide an extremely effective diversion. After that, Jefferies and his two gunmen would have to make their own chances, although Scott was still willing to offer his personal advice.

He picked up his mobile phone and tapped out the man's mobile number.

'Right, everything is in place,' Scott told him. 'There's a mob out on the streets who will be converging on the hotel within the next half hour or so. They have instructions to keep the police occupied while you make a break for it.' Scott lowered his voice to a whisper. 'Are McKinley and Dennings anywhere near you right now?'

'No,' Jefferies answered, puzzled. 'Why?'

Scott resumed his normal voice. 'Then listen carefully,' he said. 'Your best chance will be to use them as live bait. When the mob storm the hotel, send all the hostages out through the front door and instruct Dennings and McKinley to follow them out, prepared to fire if there's any opposition. There should be enough panic and confusion to let you make your own escape from the rear of the hotel or by the fire escape. Got that?'

'Yeah, sure,' Jefferies said, but his tone did not match the words. 'You really think this is going to work?' he added.

'Trust me,' Scott assured him, lying through his teeth. 'It will work. Just make sure you grab the money and get clear of that hotel while the police still have their hands full. Lie low somewhere for a couple of days and don't attempt to contact me. I'll get in touch with you when things quieten down.'

Scott signed off, knowing that he had done everything he could without getting himself directly involved. He didn't believe for a second that Jefferies had a snowball's chance in hell of getting away. But there was nothing else to lose, he told himself philosophically. If the million-to-one shot *did* come off, and Jefferies got clear, then he would at least have some temporary funds and the chance to fight another day. If not, he would be on the first available flight to Frankfurt, where he'd have to take his own chances with his superiors. His time would come again, he promised himself. One way or another.

The taxi carrying the Lethal Leek stopped at the outer perimeter of the orange plastic tapes which the police had strung across the road to cordon it off. One of the four uniformed officers hurried over to the cab, waving his arms in a clear gesture for the driver to pull back and turn around.

'I'm sorry, but this area is sealed off,' he started to explain, falling abruptly silent as the Welshman opened the cab door and climbed out.

'I'm with the SAS,' the Lethal Leek said. 'Where's my CO?'

The policeman nodded at the Heckler & Koch in the other man's hands with a faint smile on his face.

'Well, I didn't think you were with the bloody boy scouts, sir,' he said deferentially. He jerked his thumb up the road. 'And the rest of your Rambo brigade is up by the hotel.'

'Thanks,' the Lethal Leek said. He paid the cabby and ducked under the tape in search of Winston.

27

Winston had already waited the full ten minutes, and was in no great hurry to communicate with the gunmen inside the hotel again, figuring that any delay could only work in his favour. So the unexpected arrival of the Lethal Leek, and the necessary exchange of information between them, meant that at least quarter of an hour had elapsed since the last contact by the time he finally got back to the communications van.

The telephone was answered immediately this time. Winston recognized Jefferies' voice, although he still didn't know the man's name. He didn't sound quite so arrogant, but he appeared to be less nervous than before. Winston was surprised. He had fully expected the man to be showing signs of caving in, yet he seemed to have gained, rather than lost, confidence.

'Well, are we ready to discuss this thing sensibly yet?' Winston asked in a calm and reasonable tone.

Jefferies was noncommittal. 'Depends on what you have to say,' he countered. 'But there will be no release of hostages, under any circumstances.'

The very definiteness of the statement was another surprise.

Winston had the unnerving feeling that he had lost the initiative somehow, and couldn't figure out why.

The answer came suddenly, in a flash of intuition, and Winston cursed himself for his oversight. The mobile phone! The man had his own means of communication with the outside world, and had probably been using it. And somehow, in the last fifteen minutes, he must have been given a new source of hope, which suggested that some sort of rescue plan was already in operation!

Winston was thrown, but it was imperative that he did not let Jefferies know it. He forced himself to keep talking, even though his mind was racing along new paths, dealing with a whole new set of variables.

'Perhaps you'd better tell me exactly what it is that you want,' he said. 'Then we can start negotiating.'

Jefferies giggled insanely. 'What I want is for you pigs to fuck off before people start getting killed,' he said. 'But we both know that isn't going to happen, don't we?'

The man sounded drunk. Or more likely drugged up to his eyeballs. Knowing the effects of Nirvana, and the man's sudden and unprovoked reference to killings, to Winston it was another new and disturbing factor.

It was time for a change of tack. 'There's no need for anyone to get killed,' Winston said gently, accepting that he was now on the defensive. 'We can stop this thing right now. You can walk out of there any time you choose.'

A snort of derision came over the line. 'You think I want to walk out of here and straight into a prison cell?' Jefferies snarled. 'Think again, pig. When I do any walking, it'll be straight to freedom.'

'And we both know *that* isn't going to happen,' Winston said flatly, echoing the man's earlier comment. It seemed vital to find some way of denting his new-found sense of confidence. 'There are only two ways out of that hotel. In custody, or in a box. The choice is yours.'

Winston paused, giving the statement time to sink in before he played his last card. 'Oh, and there's one other thing,' he added. 'This will be the last communication over the telephone. From now on we will be using the PA system, which means that your two chums will be able to hear everything as well. You're going to have to be pretty confident that you can count on them to back you up when the crunch comes. How far do you think you can trust either of them?'

There was no immediate reply. No smart answer, no show of bravado. Winston felt a faint, inner glow of satisfaction, knowing that the silence showed he had rattled the man again, exposed his insecurity.

Jefferies was more than just rattled. A sudden feeling of panic had suddenly swept over him again. He needed Dennings and McKinley for Scott's plan to work. Without their continued allegiance and support, he had no chance at all. And the bloody pig was right – if it came down to a direct choice of surrender or death, there was only the one sensible option for either of them. As it stood, they faced only a minimal prison term for armed assault – three years at the most. Would either of them be willing to risk life by killing hostages? It was unlikely, Jefferies figured. If he only had the guts to face the same option himself, he knew what he would want to choose.

But he was not free to make that choice. The cold, all-powerful and irrational fear which lurked deep within him made it impossible. Jefferies could never even consider any sort of a prison term, and it had nothing to do with any sense of claustrophobia. It was something worse, something he had carried inside him since childhood.

Jefferies shuddered as the old memories came flooding back. He had been just seven years old, a normal, happy, outgoing child. Bright, good-looking, wanting to learn and willing to trust. And who would such a child trust if not the teacher he admired most?

But that trust had been so cruelly abused. What the innocent child had taken for professional interest had concealed a different, more insidious motive.

The sexual attack had not been serious, but it had instilled a deep-seated hatred of homosexuals in the child which had grown into an irrational fear and loathing in his teenage years. He had passed through puberty in the constant fear that he was somehow marked as a target for queers. It was this all-consuming hatred of a minority group which had led him towards extreme-right-wing politics in the first place. Now, as an adult, it was stronger than ever.

He was young, and still considered good-looking. He had heard horrible, stomach-churning stories of what happened to attractive young men in prison. Rape, sex slavery, infection with AIDS. It was unthinkable. Jefferies would rather die than face a single day behind bars.

Winston's voice came over the line again, snapping him back to the present.

'Well?' the man was saying. 'What are you going to do?'

Jefferies fought against his panic, racking his brains in desperation. The promised mob could only be minutes away now. Somehow, he had to play for time.

'All right,' he blurted out, 'suppose I were to show you I was willing to negotiate? What do you want?'

Winston was quite taken aback by the sudden and dramatic change of mood. He had obviously struck a raw nerve – but how? Why? Perhaps it was just a side-effect of the drug.

Whatever the reason, he had to act on it, follow it up.

'Release half of the hostages immediately,' he said flatly. 'Then we'll talk some more.'

'No.' Jefferies' voice rose to a scream. He needed the hostages just as much as he needed the two gunmen. In desperation he tried to think of anything else he could use as a bargaining point.

'Look, suppose I give you the location of the pub bomb?' he finally suggested. 'It's not set to go off until midday tomorrow. I can tell you where it is, and how to defuse it. You could save dozens of lives.' Jefferies paused, his voice taking on a slightly pleading tone. 'That would be a gesture of good faith, wouldn't it?'

Winston took a couple of seconds to consider the offer. It meant nothing in terms of saving lives, since that threat had already been dealt with. But Jefferies didn't know that, and the fact that he was willing to make any concession was in itself a breakthrough. In virtually every hostage or siege situation, opening the first negotiations was the hardest step to make. After that, there might be the chance of real progress.

'OK, it will do as a start,' Winston conceded. 'Give me the details.'

'The bomb is inside the fruit machine in the lounge bar of the Bull & Bush in Camden Town,' Jefferies told him. 'It is not fitted with any anti-handling devices. You simply have to disconnect the timer to deactivate it.'

Winston wondered briefly how they had managed to place a bomb inside a one-armed bandit, but decided not to press it for now. He made a mental note to make sure all the staff of the machine leasing company were questioned later.

'You realize we're going to have to check this out?' he said.

'Yes, of course.' The man sounded relieved, Winston decided, and wondered why.

In fact, there were many things the SAS man was wondering about, and he needed time to think it all through.

'I'll get back to you,' Winston said curtly, and hung up.

Stepping out of the communications van, he saw the Lethal Leek running towards him. The Welshman looked worried.

'I think we got more trouble, boss,' he said, pointing up the street away from the hotel.

Winston followed his eyeline, through the cleared area and beyond the line of the police cordon. The approaching mob, which had now bunched up into a solid wall, was surging towards the first flimsy strands of tape slung across the road. They were no obstacle at all, and Winston could already see that the thin blue line of uniformed figures would be totally inadequate to hold the mob back. More to the point, he thought bitterly, he and his men would be equally powerless.

Suddenly Winston knew, with a cold certainty, why the gunman in the hotel had suddenly seemed so confident and why the mob was there. He felt almost physically sickened by the sheer cold-blooded cynicism of whoever had conceived the desperate plan. Second Holocaust were throwing the ultimate in cannon-fodder at them, knowing that they would be unable to fight back. They were using their own young men in a ruthless and reckless gamble, counting on the essential decency of the very system they wished to destroy to work in their favour.

Winston glanced down at the MP5K in his hand. He might as well be holding a peashooter, he thought, for all the use it was. For this was London, not Tiananmen Square. There was no way that any authority in the land would sanction firing into a crowd of unarmed civilians, no matter how threatening they were. The police and the SAS alike would have no choice but to fall back or be trampled underfoot by the sheer size of the rampaging mob, who had merely to swarm into the hotel and carry off their colleagues among their ranks.

And there was damn all any of them could do about it, Winston realized in a final moment of despair. His radiophone suddenly bleeped into life, announcing an incoming call. He tugged the instrument from his belt and switched it on. A wave of noise issued from the earpiece, along with bursts of crackling static. It took him a split second to identify the sound as the engine and rotors of a helicopter. Through it, he could faintly hear the sound of a familiar voice.

'Winston? This is Captain Blake. We'll be inserting in about one minute,' came the terse message. 'The hotel does appear to have a flat roof. Primary plan is to go in down the lift shafts, unless you have any better ideas.'

Winston glanced back up the road towards the police barrier. The first wave of rioters had broken through the tapes now, and were already engaged in vicious hand-to-hand fighting with the police officers. A second, and heavier wave hovered in the background, poised to sweep in behind their cronies and march directly to the hotel unopposed. They were two minutes away at the most, Winston calculated. It was cutting things too fine.

He returned his attention to Butch Blake and snapped out a curt message. 'Hold off. We have problems down here.'

The sound of the helicopter's engines were reaching his ears directly now. He glanced up, picking out the six-seater Agusta against the background of the night sky as it slipped in between a pair of towering office blocks perhaps half a mile in the distance.

Butch uttered a sudden and muffled curse as he caught a clear view of the hotel area, and the surging mob, for the first time. 'Oh Christ! I see what you mean.'

Winston thought quickly. 'Look, I've got an idea,' he said. 'Can you drop just two or three troopers on that roof and get off again immediately?'

The answer was immediate, and affirmative. 'Can do. Then what?' In true SAS tradition, Captain Blake was ready and willing to take orders from a subordinate officer if that officer was on the spot and in a position to make a more informed judgement. It was all part of the unique flexibility and ability to adjust to changing circumstances which gave 22 SAS its edge.

'I assume you're carrying flash-bangs and tear-gas?' Winston asked, referring to the stun grenades and gas canisters which were standard armoury in Counter Revolutionary Warfare.

Winston didn't have to say any more. 'I'm way ahead of you, Sergeant,' Butch said. 'Close your eyes and put your earplugs in. It's going to get a bit unpleasant down there.'

Winston watched the chopper as it swept in towards the roof of the hotel and dropped out of sight. Seconds later it was rising again, wheeling in the sky to follow the line of the street towards the main mass of the rioters.

He moved quickly into action himself, calling over to the two Tweedles, Tremathon and Brennon. 'OK, pull back from that front door,' he told them. 'It's shake-out time.' He turned to the Lethal Leek. 'Leek, you take Miles with you and scoot round to cover the fire escape.'

'How's it going down, boss?' Tweedledee asked, as everyone moved to take up their new positions.

Winston smiled grimly. 'Just like Father Christmas,' he muttered. 'We're going to drop our friends in there a few little presents down the chimney.'

In the thick of the second wave, Pretty Boy was almost at the broken lines of orange tape now. There were no policemen left on their feet, and the street was littered with bruised and bleeding bodies. It was time to break cover and choose sides, Pretty Boy decided, although he hadn't got the faintest idea what he could do which could possibly help the situation.

Mob violence was a frightening thing, even to a man like him, who had experienced all sorts of dangers and horrors. His ears were filled with the sounds of screaming, chanting people, and the crash of glass as the rioters smashed the windows of shops and parked cars. It was like being in the middle of a war zone – but this had an unreal, bewildering quality which threatened to swamp him. The mob seemed to have a life of its own – a raw, demonic and savage power which both fed and fed on the individuals within it. It was a mass psychosis, a form of possession which could take a man over, make him doubt his own sanity.

Cheryl and Johnny were a couple of yards ahead of him. The rest of the gang had been swallowed into the crowd. Pretty Boy forced his way through the surging mass of bodies between himself and them, planning his move.

A sharp kick in the back of Johnny's leg, right behind the knee joint, made the young man sag like a burst balloon. Discreetly, Pretty Boy delivered a short, jabbing punch to the back of his neck as he fell, rendering him unconscious. Johnny crumpled to the ground in a heap.

Cheryl was only vaguely aware of the action in her peripheral vision. She whirled on Pretty Boy, her eyes wide with question. 'What the fuck happened?' she demanded, looking down at Johnny's slumped form.

Pretty Boy shrugged. 'Something hit him. A stone, I think.'

There was no time to debate the matter, and nothing they could do about it anyway. The surging crowds behind them were already pushing them onward, with inexorable pressure.

Pretty Boy stepped over Johnny's body, confident that he would be out for at least an hour. If he hadn't been trampled to death by the time this thing was all over, he'd still be around to answer a few questions. Now all he had to do was to get out of the mob to somewhere he could be more useful. It wasn't going to be easy. Then, suddenly, he heard the unmistakable sound of gunshots from somewhere behind them.

Paul Carney had come to the very same conclusions as Winston had some moments previously. There was no defence against the sheer mass of a solid mob. The SAS troopers would be swamped unless something could be done to break it up. There was only one thing he could think of. He reached inside his coat, tugged the Browning from its holster, pointed it into the air, and squeezed off six quick shots.

The sharp crack of the gunshots echoed out across the street above the general background din of rioting and destruction. Perhaps three dozen heads turned suddenly in Carney's direction, faces registering surprise, then fear. Nobody had said anything about guns. There were screams, confused shouts as individuals and small groups first froze in their tracks, their attention suddenly focused back on themselves rather than the mindless, shapeless mob. Then confusion turned to panic and began to sweep through the mob like ripples on a pond, pulsing through the seething crowd and dispersing it back into its component groups.

The reaction seemed out of all proportion to the stimulus, Carney thought, as the scattering crowd turned back in his direction. Then he heard the chattering roar of the helicopter as it swooped low over the heads of the panicking mob like a dive-bomber, pluming white, smoky trails behind it as CS gas canisters rained down into the street. A series of ear-splitting explosions rocked the air, accompanied by searing incandescent flashes which lit up the night.

The flash-bangs proved the final straw for the already confused and frightened mob. An SAS invention, they were virtually nothing more than gigantic fireworks, using grenade technology to place magnesium charges inside a non-fragmentation casing. They did little damage, but the loud bang and the fifty-thousand-candlepower flash they produced were enough to stun, temporarily blind and completely disorient those on the receiving end.

It was time to get the hell out, Carney thought, as a surging mass of humanity began to move back towards him. Jamming the Browning back into its holster, he turned and began to run back up the street as fast as his legs would carry him.

On the roof of the Courtland Hotel, Aberdeen Angus lifted off the inspection hatch of the lift shaft and peered down into its gloomy depths. Straightening, he turned to Jumbo Jackson with a satisfied grin on his face. 'All the way down to the ground floor,' he said cheerily. 'I'll bet the bastards have even put out a welcome mat.'

Roping up, the two troopers clambered through the hatch and began to abseil down the inside of the shaft. On reaching the top of the lift cage, they removed the service hatch cover and lowered themselves gently inside, dropping the last few inches on to their toes as quietly as possible.

There was now only the lift door itself between them and the lobby. Aberdeen Angus glanced at his companion, jerking his thumb towards the 'open' button. 'When I press that, dive out and hit the deck,' he whispered. 'We'll have a safer angle of fire from floor level.'

Jumbo nodded silently, understanding the man's reasoning. Firing upwards from floor level meant that the gunmen would be clear targets without any innocent hostages being in the line of fire behind them.

Both troopers set their MP5Ks for three-round bursts, tensing themselves for action. All they needed now was the sound of a diversion from Winston, and the trap would be sprung.

Winston's black face cracked into a broad grin as he watched the last of the fleeing stragglers evaporate from the streets like mist in the morning sunlight. He glanced down at his watch, checking the time. He had allowed four minutes for his colleagues to descend the lift shaft and get into position. An additional safety margin of a further minute had already elapsed. It was time, he decided.

He nodded at the two Tweedles. 'You two might as well go back in by the way you came out,' he muttered, gesturing towards the shattered bar window. 'I'm just going to make a lot of noise by the front door to draw their attention.'

He turned towards the nearest communications van, where Ted Brennon was looking at him expectantly through the open door. Raising his hand, Winston jabbed his thumb into the air.

Nodding, Brennon ducked back inside the van. Seconds later the vehicle's loudspeakers began to blast out a solid wall of sound as the Rolling Stones launched into the drum-roll intro to 'Paint It Black'. A fitting choice, Winston thought.

He turned back towards the hotel. 'Right, let's do it,' he barked.

Only Jefferies had been unaffected by the sounds of the stun-grenade explosions in the street outside, assuming it to be part of Scott's master plan. Most of the hostages had reacted in blind panic, many of them throwing themselves to the floor instinctively, despite the threat of the guns. Dennings and McKinley had just panicked, anticipating a full-scale attack and being far too concerned about their own skins to worry about anything else. They had lost what small degree of control they had possessed and were now too far down the road of self-preservation to take orders or to be of any effective use.

So he was on his own, Jefferies thought to himself. Somehow, it didn't seem to matter. The drug was buzzing in his brain, filling him with a sense of invincibility. Almost casually, he picked up the red Samsonite suitcase and began to walk towards the bar area and the emergency escape door beyond it. The sudden blast of sound from the street outside seemed like nothing more than background music.

Even the sudden appearance of Tweedledum and Tweedledee through the shattered bar window failed to evoke any real sense of threat. Jefferies raised the Colt almost as a token gesture, pointing it vaguely in their direction without really taking aim.

Not that it would have made much difference. Two bursts from their Heckler & Koch sub-machine-guns took him in the chest before his finger had time to tighten on the trigger, spinning him round like a top in a spray of blood.

Dennings and McKinley turned towards the sound of gunfire just as the lift door sighed open. Caught off guard, they were both sitting targets as Aberdeen Angus and Jumbo dived across the floor in front of them, their own MP5Ks spitting a hail of death.

The chatter of gunfire ceased abruptly, leaving only the screaming of the hostages to fill the gap. Outside, Mick Jagger hadn't even finished the second verse.

It was over.

28

It was an informal meeting, in the bar of the Paludrine Club. The full debriefing would come later.

'Well, do you think we stopped them?' Major Anderson asked.

Lieutenant-Colonel Barney Davies shrugged. 'Probably not,' he admitted. 'We didn't stop the bastards in 1945 and there's no reason to feel any more optimistic now. How do you kill off a dream – even if that dream is completely bloody insane?'

Davies managed a wry smile. 'But at least we've slowed them down, damaged their command structure,' he added. 'It will probably be a few years before they can regroup sufficiently in this country to offer any concerted threat again.'

'And we've neutralized the drug menace, at least,' Anderson pointed out.

The raid on the farmhouse factory had given the green slime the information they needed to identify Nirvana's main chemical constituents and isolate the European pharmaceutical companies producing them. A rigid import embargo would now virtually ensure that no further bulk production of the drug would be possible within the UK.

'So that's it, then?' Winston put in. 'Until the next time?'

Davies sighed heavily. 'Yes, until the next time,' he echoed.

'And Carney?' Winston wanted to know. 'What happens to him now?'

Davies grinned. 'Oh, I don't think you should worry yourself about him,' he murmured. 'I think the Special Branch, or the green slime, are sorting out some sort of job for him right now.' He paused briefly. 'They can always find a use for a good man, even if we can't.'